Muffin Top

Muffin Top

AVERY FLYNN

This book is a work of fiction. Names, characters, places, and incidents are the product of the author's imagination or are used fictitiously. Any resemblance to actual events, locales, or persons, living or dead, is coincidental.

Copyright © 2018 by Avery Flynn. All rights reserved, including the right to reproduce, distribute, or transmit in any form or by any means. For information regarding subsidiary rights, please contact the Publisher.

Entangled Publishing, LLC
2614 South Timberline Road
Suite 105, PMB 159
Fort Collins, CO 80525
rights@entangledpublishing.com

Amara is an imprint of Entangled Publishing, LLC.

Edited by Liz Pelletier
Cover design by Liz Pelletier
Cover photography by GettyImages/iStock

Manufactured in the United States of America

First Edition October 2018

"I am allowed to look sexy, feel sexy, and be in love. I am worthy of all of those things. And so are you." - Mary Lambert

This is for all of the amazing women out there, but especially you. Yes, you.
xoxo, Avery

Chapter One

Nothing good ever happened when the captain asked Frankie Hartigan to come into his cramped office at the back of the firehouse and close the door.

Frankie ran the last few calls through his head. It had to be about the asshole with the Jag. They'd had a warehouse fire down by the docks, and this knucklehead had parked right in front of the hydrant. Really, the guys didn't have a choice but to bust the car's windows and run the line to the hydrant through there. The rich dipshit had pitched a royal fit, right up until Frankie had come over, straightened his entire six-foot-six-inch frame, and asked him if there was a problem. There hadn't been. Shocker.

"Have a seat, Hartigan," the captain said as he sat down behind a desk overloaded with paperwork and manuals and—rumor had it—a computer untouched by human hands.

Frankie looked around. Captain O'Neil's office always needed its own *Hoarders* episode, but today it looked worse than usual. There was shit everywhere. The two chairs in front of the desk were filled with half-empty boxes, old standard operating procedure manuals were stacked four feet high against the wall, and the coveted firefighters-vs-cops rivalry trophy from last year's charity hockey game had the place of honor on top of the tower. Even if Frankie wanted to sit down, there wasn't a place to do it. So he did what he always did when he got brought in for a good reaming out: he stayed standing.

"I'm good."

The older man sat there, staring at Frankie from under two bushy gray eyebrows so fluffy they looked like they were about to take flight. "Is there anything you'd like to tell me before I start, Hartigan?"

Frankie did the walk down memory lane again and came up with only one possibility. He'd been a fucking angel lately. At thirty-three, he really must be mellowing with age. "Is this about the dipshit with the Jag?"

"Oh, you mean the one who plays golf with the mayor? The one who needs two new windows and a fresh detail?" O'Neil gave him a hard, steely glare that lasted for all of thirty seconds. "That little prick got exactly what he deserved, which is what I told the fire commissioner when he called to take a chunk out of my well-endowed ass."

"Well, that's the only thing I can think of." And if it wasn't that, then why in the hell was he in what amounted to the principal's office at Waterbury Firehouse No. 6?

"Good," O'Neil said with an ornery chuckle. "You never know what someone will confess to when you start off that way."

"You're a piece of work, Captain."

"I'm an old relic, but I'm here and I'm not going anywhere, even if they are making me archive or dump most of this stuff." He waved a huge bear paw of a hand at the mess.

Frankie looked around. "Yeah, I thought it looked like more than normal."

"Well, you won't be seeing it after today."

That yanked his attention back to the man behind the desk. "Are you going somewhere?"

"Nope." The captain's face lost all signs of humor. "*You* are."

For the briefest of seconds, Frankie wished he had taken the offer of a chair. Then, the familiar sizzle of the Hartigan obstinate Irish temper sparked to life.

He crossed his arms and glared at the captain. "Are you shit-canning me?"

"Nothing of the sort. It has recently come to my attention, thanks to all of my spring-cleaning efforts, that you haven't taken leave of absence in—I don't even know how long— which is totally against regulations. I can't believe human resources and professional standards haven't ganged up on your oversized Irish ass already about it. The department has gone all-in on the mental wellness aspect of firefighting safety, and that includes taking your required leave to mentally refresh yourself."

Frankie threw up his arms in frustration, wishing like hell that the captain's office was big enough to pace in. Just the idea of mentally refreshing himself was like a fart in a flower shop. "That's a bunch of touchy-feely bullshit."

"Agreed, but you have three weeks built up, and you're taking it all as of now." The captain fished around on his desk for a minute and then pulled out a sheet of paper, handing it over. "And here's the letter from up the food chain ordering you to take three weeks immediately."

Frankie looked down at the sheet of paper like it was a warm, flat beer in August. Like it was a death sentence.

"This sucks." The sheer boredom of sitting on his ass for three weeks was going to kill him. He was already to the point where he took extra shifts just to avoid having too many days off in the month to sit around the house he shared with his twin, Finian, and do the same shit he'd been doing since they got the place a decade ago. It wasn't that he needed the money—although, come on, everyone had too many bills to pay—but the firehouse was his life. The adrenaline. The camaraderie. The going out and saving shit. It's what a guy like him was made for. "What in the hell am I supposed to do for three weeks?"

The captain shrugged. "Get drunk. Get laid. Get a hobby. I don't fucking care. Just get out of my office and don't let me see that freckled mug of yours again for three weeks, Hartigan."

For once in his life, Frankie had no words. His eyebrows met his hairline and stayed there as shock washed through his body. All he could picture was the absolute misery of the next three weeks he'd spend learning origami or underwater basket weaving or some other dumb shit just to keep himself from going nuts.

Yeah, that was not gonna happen.

Marino's wasn't a nasty dive bar or an outlaw biker bar or the kind of bar where, when Frankie walked in, all the seedy patrons stopped what they were doing and started picturing the best way to dispose of his body. Those places would have been more welcoming. Instead, it was a cop bar.

And why would a self-respecting firefighter go into such a place of ill repute? Because his poor, confused baby brother was one of Waterbury's finest, complete with detective shield and annoying habit of always following the rules. Ford did, however, have the night off and a willingness to play wingman as Frankie checked through the captain's proffered to-do list—with "get drunk" being at the top.

"Can you believe this crap?" he asked, taking a drink from his first draft beer. "Three weeks."

Ford was watching the dartboard in the back, since he was up soon, but he glanced away long enough to roll his eyes at Frankie. "If you'd just taken your leave each year like you're supposed to, you wouldn't be in this spot."

Frankie flipped him the bird. "Wait, not only do I have to drink away my sorrows in this place, but you're going to tell me I told you so, too?"

"What else are younger brothers for?"

"I should have called Finn." His fraternal twin, younger by six minutes and forty-two seconds, as their mom reminded them every birthday, would have commiserated properly with Frankie in a real bar.

"Finn is in Vegas because he"—Ford shot him a shit-eating grin that made it look like he was as much of a troublemaker as the rest of the Hartigans—"wait for it." He paused, held up a finger, and took a drink of his beer, soaking the moment for all it was worth. "Took his leave like he was supposed to."

"I swear you were switched at birth," Frankie grumbled. "Somewhere out there is a changeling Hartigan who doesn't get a hard-on for following procedure."

"You already have one brother and four sisters who are like that already. I bring balance to the Force."

It was probably true. There were seven Hartigan siblings—all ruled over by Frank Senior and Katie. Frankie and his twin Finn had followed in their dad's footsteps and become part of Waterbury's bravest. The triplets, Fiona, Ford, and Faith, had chosen different routes, with his sisters going into teaching and Ford crossing over onto the Dark Side by joining the Waterbury Police Department. How a nice girl like Gina could see past that awful fault to actually fall for the guy was beyond Frankie. Fallon came next in the Hartigan order, and she was a ball-busting nurse who put all of the patching up and shit-kicking skills she learned growing up in a rowdy working-class family to keep even the gangbangers in line when they came through her emergency room. Finally, there was the baby, Felicia, the pint-sized Hartigan—well, almost a Carlyle now—who lived across the river with her billionaire fiancé and studied ants. The family joke went that the Hartigans fell into all three categories of Irish: the red Irish, the black Irish, and the so-bull-headed-their-ancestors-got-kicked-off-the-island-for-rebel-activities Irish. And that joke was funny because it was true.

"How about instead of feeling sorry for yourself for having all this paid time off, you do something productive, like figure out what we're going to do for mom and dad's anniversary," Ford said. "We all agreed to pitch in and do something big for them."

The plan had been to send them to Paris for a week, until their dad came home and declared that if their mom forced him to go to one more frou-frou French restaurant to eat snails and force-fed duck livers, he was going to choose to starve to death instead. Yeah. The Hartigans were all known for being a little bit on the loudly dramatic side, with every hill being the hill they'd die on.

"I'd say, with three weeks off, you're the perfect man for the case, Junior," Ford said, using Frankie's most hated of nicknames.

"Yo Hartigan, you're up," someone hollered from the area near the dartboard, saving Frankie from having to smack his brother upside the head on general principle for calling him Junior.

Knowing he'd been saved, Ford raised his beer in salute and strolled off to the back, leaving Frankie in unfriendly territory without a cop guide. Now, it wasn't that the cops and firefighters of Waterbury were sworn enemies, it was just that, well, there was a long-lived and healthy-ish rivalry between them, so they tended to stick to their own kind—except for the annual charity hockey game, during which they happily and enthusiastically beat the ever-loving shit out of each other in between scoring goals.

The bar got a whole lot friendlier when Bobby Marino, who was all of seventy-six if he was a day, gave up the serving duties to Shannon Kominsky. Tall with a body that made a man do a triple take and the kind of warm brown skin that he knew from personal experience was very soft to the touch, she always brightened up the bar at Marino's.

Frankie had known Shannon for years, they'd spent time together naked before, and they had both walked away relaxed and happy. If he played his cards right, tonight could be a repeat performance, complete with orgasms and her post-sex chocolate chip cookies. Some women liked to snuggle after sex. Some liked to talk. Shannon baked.

"Heya, Shannon," he said, giving her the half-lazy, half-cocky grin that had started getting him laid in high school.

And the grin would have worked, if she'd have seen it. Instead, she kept her gaze off of him as she picked up his beer, slid a coaster under it, and set the mug back down. "Not tonight, Frankie."

Damn. That brush off came brutally fast.

"What did I do?"

Now she did look up at him, but it was probably just to give him the are-you-stupid look on her cute face. "It's what you *didn't* do."

His expression must have been as blank as his brain right then, because she shook her head and her lips curled in a rueful smile.

"Call, Frankie," she said with a chuckle. "You never called."

Fuck. He shifted on his barstool. "I'm sorry, it's been crazy, but I've got some time off. Maybe you and I could—"

"Honey, it's been six months." She held up her left hand and wiggled her fingers, the neon light from the Budweiser sign above the bar catching the diamond ring on her finger. "I'm off the market."

"Damn." This was starting to happen with way too much frequency lately. Why was everyone getting married all of a sudden? "Looks like I'm too late."

"Oh sweetie, you were never in the running." Shannon leaned her forearms on the bar and brought her head close, lowering her voice as if she was about to impart an important secret. "Frankie, you're one of the best lays in Waterbury. All us girls agree."

His ego grew two sizes before the second part of her declaration registered. "You *talk* about me? *All* of you together like that?" Comparing notes? Chicks did that? Fuck, did other guys know this little factoid? Because that shit was dangerous.

"It's Waterbury. This neighborhood is like a small town when it comes to gossip," Shannon said. "But here's the deal. You're respectful. You don't promise anything you're not going to deliver. You're fun. You're honestly a good guy, but, honey, you're not the kind of guy who delivers happily ever afters." She gave him a look that walked the line between sympathy and pity. "And once you get to a certain point in your life, all of the fuck-buddy fun loses its luster and you want more, you want a forever kind of thing. You understand what I'm saying?"

Love. That's what she meant. That once-in-a-lifetime, you're-a-lucky-son-of-a-bitch-if-you-find-it thing that everyone thought his parents had, that Felicia had with Hudson, that Gina had with Ford, and that Tyler had with Everly. And for him, it was as likely to happen as him finding a unicorn, because he knew Shannon was right. He'd always known it. He wasn't a delivery driver for Happily Ever Afters R Us, which meant he was as likely to find it as he was to find...

"A fucking unicorn," he muttered.

Shannon's eyebrows went up in question. "What?"

"Nothing," he said with a sigh because how did you explain a unicorn to a woman who'd just told him he wasn't ever getting one?

Shannon shook her head at him and strutted down to the other end of the bar to take some fresh-out-of-the-academy kid's order. Annoyed with the fact that the zinger she'd delivered hit a little too close to home, Frankie turned around and perused the crowd at Marino's. Going east to west, it pretty much went cop and a badge bunny, several cops and one hot badge bunny, a group of sad-sack cops with no badge bunnies, a shitbird in a suit who looked totally out of place, and one Lucy Kavanagh, who looked like she was about to punch his lights out.

Now, *this* could get interesting.

Frankie got up off the barstool and strolled on over to provide the zaftig firecracker best friend of Ford's girlfriend some help should she need it.

• • •

If one more person told Lucy that she'd be so pretty if she just lost some weight, she was going to set them on fire.

All she wanted to do was sit in Marino's in peace and enjoy her jalapeño cheeseburger with a side of spicy fries and a Mountain Dew—yeah, that's right, full-calorie Mountain Dew, suck it, Judgey McJudgeyPants—as her own special treat after the week from hell. She'd planned to tell her bestie Gina about it. Her bestie's fiancé was a cop, hence why they were meeting for dinner in a cop bar, but Gina had to cancel at the last minute because of a bride gone bridezilla.

As Harbor City's premiere crisis communications specialists, all of her clients were of the troublesome variety, but damn, getting Ice Knights player Zach Blackburn, the

Most Hated Man In Harbor City, out of another bad press article was going to make her gray by thirty. All she wanted tonight was to enjoy a good meal and not worry about anything.

Instead, the concern troll in the shitty suit had invited himself over to let her know that if she'd only ordered a salad, she might actually walk out of the bar with someone instead of a few additional pounds.

"And what business is it of yours what I eat?" She punctuated the question by slathering a fry in Sriracha and popping it in her mouth.

"No need to get defensive there, I'm just trying to help," said the guy—who hadn't even bothered to introduce himself or—wait for it—say hi before launching into his unasked-for monologue about *her* eating habits. "I mean, come on, no woman comes into a bar alone unless she's desperate for some male company. It's all about showing up and looking decorative."

Now *that* was just some sexist bullshit right there. Who in the hell ever said that to a guy? Answer: no one.

"Really?" She pushed her steak knife farther away from her plate so she wouldn't be tempted to stab him with it. "You don't think I might just want a Mountain Dew and a burger?"

The guy went on as if she hadn't said a thing. "I'm serious. You have a great face. If you just upped the veggies and eliminated the carbs, high-fat protein, and sugar, you'd be a solid eight instead of a five."

She eyeballed the guy who wouldn't stop flapping his gums about things that had *nothing* to do with him. He was balding and wore a bad suit that only emphasized his beer belly—and *he* wanted to give *her* tips about how to look good? Of course he did.

Her chin started to quiver, and she ground her jaw tightly closed. This asshole would *not* make her cry. It didn't hurt, what people thought of her, if she didn't show it.

Yeah, keep telling yourself that, Muffin.

Lucy was a healthy weight. She had an abundance of curves, sure, but she was healthy. And more importantly, finally happy with her plus-sized body. But times like this, *assholes* like this, really had a way of stripping her hard-fought confidence. Why was it socially unacceptable to shame anyone for anything *except* their weight? Sadly, it was still open season on those who didn't look like what everyone else considered skinny.

She was used to being ignored when she walked into a department store. Or skipped in a line when someone thinner weaved around her. Or had her opinions in meetings dismissed simply because they came from a person of her size. But having someone publicly *rate* her attractiveness? That was a new low.

She briefly wondered what her "score" would be in an orange jumpsuit.

"And," he continued, totally clueless about how close to death he was, "I'm only rating you as a five because your face is nice and your tits are fucking fantastic."

That was it. She was going to have to kill a man in the middle of a cop bar on a Friday night. They better have chocolate cake in prison, but even if they didn't, it would probably be worth it.

"There you are, honey," said a deep voice she recognized just as a very large shadow fell across her table.

She looked up—way up—into the beyond-handsome face of Frankie Hartigan, who was built like a redwood tree and, rumor had it, had one between his legs.

"I'm sorry I was late for our date." He glanced over at the dipshit veggie-pusher. "Is this guy giving you a hard time, honey?"

Chapter Two

The temptation to say "Yes, Frankie, please squash him like a bug while I clap and watch" was so, so strong—like, the guys who pull semi trucks with their teeth strong. Instead, she played along with her best friend's fiancé's brother—OMG, that was now the name of her imaginary all-girl ska band—and smiled sweetly up at him.

"He was bothered by my dinner order, *honey*."

"Really?" Frankie looked down at her plate, over to the dipshit, and then right at her. There was no missing the devil in his eyes right before he turned his attention back to the other man. "What's wrong with what my girl's eating?"

Mr. In Her Business blanched. Literally. The color drained out of his face so fast that he resembled one of those swipe right before and after photos on makeover blogs. How in the hell she managed to not laugh out loud she had no frickin' clue.

"N-n-nothing," the man stuttered.

Nope. He was not getting off that easily.

She looked up at Frankie, still standing next to her chair,

his big hand braced on the back of it, and said in the clueless voice that anyone with a brain would know meant there was danger ahead, "He said I should have ordered a salad, then I might have a chance to move from a five to an eight. I'm a five because I have great tits."

Thunderous didn't begin to describe the dark look of pure vengeance that crossed Frankie's face, making even the freckles that crossed over the bridge of his nose look scary. Mr. Buttinsky made a little squeaking noise that reminded Lucy of the sound of air coming out of a balloon when someone pulled the tip taut as it was deflating. Frankie took a step forward, menace vibrating off of him in waves. The other guy didn't bother to say a word, he just took off, weaving his way at a fast clip through the crowded bar and out the front door. Lucy liked to imagine that he peed his pants a little as he did so.

"Thanks, Frankie," she said to the man still staring at the departing figure of Mr. Peed His Pants. "I owe you one."

Her ginger knight in well-fitting jeans and a T-shirt made some kind of noise that maybe was a response in the affirmative. It sounded kinda like "no problem." Whatever. She was used to that from guys. She was only of interest until a hotter, skinnier, or prettier woman came along. It was the universal fat chick cloaking device.

Determined not to let it annoy her as much as it usually would, she turned back to her jalapeño cheeseburger, spicy fries, and soda. Now she could finally enjoy her dinner in peace.

Alas, it wasn't meant to be. Frankie clunked down a three-fourths filled mug of beer on the other side of her table, pulled out the chair across from her, and sat down. Before she could even ask what he was doing, he waved the waitress over and told her he wanted whatever Lucy was eating, plus an extra order of fries and another beer. Once she'd left, he turned his attention to Lucy and gave her what could only be described as a vibrator smile. She named it that in her head—thankfully only in her head—because she now had a desperate need for her vibrator and maybe a fresh pack of batteries.

"You're not gonna make me eat alone now that we're on a date, are you?" he asked, swiping one of her fries.

She hated to stereotype, but he was really hot and, well, pretty people weren't known for being the smartest in the room. And add to that the fact that his muscles had muscles and she decided to speak a little slower than usual. "We're not on a date."

He cocked his head to one side and blinked his blue eyes at her and gave her a wink, obviously sending the message that he was just messing with her. "But that's what I told that chucklehead."

Her interactions with the oldest Hartigan had been limited to large get-togethers that involved her bestie Gina and her fiancé, Frankie's brother, Ford. They hadn't really talked before. In fact, he was the kind of hot that meant he was usually surrounded by whatever single women were there. But still, she was sure he had someplace else to go.

"I appreciate what you did. Seriously, I am going to hold that memory tight for the next time some asshole decides that he or she needs to impart unsolicited advice about my body, but you don't have to eat with me. I'm a big girl. Obviously." Yes, because making fat jokes before anyone else could was a habit ingrained since grade school, when Jimmy Evans asked if she'd make the Pillsbury Doughboy giggle if he poked her in the stomach. She'd punched him in the stomach instead. That had gone over about as well as expected.

"No really, can I stick around and eat with you?" he asked, leaning forward as if he was about to impart a deep, dark secret. "This place gives me the creeps."

"Then why are you here?"

"Long story that should take at least as much time as it does for us to eat our burgers."

Now how could she say no to that?

• • •

Frankie took a dramatic pause at the end of his story about the cops-on-firefighters brawl at the end of the last charity hockey game—one that his smack talk had started but his right hook had finished. "And that's why I was banned from Marino's unless accompanied by my brother."

Across the table from him, Lucy raised an eyebrow and shook her head. "It's clients like you who are the reason why I'm going all spicy tonight."

"You have charming, especially handsome clients?" Ego? Him? All the fucking time.

She laughed. It was a big sound, one that filled the space around them. "Some of them. Others are just scarily powerful and rich."

The curiosity was killing him, but he wanted to draw it out in order to get another one of those laughs of hers. "Don't tell me, I want to guess what you do."

She dragged a fry through the hot sauce that set his mouth on fire and pointed at him. "I'll let you have three."

The woman didn't give an inch. He liked that.

His gaze traveled over her in a slow once-over as she ate her french fries. Her basic black suit jacket hung over the back of her chair. The plain white shirt she wore only had the first button undone—not flashy by any means—but that asshole had been right, her tits were fantastic, and it was hard to miss them even though they weren't on display. Her makeup was subtle, except for the bright red lipstick, as if she couldn't help but highlight that mouth of hers that was always moving. It wasn't that she talked too much, it was that she wasn't ever, in the few times he'd met her, ever at a loss for words. Her soft auburn hair was pulled back into a low ponytail that tempted his fingers.

Thinking back to the way she'd handled that idiot earlier, he could see her delivering some vigilante justice. "Secret assassin?"

"In a way," she said cryptically. "I do kill things for a living."

"Enforcer?" It was pretty obvious just by looking at her gives-no-fucks resting face that she didn't put up with idiots.

"Sure. Some days. I have to make sure people stay in line." She emphasized her point by drawing one red-tipped fingernail across the table.

"Ringleader?"

"Only on the days that end in Y." She waited a beat. "I'm a publicist and I specialize in crisis communications."

He could see that. Lucy Kavanagh was not a woman to be fucked with. She held her own.

"So we're in the same line of work." He lifted his beer in toast and grinned. "We both put out fires."

She clinked her glass of soda against his beer mug. "Pretty much."

After that, they finished their burgers with small talk about Marino's food—the best kind of bar comfort food; the weather—good riddance to winter; and people who put fruit in beers—freaks of nature.

"So, what kind of fires are you putting out now?" he asked, not above getting a little gossip.

She started fiddling with her straw, sending the ice cubes in her soda clinking around in the glass. "I am officially on hiatus."

"Your boss make you take a forced vacation, too?"

She chuckled. "Since I'm freelance and highly in demand,

I can afford to take off time when I want."

"So what's on the agenda?" If it was anything even remotely interesting, he was going to find a way to tag along. Three weeks on his own was going to send him off the deep end.

"Not what I'd originally planned."

The way she said it set off Frankie's gossip alarm bells. Oh yeah, people might like to think it was the ladies-who-lunch type who liked to spill tea, but most of those folks had never been in a firehouse on a slow shift when there was nothing to do besides run drills and gossip. He reached over to her plate and swiped three jalapeños that had fallen off her cheeseburger. "Tell me and I'll eat all of these in one go."

She shrugged. "It's just three jalapeños, that's nothing."

Not if he had an asbestos mouth, which he did not. Anything above the mildest of salsa and his mouth was on fire. "I'm delicate."

"Oh yeah. Everyone in Waterbury talks about fragile Frankie Hartigan," she said with a chuckle.

He sat up a little straighter in his chair. He'd just meant it as a dumb joke—because he really did hate spicy food—but now? He had just enough time to think *oh shit* before his male ego took over and he popped the demon circles into his mouth. As he started to chew, he watched her eyes go wide and a smile start to curve her full lips upward, which definitely made the move worth it. Then the fiery taste hit his tongue, and it was all he could do not to spit the damn things out. Instead he reached for the water the waitress had brought along with his beer and downed it in one gulp. Yeah. Totally manly.

By the time he set his depleted water glass down, Lucy wasn't even trying to hide her smile. It was just amused, far from being flirtatious. Not the normal reaction he got from women, even when he was being an ass.

"Have some pity. I almost died from that. Tell me the truth."

She cocked her head to one side and gave him a considering look before saying, "I was going to go to my high school reunion, but thank God my sanity returned."

"What are you talking about? I went to mine. It was a blast," he said, trying to wrap his brain around her stance. "Anyway, you have one of those cool jobs with celebrity clients that you can shove in people's faces."

She snorted and gave him a hey-dumbass look. "I'm sure it was fun *for you*."

"But not for you?"

"Spend a week with all the fat-shaming jerks I went to school with when I could be getting a mani-pedi? No way."

She stopped fidgeting with her straw and looked up at him as if daring him to disagree with the assessment. He couldn't do that. Lucy Kavanagh was plus-sized. No one made it through to adulthood without getting picked on for something—he'd had his locker stuffed with gingersnap cookies in seventh grade—but anyone who looked different from the norm got it worse. But that was when they'd all still had lizard adolescent brains. There had to be another reason—and his gut was telling him exactly what it was.

"You're full of shit."

"Excuse me?" One of her eyebrows went up—way up.

The little patch of color blooming at the base of her throat confirmed he was right. "You're scared."

"I am not." More fidgeting with the straw, as if it was either that or sitting on her hands. "Fine. It's going to be couple central, and I am not looking forward to a week of being the third wheel or being a wallflower during all these activities—even a pseudo prom at the end. It would be awkward, but I'm not afraid."

"Really?" He paused and pointedly dropped his gaze to

her fingers on her straw before looking back up at her face. "Prove it by going."

She released the straw and dropped her hand to her lap. "Unlike some people," she said, giving him a look that made it all too clear she was talking about him, "I am not about to get dared into doing something dumb."

"Fine. How about getting dared into doing something fun?"

She cracked a smile. "You're trouble, you know that?"

"You're not the first woman to tell me that." He winked at her and tapped his beer mug against her soda glass.

"I can believe it," she said before popping a stray jalapeño into her mouth as if it wasn't going to set her mouth on fire.

Frankie had grown up with enough estrogen in his house to know that women were not delicate, mysterious creatures. They were like dudes, but curvier, and usually a helluva lot meaner when you pissed them off. This observation hadn't been changed by his encounters with the women of Waterbury whom he wasn't related to, either. In fact, because of the women he'd dated, he'd added the following to his all-about-women knowledge base: Don't fuck with them. Don't lie to them. Don't come until they have first.

Still, he also knew when to leave things alone, so he moved the conversation on to funny stories about their newest rookie. She had him laughing his ass off with some of her clients (unnamed, of course) who did even dumber shit than the rookie. He never would have thought a monkey could be trained to attack paparazzi, but he learned something new that night.

By the time the waitress dropped off his bill with her phone number scrawled on the bottom, he was relaxed back against his chair, having a damn good time because he wasn't worried about impressing Lucy so he could get in her pants. In fact, he couldn't remember the last time he'd broken bread with a woman and had this kind of an easy, low-key good time. Mellow didn't usually describe his interactions with women. Naked and orgasmic usually described his interactions with women, just not long enough to include actual conversation like this.

Shit. What if Shannon was right? What if he was just a good-time guy and nothing more? What if there wasn't anything more to him than orgasms? He took a drink of beer, which had suddenly gone skunky.

Lucy sat across from him digging through her oversized red purse—the woman had a whole color-scheme thing going—for exact change to pay her bill, pulling out a quarter, rooting around in the bag again, then pulling out a dime, and repeat. It was kinda hilarious.

"You know," he said. "They will make change."

She paused in her search long enough to flip him off.

He laughed long and hard as he placed a few bills on top of his check. Shit, he couldn't remember the last time a woman with whom he didn't share a last name was so totally unimpressed by him. Since puberty, the fairer sex had pretty much fallen at his feet. That wasn't a brag. It was fact. So he'd acted like any red-blooded man and had accepted the status quo as his due. He'd never given the situation a second thought—right up until Shannon's comments had struck him like a two-by-four to his thick skull.

He was thirty-three, single, and he lived with his twin brother. All of his friends were married, some more than once, and he was still fucking around at bars looking for Ms. Right Now and nothing more, as if he was still twenty-five and an idiot. So, what was he waiting for? What was he missing? Was he just destined to be the designated Waterbury fuck buddy? He didn't have answers for any of it, but that last question left a bad taste in his mouth.

It was past time for him to figure this shit out. He needed

a reset, a change of priorities. He'd step back from the scene for a few weeks and maybe then he'd figure out what was giving him this itchy little feeling that things weren't just off, that he'd missed something important. That was it. A temporary powering down of the small head to power up the big head. There was a reason why fighters didn't fuck before a big match. Women messed with a man's head. So he'd enter a little player rehab for a few weeks, just him and his right hand.

Yeah, but he wasn't one for spending a lot of time by himself. Could be a twin thing or that he was just a people person in general, but even the idea of three weeks with only himself for entertainment gave him the cold shakes.

The waitress picked that moment to stop by, and he nearly grabbed his bill back from her to tear off the section with her number on it.

Get a grip, Hartigan.

He stilled his hand in time, but that had been damn close.

"Thanks," Lucy said as she handed over the exact change plus tip.

Lightning struck for the second time in five minutes: he'd be Lucy's date to her high school reunion. It was the perfect plan because, as awesome as she was, she wasn't his type. There wasn't any teasing flirt to her. She was blunt, ballsy, and definitely not the kind of woman to relinquish control even for a second. However, she was fun as hell, and that was just what he needed to keep him busy and out of trouble. And the fact that she was definitely not into him was a bonus.

Lucy stood up and set her purse on her chair, then started to put on her jacket. Adrenaline jolted him out of his seat.

"You can't miss your high school reunion," he said, louder than he meant. "You owe it to yourself to go show them that their bullshit couldn't hold you back. You already have the killer job, and I have the perfect solution for dealing with people giving you shit."

"Really?" she asked, not even slowing in the process of getting her suit jacket on. "How's that?"

"I'm gonna be your date." He straightened to his full height of six feet, six inches. "No one gives anyone I'm with a hard time."

Lucy laughed—loud enough to make the people around them turn and look—and smacked her hand to the table.

Damn. His ego was as big as he was, but it had taken about all it could take in one night.

"Very funny," she said, wiping away a tear of laugher from her eye and catching her breath. "But I'm not going to drive with you out to Missouri for my high school reunion."

Now that was a haul. "Why aren't you flying?"

That question wiped the smile off her face. "Have you seen how people my size are treated on a plane?" She gave him a slow up-and-down. "You of all people should understand that those little seats are uncomfortable unless you're a Smurf."

She wasn't wrong. Every time he'd take his seat, he had to pretzel himself up to fit, and then the jerkwad in front of him always tried to tilt his seat back, right up until he saw the pissed-off giant behind him. Really, not flying made sense.

"So we drive." He shrugged. "How long could it take?"

"A day and a half." She picked up her purse and slid the strap over her shoulder.

He could make that work. "Good thing I am on forced vacation."

"You're suspended?"

"No." That would be easier to take. Then there would be an actual reason why he couldn't go to work, rather than because of some bullshit rule. "I haven't taken any of my required off-time, and the HR department freaked out. Don't make me sit home and be bored. Seriously. I don't do time off well. Last time I built a deck."

"That doesn't sound bad."

She was back to looking at him like he was a moron. He wasn't dumb, but he was not someone who should ever be left alone with a hammer and nails.

"I had to pay an ungodly amount to have someone come in and demolish what I'd done and build one that didn't try to defy the laws of physics." He gave in to the sense of urgency flooding his system. "Come on, have pity on me. Let me be your date."

Lucy didn't just look at him, she seemed to look right inside him. He wasn't a man who squirmed, but he did anyway. If she gave her clients that kinda look, he couldn't believe that they didn't just shut the fuck up and change their behavior immediately.

"Why do you want to do this?" she asked, suspicion thick in her tone.

Because he was running away from ghosts of women past. He needed to clear his big head, and celibacy was a helluva lot easier when there wasn't temptation involved. Lucy was a great girl, but she wasn't the kind that he needed to worry about moving his zipper. She was, without a doubt, a total ballbuster, and he wanted to keep his family jewels intact. "You saved me from a boring night at Marino's. Let me return the favor."

She narrowed her big brown eyes at him and pursed those full red lips of hers. He was holding his breath without really understanding why and didn't let it go until Lucy's mouth turned upward in a bemused smile.

"Fine," she said, chuckling as she shook her head. "Frankie Hartigan, will you go to my high school reunion with me?"

Chapter Three

Lucy added a dab of green paint to the canvas in front of her, took a sip of white wine from a small plastic cup, and tried her hardest to keep her red mouth shut. It was a losing battle. She knew it. Judging by the curious looks her best friend Tess, who sat next to her at paint and sip night, kept sending her way, she knew it, too. Glancing left, Lucy spotted her other besties, Gina and Fallon, sending her questioning looks. She pressed her lips together and turned her focus to her canvas again. It was supposed to be a tranquil creek flowing through a hilly landscape underneath a smog-filled sky—the leader of their weekly paint and sip night, Larry, was an odd duck, to put it mildly.

"What is going on?" Tess whispered. "Why are you so quiet?"

On her other side, Gina and Fallon leaned in closer. Lucy had two choices. The first was to fake a sudden case of deafness. The other was to try to bullshit her way out of telling her friends the truth. Both had an equal chance of working. Her girls knew her too well. They knew she saved all her secret-keeping for her clients and let all of her shit fly in the wind.

A counselor she'd seen in college told her that she used TMI as a defense mechanism. She'd told the counselor to go fuck himself. Yeah. He may have been onto something there.

She swished her paintbrush in the plastic cup of water she'd been warned a million times not to mix up with her plastic cup of wine. "I've decided to go to my high school reunion."

"Okay, so this should be when you should be telling us everything and psyching yourself up," Gina said, narrowing her eyes at Lucy. "Instead you haven't made a single comment about the dead birds falling from the sky in Larry's sample painting."

"I'm taking someone." There it was, out there. That should end the questioning…if she lived in an alternate universe.

Gina, Tess, and Fallon stopped painting and turned to her in unison, their eyes wide. Then they all spoke at once.

"Who?" Fallon asked.

Tess burst out with, "You've been holding out on us!"

"Tell us everything," Gina said, clapping her hands excitedly but forgetting to put down her paintbrush first, so they all ended up with little dots of gray on their smocks.

Lucy couldn't give them a hard time about their surprise. She was still in shock herself. For years, she, Tess, and Gina had considered themselves the undateables—really, they had novelty T-shirts made up and everything. Lucy was the designated fat friend. Tess, the introvert who couldn't say six words to a member of the opposite sex unless they were "I am Groot"—twice. Gina wasn't what anyone would call conventionally attractive. They'd banded together and formed a little alliance. Now Gina had a big ol' rock on the ring finger of her left hand. And Fallon? Well, she spent her days in scrubs as an ER nurse and her nights in shlubby joggers, keeping the same suffers-no-fools attitude twenty-four seven.

Needing fortification before making her announcement, Lucy shot back what was left of the discount-aisle wine in her cup. "I'm going with Frankie."

There was a beat of silence before the words came flying at her from all directions at once.

"Frankie who?" This from Tess who, present company excluded, loved her plants way more than people. She gasped. "Not Frankie *Hartigan*, right?"

Fallon let out a groan. "Oh my God, no."

"How did that happen?" Gina half asked, half squealed.

Larry cleared his throat and sent their little group a look that said shut up now. That was Larry. He loved them for being regulars while hating them for it at the same time. He liked his studio to be an oasis of quiet creativity during paint and sip nights. Lucy and her crew—like 99 percent of the other customers—came to gossip, drink, and giggle.

Lucy dropped her voice to a very un-Lucy-like level of quiet and gave her friends the lowdown on what had happened at Marino's the other night. They sat with their heads close together, paintings all but ignored, during the entire story, letting loose with a few heartfelt mumbles about what a total jerk the salad guy was and quiet agreement from Fallon that her brother should never be set loose with power tools if the goal was to build something rather than cut someone out of a wrecked car.

"Are you sure this is a good idea?" Tess asked once story time ended.

No. Not in the least. In fact, it was beginning to feel like a very, very bad idea, going by the cadre of nervous butterflies doing the Watusi in her stomach. "It'll be fine. He's going as my fake date and giant-sized-asshole deflector."

Gina tapped the end of her paintbrush on the tip of her pronounced nose. Thankfully it was the non-paint-covered end. "You'll be in the car with Frankie—alone—for two days?"

"A day and a half, really." Of being squashed in her Toyota Prius with a man who had the ability to melt women's panties with a smile. Of course, he wouldn't melt her panties because they were bigger than those of his usual targets—let's face it, they were much bigger—and made of steel, which was what happened when one had crushed on the wrong kind of guy and been burned, hurt, or ignored too many times to ever do it again. "Eighteen hours to be exact."

"Oh, that changes everything," Fallon said, all but rolling her eyes at Lucy. "Look, I love my brother, but just be careful."

"He's a sweetheart," Gina said, always the one to stick up for the underdog.

Fallon snorted loud enough to draw Larry's glare again. "No, he's a man-whore. I love my brother to death, but that doesn't change who he is. He can't commit."

"Maybe Lucy will change him," Gina said, her voice going all soft and loopy. "A road trip is so romantic."

And that is what happened when a woman fell; she started believing that it was possible for everyone. But that was *not* what Frankie had in mind. Sure, they'd had fun, but she knew how to spot attraction in the opposite sex, and Frankie definitely didn't see her that way. She was a size twenty in a size zero world. She was smart, healthy, motivated, and ambitious, but that didn't change the way people looked at her and the assumptions they made based on her size. Time to nip Gina's pie-in-the-sky dreams for her road trip now.

"It's twelve hundred miles spread out over two days. It'll be eating fast food in the car, a night in a cheap hotel, and probably a speeding ticket or two," Lucy said. "Romantic is the last thing it's gonna be."

Even if she couldn't stop wondering what it would be like.

• • •

Poker night at the house Frankie shared with his twin Finn was serious business—when it came to beer and bragging rights. The betting was limited to pocket change, and the jokers were always wild. He, Finn, and Ford were already two hands in when Fallon came through the door after a long shift in the ER, still wearing those god-awful clog shoes and a surly expression on her usual makeup-free face.

"Are you insane?" she asked without any other form of greeting. "You can't take Lucy Kavanagh to her high school reunion."

Frankie flinched. The brotherly shit-talking around the table stopped in an instant.

Fuck-nutters.

He'd been hoping to get out of town before anyone in the Hartigan clan found out about his plans in order to avoid a trip to Judgementville, population his pain-in-the-butt sister Fallon. With a family as into each other's business as theirs was, he should have known the chances of getting away clean were somewhere between null and never gonna happen.

Frankie dropped his cards on the table, face up—at least he had a whole lotta nothing in his hand anyway. Finn laid down his cards, and Ford gathered them all up and started shuffling. Both of his brothers looked from Fallon to him, shit-eating grins on their faces, ready for the show—all his suddenly mute brothers were missing was the popcorn. Smug jerks.

There really wasn't a point in denying his plans. "Why not?"

"Because she's my friend." Fallon yanked out a chair, put her jar of quarters on the table, and sat down.

Non sequitur alert. "What does that have to do with anything?"

"Frankie, I love you," she said as Ford started dealing. "But you can't make Lucy part of your ever-changing harem. She's not like your other women. She'll take it personally. You may not realize it, but under that eats-nails-for-breakfast persona is a total softie."

Annoyance had him bouncing his knee under the table. "I don't have a harem."

That got a round of disbelieving chuckles from the table. Assholes. He was related to a bunch of assholes.

"Well, I don't." He loved women, what was so wrong with that? He dated many of the women he was attracted to, and while getting to date number three rarely happened because there was always another woman out there who caught his eye, no one walked away orgasm-free or heartbroken. Everyone knew the score going in. He was nothing if not honest and upfront. And what had he gotten for that honesty? A reputation as a guy who was good for only one thing. That was starting to really piss him off. "Anyway, if I did, Lucy wouldn't be part of it."

"Why's that?" Finn asked as he picked up his cards.

He glanced down at his cards and found another crapfest. "She's not my type."

Fallon snorted and threw two cards on the table facedown in the universal sign for hit me with two fresh cards. "You mean she isn't all boobs, ass, and tiny waist, weighing in at under one hundred and twenty pounds."

"That's not it," he said, not bothering to keep the pissed-off edge out of his tone.

His sister should know him better. He was an asshole, but not that kind of asshole. The truth was, Lucy would eat him alive. People might say firefighters were adrenaline junkies who rushed into danger when others ran away, but every one of them had finely tuned survival instincts. He knew just where that line was, and for some reason Lucy Kavanagh set off every warning bell he had. That hadn't stopped him from thinking about her at inopportune times—like in the shower when he was taking care of his morning hard-on—but that only reinforced that his dick could not be trusted at the moment.

"Really?" Fallon asked. "Then what is it?"

"I'm on the bench, so no woman is my type."

Ford laid his cards facedown on the table and gave Frankie the cop stare down he'd been practicing since birth. "What do you mean?"

"I mean that I've benched myself." Finn, Ford, and Fallon all stared at him like he'd grown another head. Guess he was going to have to spell it out for them. This wasn't going to be weird or awkward at all. "I'm taking a break from sexual activities."

"Did you catch something?" Finn asked.

They might be twins, but it was definitely fraternal, not identical. While Frankie had rarely met a risk he didn't want to see if he could survive, Finn was the kind of guy who never did anything by chance. Of course he'd figure Frankie had blown off protection, which he did not do. Ever.

"No, I do not have an STI." He bit out each word at his brother.

Fallon eyeballed him. "Did you fall down and break your boner?"

Frankie flipped his sister off. And to think that question came from the registered nurse in the family, who had to know that wasn't possible. At least he didn't think it was. Fuck. He was not going to Google that. Some things a man didn't need to know.

"Then what is your thinking here?" Ford asked.

"Let's just say I'm expanding my horizons, and this three-week break from work might be the perfect time to take a break from other things, too."

Everyone sat in excruciating silence for all of about five seconds before Fallon let out a huff of disgust. "Franklin Delano Hartigan, you shithead."

"What the hell is that for?" he asked. Not that he wasn't, but he did like specifics.

"That's why you agreed to go to Lucy's high school reunion," Fallon said, shaking her head. "I've been trying to figure it out since she told me, and now I understand. You shallow jerk of a man, you think that by spending a week in the constant company of an extra-curvy woman that you're taking yourself 'out of temptation's way.'" She air quoted the last bit sarcastically.

"That's some bullshit," he said before he could think better of making the admission. His lack of attraction to Lucy had more to do with total non-compatibility rather than physical attraction. "You don't know what you're talking about."

Everyone just stared at him, their cards ignored. Why had he opened his mouth? He should have just let his family think that he was the same kind of asshole as the piece-of-shit at Marino's giving Lucy a hard time about her cheeseburger. It would have been a helluva lot less awkward.

"So, you find her attractive?" Finn asked, sounding a lot like their scientist youngest sister, Felicia, when she was in the middle of gathering data for a study—except instead of getting information on ants, it seemed like Finn had focused in on his twin.

Fallon glared at him. "If you say she's got a pretty face for a bigger person, I am going to stab you with the closest pointy object."

"Look, I can't help who I'm attracted to. I have dated all sorts of women," he said, unable to keep the defensiveness out of his voice. "It's not that I'm excluding anyone, it's just that I am drawn to who I am drawn to."

And women who were never going to buy the lines he was selling were not one of them. He liked his balls attached and swinging under his dick, thanks very much.

"Bullshit." Fallon sat back in her chair and crossed her arms. "It's that you take some folks off the list before you even give them a chance."

"You want me to bang Lucy Kavanagh?" Where in the hell was this conversation going?

"No," Fallon exclaimed. "I like her."

He tossed his cards onto the table in frustration. "And you can't like people I fuck?"

"If that was the case," Fallon said, her voice rising, "then I'd have to not like almost the entire female population of Waterbury."

And if Frankie needed any confirmation that he needed to take a time-out from women—all women—then this was it. Even his sister thought he was a man-whore and nothing more. He looked at his brothers, who had transformed their faces into carefully neutral masks, which told him everything he needed to know.

"How about everyone steps back and takes a deep breath," said Finn, ever the peacemaker. "You two are getting pretty fucking worked up when you're both right."

Frankie and Fallon stopped shooting death glares at each other to turn their combined ire onto Finn. "What?" they asked at the same time.

"Sexual attraction is what it is. We don't control it," Finn said, talking slowly because he was obviously trying to pick his words carefully. "But we, as humans, do tend to separate the world into them and us, which can alter our perspective about who we should even consider as possible sexual partners. The research on physical attraction is actually pretty fascinating."

He looked from Frankie to Fallon to Ford, and they must have each had the same shocked expression, because Finn flipped them off. "What? I can read."

There was a beat of silence, and then they each started laughing, the tension seeping out of Frankie's shoulders as he relaxed back against his chair. His gaze caught Fallon's. They were too much alike in a lot of ways, quick tempers, impulsive, embracers of chaos, and—yeah—adrenaline junkies. But they were both the kind of people who stuck up for the kid getting picked on. For him, it was probably because he was the oldest of the Hartigan siblings and that had been his role as long as he could remember.

For Fallon? Well, the world wasn't always easy for a woman who didn't conform to what was expected. She'd gotten so much shit growing up about her brash personality and tomboy ways that defensiveness was pretty much her starting point in any discussion. And that attitude showed up when she was going mama bear for her friends. He could understand that.

"Look, I know Lucy's your friend," he said. "I like her but not that way. I'm going because it will give me a break from my usual routine in Waterbury, and I could use that to get my head clear. And she deserves to rub her awesome life into the faces of those assholes from high school. It's a win-win for both of us."

She pursed her lips but didn't call him an asshole again, so that was progress. "You're sure everything else is all right?"

"Yes." He grinned at her. "And my dick still works."

"No, I mean this is a big change from your standard operating procedure," she said, not even cracking a smile at his joke. "You're a pain in the butt but you're *our* pain in the butt, so we're here for you if you need us."

Like he'd ever doubted it. They might fight. They might call each other out. They might be loud and obnoxious and way too involved in one another's lives, but they were family and that's how they rolled—all in it together.

"I'm thirty-three," he said, gathering up everyone's discarded cards on the table and shuffling them. "I'm just ready for a change."

Finn chuckled and took a sip from his beer. "Frankie's going to Missouri to find himself."

They all laughed, the equanimity of the Hartigan poker table back to normal. And that was about as much touchy-feely chatting as he could take, so he told Ford it was his turn to get fresh beers from the fridge and deal out the cards, figuring he could use the winnings he was about to make to pay for tolls on the drive to Missouri.

And that was what put the smile on his face, not the idea of spending a day and a half on the road with Lucy Kavanagh. Not at all.

Chapter Four

Lucy pulled into the driveway of the bungalow Frankie shared with his brother at six a.m. It was too early to be up. Thank God for Mountain Dew, lots and lots of Mountain Dew. She put her Prius into park, took a drink from her second soda of the day, and then got out of the car so she could move her suitcase over in the trunk to fit Frankie's bags. She didn't even get her driver's side door shut before Frankie's voice stopped her in her tracks.

"There is no way in hell that I'm going to fit in that toy-sized car."

She whipped around. Frankie stood on his front porch in jeans he filled out way too well, a Waterbury Fire Department T-shirt that only seemed to make his already broad shoulders seem more so, and an Ice Knights hockey baseball cap that drew her attention to the look of utter disbelief on his face.

"It's bigger on the inside." Okay, not a whole lot, but she wasn't going to admit that.

"Are you kidding me?" he asked with a shake of his head as he strutted down from the porch and toward the driveway.

"That is *not* a Tardis."

Not the comparison she'd expected from him, and she couldn't help giving him mental points for the *Doctor Who* reference.

"I fit comfortably and I'm sure you will, too." Honesty time. She'd never driven her compact car any farther than her daily commute, but she'd already mapped out the charging stations along their route to Antioch.

"Perhaps you haven't noticed, but I'm not pint-sized." He stopped next to her, his shadow practically throwing her entire car into the shade.

She put a hand on one of her hips. "Perhaps you haven't noticed, but I'm not, either."

His gaze pivoted from her car to her face. The disbelief in his eyes at the size of her car turned curious as he looked at her and moved on to what looked like—but probably wasn't—heated appreciation as his focus moved down her body to the spot where her hand was on her hip. Of course it wasn't that kind of look, though. Even if it was, it was just because Frankie couldn't help himself. The man flirted the way other people breathed.

Normally, that kind of guy—the player—always left her feeling icky. Really, who wants to be with someone who had more notches on his bedpost than Santa had names on his naughty list? There was just something gross about it.

Still, she couldn't help but shift under the attention from Frankie and pray like hell that she didn't match her red V-neck T-shirt right now.

Hypocrite much, Lucy?

"I'll cover all of the cost of gas if we go in my car," he said, his gaze back up to her face.

Nope. That wasn't going to happen. "I invited you. I'll pay."

"So glad you agreed to take my car." How he managed to

make the gotcha grin on his face look sexy, she had no clue. "You can park your golf cart in the garage while we're gone so the neighborhood preschoolers don't boost it."

Wait. What? Had she? Damn it. He was already hitting the code on his garage door, revealing a bright scarlet Chevrolet Impala that was waxed to a high shine until it gleamed even in the garage. Oh hell. It just had to be red. She was such a sucker for anything but eyeshadow in that color.

She should put up a fight about it, but…red Impala. "You are way too used to getting your way."

"It's because I'm so charming," he said, crossing his arms across his chest and making his poor T-shirt strain around his biceps.

Something in her head popped and fizzled as she stared at his arms. Not just his biceps, but his thick forearms. The longer she stared, the more she needed to grab her second morning Mountain Dew from the cup holder in her Prius, because she was seriously overheated in the way that sent a delicious tingle through all her most sensitive spots.

"I'll take your silence as agreement," Frankie said.

Rolling her eyes, she told her lady bits to chill the fuck out. "You get your way because you're a bulldozer."

"That, too." He shrugged his broad shoulders. "Now, pop the trunk so I can get your bags."

Lucy sighed. The man *was* driving halfway across the country to go to her high school reunion. She could let him win the battle of the cars. She pressed the trunk release on her key fob.

He ambled over and peeked in. "Two suitcases? We're only going to be gone for a week."

"Exactly, I economized to fit everything in only two." Men never understood everything that went into packing for a week away as a woman.

"Does this one have bricks?" he asked, lifting the smaller

but heavier of her two matching red suitcases.

"So funny."

It was her shoes—lots and lots of shoes. She had a bit of a DSW problem. They loved her there—as they should, considering how much of her paycheck they now owned.

Frankie carried her bags, which she'd wobbled under the weight of when she'd loaded them into her trunk, as if they didn't have a thing in them. Then he put her bags in his much roomier trunk and pulled the Impala out of the garage, easily maneuvering around her Prius on the driveway. She got behind the wheel of her car and drove it into his pristine garage, where all the tools hung from pegboards on a perfect line of hooks. The yard equipment was located in one corner. The trash can and recycling bin didn't even have a speck of dirt on them. The sight soothed some of the nerves eating away at her stomach lining. She might work neck-deep in chaos thanks to her high-maintenance clients, but she was a woman who loved the sight of everything put in its place.

Still, the garage was definitely not what she'd been expecting from Frankie Hartigan. His twin must be responsible. She glanced at the man rocking out in his car— yes, there was head banging—with the windows rolled up, but the *thump, thump* of a hard and fast drumbeat still managed to escape the confines of the Impala. He must have spotted her watching him, because he gave her a sexy grin and a cocky wave before sliding on a pair of aviators.

The garage was definitely his brother's domain. There was no way the giant ginger she was driving cross-country with was a neat freak. The idea of it was ludicrous. She grabbed her still mostly full Mountain Dew, her favorite red lip gloss from its designated spot in her second cupholder, and her phone charger, then walked out of the garage and over to where Frankie now stood next to the open passenger door of his Impala.

After she got in and he closed the door behind her, he walked around the front and she took in the immaculate interior of the Impala. If possible, it was even cleaner than the garage. She just might need to reevaluate her road trip partner, because it seemed there was more to Frankie Hartigan than the consummate wild man he liked to show everyone, and there was nothing she loved more than figuring out the solution to a riddle. It's why she'd been drawn to crisis communication rather than the other marketing specialties. She liked solving puzzles.

Thinking of which, Frankie picked that moment to get behind the wheel and turn the key in the ignition. The engine didn't purr. It roared, all pent-up power and badassery.

"Let's get this show on the road," she said, needing to reassert her dominance before the wave of testosterone and muscles overwhelmed her. "We've got eighteen hours ahead of us."

"No way," he said as he reversed out of the driveway. "We'll do it in sixteen."

"I've made this drive before." Too many times to count. "And it's definitely eighteen."

He turned that cocky grin on her again. "But you've never driven it with me. Buckle up. Miss Scarlett's about to take you on the ride of your life."

• • •

And they were on track for sixteen hours to Antioch, Missouri, right up until Frankie spotted the red and blue flashing lights in his rearview mirror while they were on the interstate somewhere in the middle of nowhere west of Pittsburgh.

"Oh, Miss Scarlett," Lucy said as she patted the tan leather on the Impala's dash. "This stop is going to cost you and make it that much harder to make the drive in sixteen hours on the road."

About two hours into the drive, she'd started giving him crap about naming his car and had been putting it into conversation at every opportunity. There was no way her biting sense of humor was going to miss the opportunity to get in her digs while he pulled the registration from the glove box. He couldn't blame her. He'd have done the same thing.

"Do you know why I pulled you over today?" the cop asked as soon as Frankie had rolled down the driver's side window.

Some people would try to finagle their way out of the ticket. Not him. He knew well and good that he had a lead foot and that for anytime he got caught laying it down, there were another dozen when he didn't. It had been a while since he'd gotten a speeding ticket, so he knew he was due.

"Eighteen over the speed limit," he replied, because more than twenty on the interstate always came with the possibility of getting arrested, and he liked his air fresh and his sky fully visible.

The officer didn't even crack a smile at Frankie's honesty. He just took his license and other information and went back to his cruiser to write up a ticket.

Lucy pivoted in her seat. "I take it this happens a lot."

"I'm a big guy. My foot weighs a lot."

One side of her ruby red lips curled upward. She was wearing big black sunglasses that covered her eyes completely, but he still knew there was a lot of sass in them. The woman had it in spades.

So far on the drive, she'd schooled him on Ice Knights hockey trivia, tried to win an argument on the best action movie of all time—it was the Steve McQueen classic *Bullitt*, no matter how much she argued for *Die Hard*—and had told him stories about her unnamed clients, which had him sharing stories about the people at his firehouse. When he'd told her about the prank with a snapping turtle a rookie had found in his locker after coming back from the shower, she'd almost spit out her Mountain Dew.

They'd been in the car for five hours and most of it had been spent talking. Now, he was a talker so that wasn't weird, but he usually didn't spend that much time talking to women he wasn't related to, so that put this in new territory. He wasn't sure how he felt about that.

Sure, he'd still taken a few sly peeks at the bountiful cleavage shown off by the modest V-neck of her T-shirt—hello, he was just a dude—but he'd kept his hands to himself. That didn't mean he hadn't thought about what she'd look like without that shirt during the lulls in their conversation. It was hard not to. That asshole at the bar had been wrong about a lot of things, but he hadn't been wrong about the fact that Lucy had gorgeous tits. Somehow without him meaning to, his gaze had slid back over to her, taking in the full curvy package.

That was exactly the last thing he needed to be doing. His dick was not in charge. Shannon's words about him only being a good-time guy echoed in his head. Fucking A. He clenched his eyes shut and sucked in a deep breath. What in the hell was wrong with him? Could dudes be nymphomaniacs?

Of course, that's when the unmistakable crunch of cop shoes on gravel sounded, forcing him to open his eyes and bring his attention back to his window. Never had he been so glad to see one of the boys in blue—or in this case tan and brown.

"So here's your license and registration back," the cop said, handing him that along with an all-too-familiar piece of paper. "And your ticket. There's information on the back about how to pay or dispute it."

"Got it." He nodded. "Thanks."

"Just be sure to slow down," the officer said with the tip of his wide-brimmed hat.

He watched the officer walk back through the rearview mirror. Sure, he was delaying the inevitable shit-talking smackdown that the woman in the passenger seat was about to deliver, but he did have an ego and he was about to be out three bills.

"Eighteen hours," Lucy said, teasing him like only his family did. "I should've made you bet dinner on it."

"Miss Scarlett isn't done showing off yet," he said as he turned the key in the ignition.

Then he turned it again.

And again.

Miss Scarlett turned over, but the engine didn't roar to life. He counted to ten and tried again. The engine turned but nothing happened after that.

"Please tell me you're just giving me shit," Lucy said, lowering her sunglasses and showing off her mossy green hazel eyes.

He sure wished he was. "Nope."

Holding his breath as if that would help, he tried again. Nothing. Miss Scarlett was officially not speaking to him. What was it with the women in his life lately? Grudgingly, he admitted defeat and took the keys out of the ignition. There was only one thing to do.

"I'll be right back," he said before getting out of the car and walking back to the cruiser still parked behind them.

An hour later, he and Lucy were sitting shoulder to shoulder in the front cab of a tow truck, pulling into the Black and Gold Garage that was decorated with window clings of the ice-skating penguin mascot of one of the Ice Knights' most hated hockey rivals.

"That's not a good sign." Lucy jerked her chin toward the penguin.

It wasn't. Thirty minutes later, after finding out that Billy, the shop's one mechanic, was home with a sick kid and wouldn't be back to look at Miss Scarlett until the morning, he and Lucy were on the front steps of Katy K's Bed and Breakfast. Everything screamed delicate and cute, from the intricate wooden scrollwork on the wraparound porch to the baby pink bistro table and chairs set in the middle of a garden bordered by shrubbery shaped and trimmed to look like *Alice in Wonderland* characters. It gave him the heebie-jeebies. Still, it was their best shot at overnight accommodations, according to the woman behind the repair shop's counter.

He lifted his hand to knock on the front door, but it swung open before his knuckles could hit wood, revealing a woman who was five foot nothing, maybe a hundred pounds soaking wet, and was wearing a necklace with a ginormous wooden cross hanging from it.

"You must be the sweet couple Maureen called me about," she said. "I'm Katy Kendrick and I have good news and bad news. Which do you want first?"

"The bad news," he and Lucy said at the same time.

"This is our busy season, with it being high school reunion time and all, so the only room I have available is our smallest one, and we've been using it for storage so it's pretty crowded with boxes."

Room? Just one? That wasn't great, but it definitely could be worse.

"Not a problem," he said. "We're just grateful to have a place to sleep tonight."

"Wonderful." Katy looked up at them with a sweet look on her face that made him think of puppies and unicorns. "And I just love your wedding ring." She ducked her head toward the sapphire ring on Lucy's left ring finger. "We run a good, Christian establishment, so it's such a relief you're a married couple. I'm not sure what we'd have done otherwise."

He froze. Solid. Like one of those people cursed in mythology. He would have thought he'd learned to bluff with all the poker he'd played, but no, he sucked at lying almost as much as he sucked at building decks.

"Three years and he still insists on carrying all of my luggage. Can you believe it?" Lucy said, smooth as a velvet Elvis painting as she slipped her arm through Katy's and led the woman into the house, leaving him with the three suitcases on the porch. "So, tell me about this adorable B and B."

The rest of what they were saying was lost as the two women walked down the hall while Frankie watched, a little awed and a whole lot scared. Not shrivel-his-balls scared, more of like that thrill of oh-my-God-yes that happened right before he walked into a burning building when everyone else was running out. Fallon was right, Lucy was not to be messed with, but not for why his sister thought. It wasn't that Lucy wouldn't survive—he might not.

That odd awareness buzzed through him as he picked up the bags and carried them inside to where the women were standing just inside a room at the top of the stairs.

"I know it'll be a tight fit," Katy said.

Lucy turned and gave him a look that managed to say "oh shit" and "keep your mouth shut" at the same time. Now that was a skill. He found out the reason for it a few seconds later when he peeked over the top of the women's heads. The room was small, but that wasn't the problem. It was the practically wall-to-wall boxes that left a narrow walkway from the door to the connected bathroom and around the double—yes double—bed in the middle of the room.

"Don't you worry about it," Lucy said to the other woman. "This is far from a crisis."

Frankie took another look at the bed, trying to figure out how he could fit his six-foot-six-inch frame on it, let alone how the two of them would fit on it without becoming a pretzel of intertwined limbs and some serious spooning. The mental image of having Lucy's soft curves against him had an immediate and very hardening effect.

Not a crisis? Unless the bathtub was big enough for his ass, that was exactly what this was.

Chapter Five

"Don't even touch it."

Frankie glanced down at the bill the waitress at the diner had dropped off along with his slice of pecan pie. And this is how it was going to go with Lucy. He shouldn't be surprised. The woman didn't have an easy bone in her body.

"Why not?" He toyed with the edge of the bill. He couldn't help it. He liked watching her get all fired up.

She narrowed her eyes and reached for the receipt. "I'm covering food and board during this trip."

"Are you saying that I'm a kept man?" he asked, not letting go when she tugged at the narrow piece of paper signed with hearts and ten digits that looked like a phone number.

Lucy snorted and tugged again. "That would indicate someone wanted to keep you."

Now that sliced like his fork through the delicious goo hiding underneath the pecans in his pie. It must have shown on his face, too, because Lucy's bright red lips drooped just a bit.

"Of course, your problem is too many people want you,

right?" she asked, her words without their usual bite, but she still managed to slide the bill from his grasp.

He picked up his fork and pushed it through the pie with enough force that his fork clunked against his plate. "I don't have a problem."

One of her eyebrows went up, then another. "Then what are you running away from?"

"Who said I'm running?" He shoved the pecan pie—his favorite of all the pies—into his maw and chewed it without tasting even a hint of gooey goodness.

She kept the bill in her left hand as she dug through her purse with the right, probably looking for exact change. "No one goes to a high school reunion unless forced or they've won the lottery, and you're driving a bazillion miles to go to a virtual stranger's high school reunion."

"You're not a stranger. I've known you for months." If by known, he meant that they'd been in the same room and spoken all of about twenty-five words to each other.

She dropped a quarter, three dimes, and two pennies on the black plastic check holder, along with several bills. "You've known of me. That doesn't mean we actually know each other."

There she was, Lucy Kavanagh, the woman who saw through all of the bullshit and called his sizable ass on it. She reminded him more of his sisters than any woman he'd ever dated, and that was just weird. Needing to clear that out of his thick skull, he opened his mouth.

"Okay," he said, not thinking about what was going to come next. "Give me the down and dirty, and I'll give you mine."

She cocked her head to one side and considered him as if he was one of her problem clients. This could go either way, really, but that was the fun in diving in headfirst without testing the water—as long as you didn't get knocked unconscious, it was an adrenaline rush. Mind seemingly made up, she zipped her purse closed and locked her focus on him in a way that had him squirming.

"I grew up in Antioch, Missouri, the only child of a retired underwear model, yes really, and the local doctor," she said. "I had a pet lizard named Scales McGoo growing up and took piano lessons every afternoon. To this day, I will shiv anyone who tries to make me play 'The Entertainer'—the ragtime song, not the old Billy Joel one. I graduated top of my class, was captain of the debate team, and went on to college a few hours away. I majored in public relations, held down a full-time job while going to classes, and didn't lose my virginity until a week before I graduated college, when I had an awkward one-night stand with the bartender at the local dive bar where all of us students went."

She took a quick pause to take a drink while he tried to process the rapid inflow of information.

"I love my job even though I want to kill my clients some days, I live in a gorgeous apartment with a beautiful view of the Harbor City bridge, and six months ago I went on what I thought was a date but turned out to be a sales pitch for an MLM scheme selling weight-loss supplements. Can you believe that the guy actually had a great return on the diner outlay when he pulled that crap because his so-called dates were so humiliated that they agreed to a subscription just to get away from him faster?"

She took a long sip of her Mountain Dew float through the bright green bendy straw and then continued.

"My favorite color is red. I'm a Virgo. I would give up my DSW rewards card for a week on a private island where I can lounge on the beach without anyone giving the fat girl in the bikini a second look. Oh, and I believe anyone who leaves voicemails instead of texting like a normal human being should be smacked." Another pull from her float. "Okay, your turn."

Fuck-nutters. It would take him a week to catch up to all of that.

"What did you do to the guy?" he asked.

Confusion put a *V* between her eyes. "The bartender?"

"No." Bartender? Who didn't have a bumping uglies with bartender in their history? "The supplement asshole."

She got an evil grin on her face that almost made him feel sorry for the douchebag. "I ordered two of everything on the menu and stuck him with the bill. I figured that probably came close to negating every penny he'd earned from his other dates. Now, stop stalling. I believe you promised me down and dirty."

Challenge accepted. Taking a deep breath, he plunged in.

"I'm the oldest of the seven Hartigan kids," he began. "That's how the entire neighborhood referred to us then and still calls us now. Dad's a firefighter and Mom's a teacher. I did okay in school and never wanted to do anything after graduation except the firefighter academy. I did *not* graduate top of my class, my brother Finn did." Him? He'd been in the highest 30 percent, but it had come so easy to him that he hadn't put that much effort into it. Top third was good enough. "I lost my virginity my freshman year in high school when I took Connie Wagner to her senior prom." She'd asked him, and things had just rolled forward from there. "I believe in driving fast, playing hard, and working until the job's done. I might be the head pot-stirrer in the family, but I'll smack the shine off of anyone who even tries to bust the chops of anyone in my family."

Not that he'd admit it out loud to anyone who shared his DNA, but there had been days when Fallon had been in high school that he'd picked her up from school just to give the shitheads giving her a hard time a message. All he'd had to do was look at the little punks and they'd just about pissed their pants. Of course, Fallon had just rolled her eyes at him when he'd turned the same look on her and informed her that he was not happy to have to come get her from school but Mom hadn't given him another choice.

"I don't really date so much as I hook up, and the night we had dinner at Marino's was when I found out that I'm the kind of guy someone bangs but they don't take home to meet the parents. That little punch to the ego got me thinking, and until I figure some things out, I am on the sexual bench, something I'd very much appreciate you not share with anyone else."

That last part he hadn't meant to say out loud, but Lucy had that effect on him. She made him work for it, and the unvarnished truth just sort of came out. Man, if she had that impact on him, he couldn't imagine what spilled out of her clients' mouths when she'd sat them down and gave them that look. It was the one she was giving him right now.

Leaning forward with a neutral accepting look on her face, her forearms on the table, she gave off the air of someone who wanted to hear all about a person's fuckups and would help fix them. "Sexual bench?"

"I'm temporarily celibate." Fuck. If only the diner waitress had given him a stapler to use on his mouth instead of her number, he wouldn't be stuck here watching Lucy have a non-reaction to his announcement, which was a reaction all in itself.

"How often do you usually have sex?"

"Few times a week." Sometimes the same woman. Usually not. It had been fun when he'd been young and dumb. Now? Things were different. He couldn't put his finger on the reason why, but it was.

"And how long has it been?" she asked, her voice as bland as if she'd been asking about the weather.

"A week." He shoved another bite of tasteless pecan pie

into his mouth.

Finally, her facade cracked and she grinned at him. "No wonder your forearms are so muscular. It must take a lot of wrist action to make up for all of that."

He almost choked on his pie. That was not what he was expecting from her. Did she ever say what he'd presumed? The answer to that was a big negative.

"What?" she asked and shrugged her shoulders. "I'm dateless, not orgasmless. There's a reason why sex toys are a fifteen-billion-dollar global industry."

He shook his head, since his ability to speak wasn't working at the moment. It wasn't the first time in his life that he'd been rendered speechless, but it didn't happen often—unless, of course, he was around one Lucy Kavanagh.

She nodded and went on. "The stats say twelve percent of women masturbate with a sex toy at least once a week, but come on, that's gotta be underreported. Amazon has something like sixty thousand adult items in stock, plus there's places like Babeland and Adam and Eve. And it's not just women. Twenty percent of men say they've used a vibe." She gave him that teasing grin of hers again. "Have you used a vibrator?"

He shook his head. Sure, he'd started the "down and dirty," but he'd never expected her to really take it there—if only verbally.

"Oh Frankie." She reached out and patted his hand as if he were some sweet, young, naive thing, which his male ego insisted he most definitely was not. "You are missing out."

"How do you know all this?" And what else did she know?

"I am a curious, sex positive, grown-ass woman," she said, her shoulders tensing and her chin going up as she withdrew her hand. "Or were you thinking it was just the old line about fat girls having to be more creative and enthusiastic in bed because it was the only way we got laid?"

She said the question in the same teasing tone she'd been using for the past five minutes, but there was no missing the line of tension wound through it. It had his muscles tightening in response as she watched him, waiting for his answer, no doubt having already answered it in her head.

"Why do you do that?" he asked.

"What?"

"Go straight for the worst thing someone could be thinking like you're launching a pre-emptive strike?"

"Experience." She stood, hooking the long strap of her purse over her shoulder, her hands shaking just the slightest bit. "Look, I'll let you in on a secret to survival for someone like me. If you prep yourself for the worst, you won't be disappointed, and if you own the insult before it can be uttered, you can't be hurt."

Frankie hadn't gotten this far in life without learning to read women, and what he got from Lucy's fuck-you stance was that sympathy was the last thing she wanted. No doubt she'd heard enough empty platitudes in her life.

Still, he couldn't help but ask, "Aren't you afraid of missing out on something because you don't give people a chance?"

"Haven't met anyone yet who was worth taking that chance on, so it looks like we're both celibate for the moment." She picked up her float from the table and held it out to him in a toast. "To no nookie."

It was not a toast he ever thought he'd be raising a glass to, but then again, he never thought he'd ever be cockblocking himself. So he clinked his glass against Lucy's, then watched as she wrapped her full lips around her straw and sucked, and he failed horribly at willing his dick not to react to the sight.

For the first time, he started questioning this whole "bench" plan.

• • •

Calling what was in their en suite bathroom back at the B and B a bathtub was an insult to bathtubs everywhere. It was just about the regular width of a tub, but only half the length of a normal one. There was no way either of them were going to make it a night sleeping in that thing—not without the mother of all shoehorns and probably a firefighter with the jaws of life to get them out the next morning.

"You're not gonna make me say it out loud, are you?" Frankie asked as he stood behind her in the bathroom doorway.

She let out a sigh and mentally girded herself up for the shitty reality of the situation. "No."

"That leaves the bed."

Whirling around, too desperate to find another solution to even think about exactly how close they were, she ended up with her nose almost touching Frankie's chest. She inhaled a few million lungfuls of his delicious scent as she tried to remember how to form words. Being this close to him just did that to her. It really, really wasn't fair that he smelled so good when he already looked like he did.

That way lay bad decisions. Decisions totally and completely endorsed by her girlie bits. "There has to be another option."

He took a step back, pivoting as he did so they both were staring out at the cramped and crowded room. Boxes marked Christmas, Halloween, Easter, St. Patrick's Day, and other holidays were literally stacked up to the ceiling along every available wall space. That left a narrow walkway between the boxes and the double bed that led to the bathroom and the door. Her suitcases and his duffle barely fit stacked on top of each other in the bathroom between the toilet and the pedestal sink. The floor could work, as long as Frankie laid on his side and could manage to shrink himself down to the size of a normal American man.

"If you can spot another option, then I'm good, but I'm practically walking sideways just to get through the room," he said.

"I can take the floor." There was no way she could make him take one for the team for that. As long as he didn't have to get up in the middle of the night and walk to the bathroom, they could make it work.

He snorted. "That's just dumb."

She turned to face him, daring him to repeat that. Lucy was a lot of things, but dumb wasn't one of them. "Excuse me?"

At least he had the decency to look contrite about his word choice. "Look, I don't have cooties, and I'm not going to jump your bones if we share the bed."

Of course not. Heat crept up her cheeks, and she desperately hoped he didn't notice. Her gaze dropped to her wide-width sandals, which she had to special order, and the jeans she ordered from a specialty shop and then had to get altered because it wasn't enough of a pain in the ass to find clothes and shoes that fit—the powers that be made it a more expensive process than for the so-called regular-sized women. There was no way in hell that she'd ever be Frankie Hartigan's type. It shouldn't hurt, and God knew she didn't want to be his type anyway, but the high school reunion already had her on edge, and the off-handed, no-duh rejection just sliced straight through her defenses.

"Fine," she said, forcing a light, "whatever" tone she sure wasn't feeling into her voice. "But I get the right side."

And that turned out to be the easy part of the night. Laying down in the dark next to Frankie was much harder. She'd never been more aware of how she laid down in a bed, where she put her arms, and the fact that her sleep shorts turned into wedgie shorts the moment she shifted even the smallest amount.

His breathing was soft and even. The man must have been born under a lucky star to be one of the people who crashed out as soon as their head hit the pillow. It was definitely another mark against him. She let out an annoyed—but quiet—huffy sigh.

"You are seriously fucking with my meditation," he said, his voice a grumbly low rumble in the dark.

Medita— Her eyes snapped open and she rolled onto her side to face him. "You meditate?"

He didn't move. His eyes stayed closed, which gave her the opportunity to check him out—something that was especially easy because he'd stripped down to boxers and a T-shirt and slept on top of the covers while she'd been trying to fall asleep under the sheet. The man's thighs were phenomenal. She'd never been much of a leg woman, but seeing the tree trunks Frankie stood on gave her a new appreciation. Was she a total dog for checking him out when all he was trying to do was *meditate*? Yeah. So what?

"Tell no one about this," he said. "And I won't drive off in the morning and leave you behind in this one-B-and-B town."

She rolled her eyes at him, which for some reason was harder when she was laying on her side, because there was no way he'd do that. Frankie was a lot of things, but a total asshole wasn't one of them.

"Tell me everything." Because finding out the Mr. Manly Man firefighter meditated was way better than staring at the ceiling and wondering if the B and B owner had fixed the leak that had caused the brown stain or if their upstairs neighbors were going to fall through and land on their laps— and thoughts like that were why it took her forever to fall asleep. It sure wasn't because of the man beside her.

Uh-huh, sure it's not.

"Fallon got me started on it to help me fall asleep," Frankie said. "Otherwise I'm up until three in the morning."

"Even during"—she paused dramatically—"sleepovers?"

He opened his eyes and turned over then, and one side of his mouth curled in a half smile. "Is that your delicate way of asking about what happens after I fuck?"

"Past tense," she said, her voice breathier than before, but she couldn't help it. Their faces were only inches apart, and they were in a bed, for the love of stilettos, which meant she'd gone from just being awake to being *aware* and awake. "Fucked."

His gaze dipped down to her mouth. "You're a real hard-ass."

Her pulse picked up, and a swarm of horny butterflies took off in her stomach. "Stop trying to avoid the question."

He glanced up from her mouth, and she got the full force of those blue eyes of his. It didn't matter they were in a darkened room, at that moment she would have sworn on a stack of designer shoes discovered in the 70-percent-off section of DSW that his eyes got darker as he stared at her. Then a lazy smile curled his lips—the kind that probably set girls' panties up in flames. Not hers, of course, because he was Frankie Hartigan and she was not his type, but *oh my*, it was something.

"Yes, I have trouble sleeping," he said, his voice lower, rougher than just being pulled out of his nightly meditation should have accomplished. "Even after I do dirty things to members of the opposite sex until we are both a sweaty, drained mess of satisfaction on the bed or couch or kitchen counter or hall floor or wherever it is that we got it on."

She pictured that and her core clenched, because who wouldn't have gotten the mother of all pornographic mental images after that?

"Usually men sack out after orgasm," she said, letting her brain go on autopilot because somehow she'd lost total control of this conversation. "They've linked it to the release of a cocktail of brain chemicals and the hormone prolactin that's released during ejaculation. So you should get at least a good post-sex nap. Of course, studies have also shown that men with lower prolactin can recover from sex faster for another go. Have you experienced that?"

He chuckled. "How do you know all this?"

"Everybody's got to have a hobby."

"And your hobby is sex?"

"Not really, but my dad's a sex therapist so I grew up in a house where it was treated as just another part of life instead of something dirty or weird," she said, her pulse still going a million miles an hour but her brain finally coming back from mental porno overload. "And yours seems to be trying to change the subject. Refractory time, how much do you need?"

"Not a lot," he said without hesitation.

Oh, momma. She filed that information away for later jilling off fantasy time. "Well, I'm not a doctor or a scientist, but you probably have lower prolactin, so that's why you're not going to Snoozeville as easily after knocking boots."

"Knocking boots?" One eyebrow went up. "What are you, a nineties R&B junkie too?"

"I am a woman of unbelievable depths."

"So how about you? Do you go straight out after sex?"

It was a fair question after how she'd deep-dived into him, but that didn't mean she was going to answer. "A lady never tells."

"Does that mean I'll have to find out for myself?" he asked with a raised eyebrow.

And the horny butterfly battalion went into overdrive. *Fucking A.* "N. O. Remember? You've temporarily renounced sex."

His eyes did that thing again that made her ovaries volunteer as tribute. "Right. No sex." He glanced down at her mouth and then back up. "Goodnight, Lucy."

He rolled over, leaving her to stare at his back as she reminded herself that "no sex" really meant "no sex with her." Still, after that little convo, there was no fucking way she wasn't going to be kept up all night by thoughts of sex with Frankie.

Tomorrow was going to be even rougher on no sleep.

Chapter Six

Lucy cracked her eyelids, the hint of a dream still hazy in her memory—something about the rain that had left her hot and yearning—and turned toward the left side of the bed. No one was ever going to confuse her with a morning person, but she wasn't so out of it when she woke up that she wasn't going to remember the hunka hottie she'd gone to sleep next to. Really, she'd have to be near death to forget how she'd spent way too much time listening to him breathe before she'd finally drifted off.

Sitting up, she took stock of their room. Frankie was gone, but the sound of the shower coming through the closed bathroom door gave away his location. That turned out to be a really good thing because—per usual—her boobs had escaped the confines of her tank top while she'd slept. Thank God she'd woken up with the sheet up to her chin, because looking like she was going for Mardi Gras beads was not how she wanted to start off her day when she'd be trapped in the car with Frankie for the next twelve hours. Thinking of which, she grabbed her phone and hit the contact number to

FaceTime Doctor Daddy. Yes, it was a weird nickname, but so was her dad.

Her dad picked up almost immediately. Unlike her, he was a complete morning person, as proven by the fact that he was dressed and ready for the day at five thirty Antioch time. "How's my favorite girl this morning?"

"I'm here." She tried to avoid looking at the little box with her picture in his because she hadn't done as good of a job as she'd thought taking off her mascara before bed.

"What happened?" he asked.

"We hit a bit of a snag. Frankie's car broke down, but it should be all fixed up this morning. We should be in tonight, but it will be really late tonight."

Her dad made a tut-tut noise. "Just drive safe."

"We will." A low growl sounded, and the tips of two pointed ears appeared at the bottom right hand of the screen. "Is that Gussie?"

She'd done her best to pretend the French Bulldog was going to a kennel for the four days she'd be home. It wasn't that Gussie was a mean dog or even a bad dog, it's just he had some nasty habits that made being around him awkward to say the least.

"Yes, it is," her dad said as he looked down at the dog who was almost completely out of camera range. "Look at my boy. He's such a good boy."

Her dad might think so, but the Frenchie wasn't a good boy, he was a total dog. Right on cue, she could see his pointy little ears bobbing forward and back. Lucy closed her eyes. She didn't have to see more than just the tips of the dog's ears to know what he was doing. Gussie was humping the stuffed reindeer a patient had given her dad that the dog had fallen in lust with at first sight.

"Dad, do you have to let him do that?" she asked, her cringe reaching all the way to her internal organs.

"It's better not to interrupt, Lucy. It's a totally natural thing."

Platitudes like that were what she'd grown up hearing, thanks to the fact that her dad was a sex therapist. That didn't change her mind at all. To make it even worse, two things happened right then.

One, Frankie walked out of the bathroom wearing only a white towel he was holding mostly together with one hand.

Two, her dad bobbled his phone, changing the angle so there was no missing Gussie as he...ahem...finished.

"What in the hell?" both men asked at the same time.

Lucy slammed the phone to her more than ample chest, glad her cleavage was good for more than storing cash and the occasional tube of chapstick.

"Why aren't you dressed?" she hissed at Frankie as if her dad hadn't already gotten an eyeful.

"Because I just came out of the shower," Frankie said, looking at her as if she'd just grown a second head. "Why are you watching dog porn?"

Her jaw dropped. What the hell? "It's not dog porn, you sicko. I'm talking to my dad."

"And *he's* watching dog porn?" Frankie asked.

"No." Oh God, how in the world did she explain this? "Gussie is just...enthusiastic."

"And he's got a schedule he likes to stick to." Her dad's muffled voice came from the phone's speaker crushed against her chest. "More importantly, why is your so-called only a friend naked in your room, young lady?"

"Dad," she said with an annoyed sigh as she moved the phone so she wasn't smothering it and angled it so her face took up the entire screen. "I'm a grown woman. I've seen plenty of naked guys before. This is not a big deal."

Frankie let out a grumble of a complaint. "If you'll excuse me, I'll just take my seriously damaged ego and go get dressed now." He grabbed his jeans off of a stack of boxes where he'd left them last night and went back into the bathroom.

Lucy let out a deep breath that sent her bangs flying upward. What she wouldn't do for a vat of coffee and a return to simpler times when phone calls were voice only.

"He's just a friend, Dad," she said. "We had to stop earlier than expected because the car's fuel pump went out, and it's a really small town with one B and B that only had one room available."

"Sorry for my reaction, it was just unexpected," her dad said as he adjusted his bifocals and got his doctor face on. "Sex is a natural and beautiful part of life, not something to be ashamed about. I remember with your mother—"

"Dad!" she exclaimed, whipping her head around to make sure the bathroom door was still closed, which it thankfully was.

"Fine. Well, I look forward to meeting"—he made air quotes—"your 'friend' when he has clothes on tonight."

She opened her mouth and shut it right away. There wasn't any point in trying to set her dad straight. He was a die-hard romantic and always had been. At least she'd inherited her mom's more cynical outlook on all things romance.

"I'll text when we're a half hour out," she said. "Don't wait for dinner, though."

He nodded. "I won't, but I will save you plenty of tofu."

Yay—not.

"Bye, Dad." She blew her father a kiss and hit end.

And to think waking up with one boob hanging out just might have been less embarrassing than that call.

・・・

The mechanic must have been an early riser, because by the time Frankie and Lucy had walked from the B and B—with him carrying all three pieces of luggage despite her protests—the fuel pump was fixed and Scarlett was parked in front of the shop, looking almost as good as the sight that had greeted him when he'd woken up this morning.

Rolling over and getting an eyeful of Lucy's pink-nipple-tipped tit that had spilled out of her top while she'd slept had been a little like getting new equipment at the firehouse—awesome and awe-inspiring. At first, he was rendered immobile by the sight. Lucy's boobs weren't just amazing. They were lickable, and squeezable, and nibble-able, and so-many-more-dirty-things-able. Seriously, a man—specifically him—could spend a lot of time displaying the proper amount of devotion to Lucy's tits. That wasn't going to happen, though, and she deserved better than to have him getting an eyeful. Raising the sheet to cover her was the right thing to do. There was no way he wanted her to wake up and realize what had happened. So he'd yanked up the sheet, gotten into the shower, and blasted himself with ice-cold water.

"I need you to let me cover this," Lucy said when they walked inside the mechanic's shop.

He set their bags down near the counter and rang the bell to let the mechanic know they were there. "That's not gonna happen."

"Why not?" She narrowed her eyes at him and crossed her arms.

"Because it was only a matter of time with that fuel pump." He would not check out her rack. *He would not.* His gaze went straight to her boobs. He quickly rubbed his eyes and refocused on the bell on the counter. "The fact that it happened on this drive means nothing."

"You do know that letting me pay for the repairs your car needed during a road trip I asked you on won't permanently shrivel your dick, right?"

The door connecting the garage bay to the office area

opened up, and a wiry man in blue coveralls strode in with a folder in his hand.

"So I'm paying," she said, plopping her giant purse onto the counter and unzipping it.

"Nope." He put his hand on hers, stopping her. "You're not."

They silently eye-fought while the mechanic opened up the folder and slid the printed invoice across, all the while looking at him and Lucy as if they were sixteen shades of crazy. Frankie smacked his hand on it before she could. She shot him a dirty look but didn't voice a protest. Sure, it was a small victory, but he was still relishing it an hour later when the small town wasn't even a speck in Scarlett's rearview mirror.

"So, what's our cover story?" he asked as they sped through Illinois, needing to break up the monotony of the scenery and the excitement of his fantasies, which were making driving uncomfortable.

She turned in her seat and flashed an ornery smile his way. "You wrecked your car checking out my ass while I was crossing the street."

Yep. Lucy would have her revenge for him paying for the fuel pump. Had he expected her to react any differently? That would be a big nope.

"How can you say something like that about Scarlett?" he asked as he smoothed his palm across the dashboard. "She can hear you."

Lucy rolled her eyes. "You are such a pain in the ass."

"Why don't we stick to the truth as much as possible," he said. "Makes things easier to remember."

"Good point." She pursed her full red lips together and looked out at the endless fields of corn or soybeans or wheat or whatever in the hell it was that people grew out here. "We met because your brother is dating one of my best friends."

"And you couldn't keep your eyes off me and decided to make it your mission in life to have you wicked way with me."

She shook her head and put her sunglasses back on, pivoting in her seat so she was looking out the front windshield. "No way. You pursued me. I turned you down four times before I finally agreed to go out with you—just for coffee."

A coffee date? Really? Women loved him, they didn't make him go the is-he-a-serial-killer route with an afternoon date. "I'm not sure my ego is going to survive this trip."

"Your ego is the only thing bigger than you are. It could use a little downsizing," she said with a chuckle. "Now back to it."

"Obviously our coffee date lingered into dinner after you realized that you had a thing for devastatingly hot firefighters." *Nice recovery, Hartigan.*

"More like you intrigued me with stories about your extensive My Little Pony collection."

It was a good thing the road in this part of the world was flat, straight, and uneventful because he had to turn his head, his mouth gaping open a bit, to stare at her. My Little Pony? Oh, she was getting mean now. He'd never thought of himself as the testosterone-filled caveman type, but yeah, that plus the coffee date was getting to him. He was about to open his mouth when he saw her lips twitch. The woman was busting his chops, and she was doing it on purpose. He clamped his piehole shut and turned back to the highway.

"Don't hate on Sparkle Nose."

She let out a laugh that filled the car. "That's not a real My Little Pony horse name."

"It should be, and I'm sticking to it." Oh yeah. She may have started this ridiculousness, but he was running with it. Never challenge a Hartigan. "Sparkle Nose is the best. I think I should get a temporary tattoo."

"I agreed to a second date because you made me laugh, and that was all she wrote."

Not what women usually said about him, but wasn't that a big part of why he was here in the middle of the farm belt right now? "How long have we been together?"

She tapped her red-tipped nails over the inner seam of her jeans, obviously thinking over the options. "Six months. Enough time to really get to know each other but not so much that we've gotten past the cow-eyes thing."

"Cow eyes?" he asked.

"You know when you get that goofy smile on your face when you see the person?" She must have realized he had no clue what she was talking about, because her eyes widened. "Oh my God. You haven't really crushed on someone before? With all of the women you've dated, you haven't gotten the stupid cow eyes because just looking at the person makes you all gooey and happy on the inside?"

Frankie didn't have to think about it. "No."

"So what, you just banged 'em and left 'em because they were totally interchangeable?" she asked, her astonished tone taking some of the sting out of her words.

"Not even close." He loved women, all of them. He'd just never been in love with one woman. Maybe it was a defect, a character flaw that had kept him on the field so much longer than almost anyone else in his orbit. He was the player who couldn't retire even though it was way past time.

"Explain it, then."

There wasn't any judgment in her words, just an honest, straightforward curiosity that had the words coming out of his mouth before he could consider whether he should.

"I like women. I like the women I've dated. I was attracted. They were attracted. Sure, the physical had something to do with it, but the why of the attraction was different for each one. It could be their laugh, their weird drink order, or the way they saw the world. So, we'd go out a couple times, have sex, and everyone was satisfied. No one got hurt. End of story."

Silence hung between them, filling the inside of the car like a third passenger.

About two miles later she broke it. "That was enough for you?"

"It was." The last word being the operative one.

"And now?"

He let out a sigh. "That's what I'm trying to figure out."

And he had miles and miles of road ahead of him to do that. Too bad that by the time they pulled off what seemed like the thousandth highway they'd been on that day and onto the darkened streets of small-town Antioch, he hadn't figured out a damn thing. After an extra-long day on the road, the only sound in the car was the GPS as it took him through the sleepy streets until he pulled into the driveway of a two-story blue house with white shutters and a wraparound porch, complete with flowers hanging in baskets and a swing. Light streamed from the house's windows, and Lucy's shoulders relaxed, a small smile that looked a lot like relief curling her lips.

"I should warn you about Gussie," Lucy said after they'd parked and he'd grabbed his duffle and her two suitcases from the trunk. "He's a little excitable."

Frankie was still trying to figure out who Gussie was—he'd thought her dad's name was Tom—when the front door opened. A blur of black flew out from inside, making a beeline straight for him. By the time he realized the streak was a dog, it was already leaping into the air and going straight for Frankie's balls.

Chapter Seven

There were many benefits to growing up as a Hartigan. One was the fast reflexes a person developed when they were one of seven kids. Dodging a dog who thought he was a missile was nothing compared to getting out of the way of a flying towel or book aimed at his oversized noggin by one of his siblings.

"Oh my God," Lucy yelled. "Gussie, no!"

In a move of incredible dexterity, she intercepted the dog, scooping him up in midair and pressing him to her chest. The dog, which Frankie could now identify as a French Bulldog, since it was no longer gunning for his family jewels, must have realized who held it because he let out the happiest of yaps and began licking her face.

Frankie was still watching her when a man who looked like he'd just walked out of The Dad Catalog hustled out of the front door and down the porch steps.

"I am so sorry about that," he said. "Gussie is convinced that we are in a state of siege, and he's actually a German Shepherd charged with protecting us against any and all strangers."

"Translation," Lucy said as she did her best to avoid Gussie's tongue. "He's a spoiled dog who's half evil."

The somewhat-evil dog in question was still slathering his attention on Lucy with total love and devotion, oblivious to the insult sent his way by the woman holding him. She wasn't helping her cause of getting the dog to stop at all, either, because she kept making kissy noises and talking baby talk to it in a low tone.

Lucy's dad held out his hand. "Tom Kavanagh. You must be the fake-but-still-walks-around-my-daughter-naked date."

Well, that was one way to put it. He dropped his duffel to the sidewalk so he could shake Tom's hand. He'd meant it to be a friendly gesture. Tom meant it to send a message, judging by the fact that the man was trying to break his knuckles with the strength of his grip.

"Dad," Lucy said, delivering a kiss to her father's cheek as she passed them, still carrying the besotted dog. "He was wearing a towel."

Tom's aw-shucks smile didn't waver, but his hold tightened. "You're right, Muffin. My mistake."

Then he turned, hooked his arm through Lucy's, and led her into the house. Shaking his head, Frankie picked up his duffle and followed them inside. He sat Lucy's two suitcases and his bag down in the large entryway. It was all warm woods and peaceful greens and browns in here, from the hard floor to the ceiling. Off to the left, a door opened into a room with a large desk, several diplomas on the wall, and a chair facing a love seat. Beyond the open door straight ahead of him, though, the house was a riot of bright colors and huge windows that looked out onto a vast, tree-filled backyard. It was almost like the spaces were inhabited by two different people.

"He's got the look," Lucy said, setting Gussie down on

the rug and stared adoringly up at her.

Her dad nodded. "That he does."

"What look?" he asked.

"The one where people are trying to mesh two very different decorating styles into one home," she said.

Okay, he was guilty there.

"The front is my dad's office. He's a sex therapist, and the warm, calming colors tend to help his clients relax."

"It's true. There have been studies about the power a muted green can have on the psyche," Tom said.

"And in here, nothing's changed since Mom left, so it pretty much looks exactly the way it did twenty years ago." She cut a knowing look at her dad. "Not that a psychologist would have anything to say about the meaning of that."

"What it says," Tom answered as he walked to the open kitchen and pulled a trio of mugs from the cupboard, "is that I hate to redecorate and your mom did a great job, so why mess with perfection?"

"You should go sit on your couch and answer that one," Lucy said and gave her dad a hug before turning on the stove to heat the kettle already on it. "Hot cocoa or chamomile?"

The question just hung out there while Frankie stood staring at the two of them, feeling a lot like he'd walked in on the middle of a conversation that those two had been having for years.

"Frankie," Lucy said, snagging his focus away from trying to unwind the dynamics between father and daughter. "Which one will help you relax more after the drive? Taking a mug out onto the back deck after a hell drive like we had is a family tradition."

"Hot chocolate," he said without hesitation, because chamomile tasted like a rookie firefighter's damp socks. Not that he'd actually *eaten* a rookie's socks, but that tea was exactly what he imagined them tasting like.

A few minutes later, he was out on the deck, standing next to Lucy and her dad and listening to the bugs chirp or whatever it was out there making that noise—he *was* from the city, even if Waterbury wasn't Harbor City—and drinking hot chocolate that hadn't been made from an instant packet, and wondering how in the hell he'd been missing out on this fucking fantastic drink for his entire life.

"It's a family secret," Lucy said as her dad gave him the evil eye over the top of his mug of…wait for it…chamomile.

"What is?" he asked, wondering if he could get away with licking the inside of his mug just to get every last drop.

"The hot chocolate. It's my mom's recipe."

There was something in her voice when she said it that made him want to reach out and…what? Hug her? He didn't have the right. They weren't friends, despite the strange circumstances they were in. They weren't lovers. They inhabited some weird space adjacent to all of that, and it didn't have a name or solid boundaries. So he kept his hands to himself.

They sat in silence for a while—or as close to it as you could get while all of the insects in the entire world, at least that's what it sounded like to his city ears, chirped and buzzed—before collecting their mugs.

"I'm sure you two are tired from that drive today," he said. "Muffin, your room is all ready for you." He turned to Frankie. "I've got you set up in the room above the garage."

"Dad, that's not even in the house," she said with a gasp, her big eyes going round. "We can't put a guest out there."

The older man shrugged. "I turned the spare room into a workroom for my fishing lures. There's magnifiers, threads, and bobs everywhere. No one wants to sleep there."

Lucy looked like she was about to argue, but Frankie took her hand, trying—and failing—to ignore the spark of attraction that sizzled up his arm when he did. Where did that come from?

"It's okay," Frankie said with a smile, ignoring the pang of disappointment. "That gives you some privacy to visit. It's not like you see each other all that often."

One of her eyebrows went skyward, but she didn't argue. No doubt she saw right through his bullshit, because she always seemed to.

"Dad, we're not having sex," she said. "In fact, Frankie is temporarily celibate because he thinks his man-whore ways have limited his ability to form relationships."

If the bugs or frogs or whatever they were in the woods were still chirping, he didn't hear it anymore over the rush of blood in his ears. "I never said that was the reason."

"You didn't have to. But it's true, isn't it?"

Fucking A. This woman. "Maybe."

"Now, that is interesting," Tom said, stopping outside the French doors and, for the first time since they'd arrived, not looking at Frankie as if he were the barbarian at the gates. "I'd love to talk to you more about this. Are you an early riser? I could fit you in before my first morning appointment tomorrow."

Oh yeah, because that's what his Irish ass was about to do—talk about his feelings about sex. Somewhere, one of his ancestors rolled over in his Catholic grave at even the idea of it. "I appreciate the offer, but I think I'll be fine after a few weeks on the bench to get my head straight."

"You should take him up on it." Lucy hooked her arm in his and looked up at him as if she hadn't just slid a shiv right into his tender parts. "He's considered a national treasure in the sex therapy community."

"I'm sure he is, but all the same…" He let the rest of the sentence drop, wishing like hell he was already in the room above the garage.

"Don't pester him, Lucy. He'll find his own way," Tom

said, his expression taking on some of its papa bear effects again as his gaze dropped to where she was touching Frankie. "And in the meantime, I'll help you carry your bags to your room. Frankie, I'll show you the door to get to the garage apartment on the way."

Lucy didn't look like she was ready to let it drop, but after a second she did and they followed her dad inside.

"This isn't over," she whispered under her breath before slipping her arm out of his, picking up her suitcase and heading off down the hall.

• • •

Not for the first time in her life, Lucy cursed her big mouth, which was almost as big as her ass and twice as troublesome. However, this time she was determined to keep it shut for at least as long as it took her to get from her old room to the garage apartment.

She'd considered apologizing to Frankie via text, but it seemed kinda cold. Plus, she'd have a much better chance of getting him to actually talk to her dad if she said she was sorry in person. It was a helluva lot harder to ignore her when she was standing right there as opposed to a text.

She just had to treat this as if she was talking to one of her clients so he'd understand the brilliance of her plan, and not as if she was talking to a guy who made her panties damp every time he looked at her, despite the fact that he'd probably seen more panties than she owned. Nope. That wasn't factoring into her decision to tiptoe past her dad's room as if she was fifteen again and go talk to a cute boy. Not. At. All.

By the time she climbed the stairs to the guest suite above the garage, she had a plan of attack. Really, this was for his own good. If there was anything a child of a therapist knew, it was the value of figuring out the reason why behind a behavior. Frankie just needed to do a deep dive and figure his shit out. Helping him do that would be a much better form of repayment than gas money for coming with her to the reunion.

Frankie answered on the second quick tap on the door. He was in a pair of loose shorts that hung low on his hips and nothing else. She shouldn't look, but his brawny form filled the door and she didn't have any other place to look. So she perused. She took in. Okay, she totally gawked—who wouldn't when presented with that much hotness? Part of her knew she should look away. After all, the man had given up more than a week of his life to come to her reunion. He deserved some appreciation of the non-eye-fucking kind. Instead of eyeballing him like he was as gorgeous as the perfect pair of heels that were cute and comfortable, she should be keeping her eyes on his face and not his broad shoulders, reddish gold hair dusting his pecs, or the way his shorts left very little to the imagination about how very *not* little he was.

She was a horrible person, she knew that. However, she also knew that Frankie's happy trail matched his ginger hair. That item of information would get stored away for future jilling off material.

See? Horrible person who should know better and is looking anyway!

"Everything okay?" he asked.

"No." She steeled herself for the words she had to say. "I need to apologize, and I hate apologizing."

His mouth wavered as if he was trying to stop a smirk from emerging. "I'm shocked. You seem like the kind of person who just loves saying she was wrong."

From anyone else, the sarcasm would have scratched its way under her skin and down to her don't-fuck-with-me marrow. But from Frankie Hartigan? The man couldn't even do mockery without turning it into flirting. It would be annoying if she didn't enjoy it so much. It was nice being the object of someone's "A" flirt game. It wasn't that men didn't hit on her. They did. It was the type of men who made a move on her that made her dating prospects so poor. Suffice it to say that fat fetishists and guys who thought she didn't have options and would go for their still-living-in-their-mom's-basement asses tended to clog up her dating app inbox. But guys like Frankie? This was just FWC: flirting without consequences—especially since the man was on a no-sex diet.

"You're not going to make this easy, are you?"

"No." He grinned at her. "I'm enjoying it too much."

Since sliding through the doorway while he blocked 90 percent of it wasn't an option, she put one hand on her hip and gave him her best don't-waste-my-time glare. It usually made her clients—even the fuming mad ones—step out of her way. Frankie just folded his arms across the wide expanse of his chest, totally unperturbed. Of course he did.

"May I come in?" she asked, resisting the urge the play with the hem of her shirt to give her hands something to do. "We need to talk."

"That sounds serious." He took a pivot step, giving her enough space to pass by him and walk into the room.

To distract herself from taking an extra sniff—and yes, she was still horrible, and no, there wasn't anyone who could judge her more harshly than she was giving herself the side-eye at that moment—she looked around the room. It might be above the garage, but it was a great space, the back wall composed of windows overlooking the woods that in a few miles became a part of the Dogwood Canyon Nature Park.

The view outside was almost as good as the one inside the room.

Not that she was looking, because that was a very not-good idea. She liked sex as much as any other woman—maybe a little more compared to some folks—but making a run at someone like Frankie Hartigan wasn't smart. Taking a few steps away from him meant getting closer to the bed, but it was better than standing next to him and having her pheromones going crazy.

"It's about you talking to my dad," she said, stopping a few steps shy of the bed. "I really think he could help. You've got to admit, you've gone from one extreme to the other."

He snorted. "No offense, but I'm not talking about my sex life with your dad."

What was it about sex therapists that freaked people out so much? It wasn't like 95 percent of the population was allergic to orgasms and the kind of intimate connection that came from sex.

"Why not?" she asked. "It's his job, and he could help."

"I'm pretty sure I can do that on my own," he said and looked purposefully at the open door. "But thanks for stopping by."

There was no missing that don't-let-the-door-hit-you-in-the-ass-on-the-way-out dismissal, but she wasn't giving in that easy. If she was that kind of woman, she wouldn't have been able to get Harbor City's most hated hockey player to agree to doing a series of visits to sick kids at St. Vincent's Hospital. There was definitely a reason why Zach Blackburn called her B.B. after he finally agreed to her plan to start rehabbing his image so the team wouldn't kick his tattooed self to the curb come free agency time. They both knew B.B. stood for Ball Buster. She didn't give a shit. She embraced the nickname a lot more than the one everyone had called her since she was a kid—Muffin Top. Her dad hadn't meant it to be mean and had given it to her when she was just a baby. He just had no clue what it was like to be a fat woman in society's eyes—which brought everything back to the whole reason why the redwood of hotness known as Frankie Hartigan was standing in front of her.

"Fine, we can talk about the plan of attack for this week." She made her way farther into the room, moving toward that wall of windows while stating her point that she wasn't going until she was good and ready without saying a word about it. "We need to walk a fine line between being believable and shutting up everyone's mouths."

He crossed his arms over his bare chest and raised an eyebrow. "What do you mean by believable?"

What did he think she meant? That people were going to take a look at her and then at him and then figure something was rotten in Antioch—and they'd be right. If going to her reunion alone was going to be bad, going to her reunion with Frankie and having everyone realize it was a farce would be about a million times worse. Humiliation was very much not her thing.

Her shoulders sank, but she refused to look away from him. She'd own it and take its power, just like she had with her size. "The last thing I want is for people to realize the truth."

"The truth?" The vein in his jaw twitched as he stalked toward where she stood with her back to the windows, annoyance as plain on his face as the dusting of pale freckles across his shoulders. "That I'm just arm candy?"

It came out more like a curse than a question—as if it was the last thing he wanted to be, which it probably was. Who wanted to be *her* arm candy? Definitely not someone like him.

She didn't mean to take a step back, but there was a dangerous heat swirling in his eyes, turning them a darker shade of blue that kicked her heart rate up and turned her mouth dry. "That this is a pity date."

His gaze dipped to her mouth and then lower to her sleep tank top and shorts, which more than covered everything plus some—and had cats on them—but her PJs seemed to shrink under the intensity of his focus. "I wouldn't call it that."

Oh, she knew what he was doing. The man flirted as easily as he laced up his shoes, but that didn't mean she was going to fall for it. "Look, I'm a big girl, I can take calling things as they are. I'm not ashamed of my size. I *would*, however, be very embarrassed if it got out I had to bring a fake date to anything, much less my high school reunion, okay?"

Taking another step nearer, he stood so close that while they weren't touching, they might as well have been. Her heart rammed against her ribs, and a riot of excited butterflies zoomed around her belly. She could just picture how she must look to him—a flushed plus-sized woman in cat pajamas. Her inner sarcasm bitch declared it totally sexy.

One side of his mouth curled up, and he raised his one arm, putting his palm against the glass behind her. Then, with deliberate slowness, he did the same with the other arm, effectively bracketing her with his sinewy arms. His pecs were at eye level, and that was very not fair, so she looked up and up some more to his face. The man was too tall, too big, too overwhelming for his own good. It wasn't that she was trapped. Far from it. Her mutinous body didn't want to move an inch. It wanted more. It wanted to feel him pressed against her, his mouth molded to hers, and his hands everywhere.

"Maybe you noticed," he said, his voice holding none of the humor his one-sided smile denoted. Instead it was hot, hungry, needy in a way she could identify with all too well. "I'm not exactly small, either, and a pity date this is not."

The rough edge in his words did floppy-floppy things to her insides as she wet her lips in anticipation. No! Not anticipation. Because they were dry. That was all. "What is it, then?"

His jaw tightened, and his gaze jerked away from her mouth. "A lesson in frustration."

She flinched. It couldn't be helped. Sure, she wasn't his type, he wasn't hers, and he was on a sex suspension, but still—ow. "That bad, huh?"

"You have no idea." He shook his head as if he was trying to grasp it himself and let his arms drop before taking a step back.

Annoyance—and to be honest, a little embarrassment at how badly she wanted that kiss he obviously had no interest in giving—snapped her spine straight. Well fuck you very much, Frankie Hartigan. So she wasn't like her underwear model mom or the other women she'd seen him cuddled up with on every day that ended in Y. Too fucking bad.

"Well, I'm sorry it's so difficult for you," she said, not giving two shits about the peevish tone of her voice. "But this whole thing was *your* idea."

The bastard didn't even look the least bit sheepish about being such an ass. "I don't know what I'm doing right now, and being with you isn't making it easier."

Boo-fucking-hoo, Mr. Big Boy Firefighter. "This trip *was* your idea."

"I'm not talking about the damn trip." He ground out the words. "I'm talking about the fact that I'm here with you"—he waved a hand toward her, gesturing at her tank top and sleep shorts—"like this."

Like this?

Like.

This.

She glanced down at her pajamas. They weren't her normal late-night-with-a-guy nightie and panties, but why in the hell would they be? She was in her dad's house with a guy who she didn't have even a sliver of a chance with even if she wanted to—which she didn't.

"Are you fucking kidding me?" she asked, her defensiveness getting in the driver's seat and flooring the gas. "These are my I-don't-give-a-damn jammies. They aren't about you. Not everything is about you, Frankie Hartigan.

Just because you're having pussy withdrawal and you don't like me in cat-themed PJ's or whatever—" She took a deep, calming breath. It wasn't his fault he wasn't attracted to her. She sighed. "I am who I am, Frankie. That's not going to change."

Frankie's expression gave off the impression that she was talking a different language—one he'd never even heard of before. Her foot slid off the metaphorical gas pedal. She searched his face for any hint of disgust or censure and found none. The buzzing in her ears quieted, and the heat that had rushed up from her toes cooled until it was just a pool of clammy regret in the center of her palms. She'd totally overreacted, brought her own baggage and had laid it at his Frankie's feet. Here was the guy who'd given up a week of his life to be her fake date for her high school reunion. And she was pissed because he hadn't wanted to kiss her as much as she wanted him.

Shit.

Her friend Gina was right. She really needed a filter.

"I'm sorry. For everything," she said quickly.

Slipping around him before she could say anything else stupid, she hustled out of his room, down the stairs, through the small hall that connected the guest suite to the kitchen and to her own childhood bedroom, trying her best to outrun the embarrassment burning her cheeks.

It didn't work. It never did.

Of course, she might get lucky and the house could get hit with a meteor tonight. Or aliens could invade. Or, you know, Godzilla could attack. All were preferable at the moment to the sun rising on a new day that would involve sitting across the kitchen table from Frankie Hartigan.

Chapter Eight

The next morning, Frankie set his bowl of cereal on the small kitchen table and sat down across from Tom. Lucy was nowhere to be found. She'd come into his room last night in that form-fitting tank top and short shorts, and his brain had taken a distant second place to his cock. All he'd wanted to do was *everything*, and he couldn't. The fact that he'd reacted that way to Lucy was just one more mark against his ability to think about a woman without his dick getting involved.

She'd made some ludicrous comments about him not liking cats or something. Honestly, it'd been hard to follow what she was saying over the sound of his heartbeat hammering in his chest. He'd focused all his attention on willing his little head not to make his attraction to her known. It wasn't like she'd given him any signals she was into him, either. Jesus. *Get a grip, Frankie.*

Before Shannon had dropped her little truth bomb, if she'd given him the slightest green light, he would have just fucked Lucy six ways to Sunday, gotten her out of his system, and moved on. Now, instead of waking up with a sexy woman and breakfast in bed, he was pouring almond milk into his organic, multigrain cornflakes. His dick *and* his stomach were very disappointed with the entire situation.

"What is it that you do in Waterbury, Frankie?" Tom asked as he took a drink from a brownish-green smoothie in a plastic cup with a picture of a French Bulldog in sunglasses on it. "Do you work at Lucy's firm?"

"No, I'm a firefighter." He took a bite of the cereal. Okay, it wasn't dusted in sugar and floating in whole milk, but it wasn't cardboard, either. He could live with that.

Tom steepled his fingers and tapped them against the dimple in his chin. "And how did you choose that line of work?"

"It's a family tradition." He shrugged and took another bite. "Every Hartigan male, with the exception of my brother Ford, has joined the fire department for three generations."

The only noise in the kitchen was the sound of the cereal being crunched up in Frankie's mouth and the stuttering slurp of Tom getting up the last of his smoothie through the extra wide straw. Weird? Not at all. Frankie had breakfast with the dads of all the women he almost kissed and then spent the night fantasizing about. Didn't everyone? Wow. That much mental sarcasm was usually Fallon's territory. He needed to shovel the organic flakes down before he got hangry and things really went off the rails.

"Ahh," Tom said in that way that just screamed, *lay on my couch and tell me about your mother.* "You're not a risk-taker."

Frankie almost choked on his cornflakes. What in the hell? "I run into burning buildings for a living, I wouldn't say that."

"I'm talking emotional risks," Tom said. "That would explain the sexual situation you find yourself in."

And this had just gone from weird to totally bizarre. He

was *not* afraid of risks and he was *not* having this conversation with Lucy's dad at the breakfast table. He *was not* afraid of women or relationships. He loved women and knew he wasn't relationship material. That's the part Shannon had gotten right. He was his father's son—the part of his dad no one knew but him.

Still, Tom's statement sliced through him like an ice pick between the ribs. His throat closed up, his gut churned, and his pulse pounded in his ears like it hadn't since that day when he'd walked in on— No. He wasn't going to go there. Not now. Not ever again.

"No offense," he managed to get out between clenched teeth. "But I'm just here for the cornflakes, not therapy."

"You're right." Tom pushed his chair back and got up. "Sorry. Occupational hazard." He picked up his cup and took it to the sink, where he rinsed it out and put it in the dishwasher while saying, "Never mind my questions. I'm sure you'll work it all out on your own."

He would. He was a man of action and he'd taken it, cutting himself off and getting himself out of temptation's way. At least that had been his plan—right up until Lucy showed up at his house in that ridiculous electric car and had given him shit about Scarlett. What did it say about him that he'd gotten turned on not just by what he could imagine that sweet mouth of hers doing to him, but also by what she was actually saying? It said that even this brief conversation with Dr. Sex Therapist had fucked with his head.

He needed to get out of here.

The only reason he was even sitting down for breakfast was to get a peek at the woman who'd completely screwed any chance he'd had of getting eight hours of sleep last night.

"Lucy set this up, didn't she?" The woman was trouble— and not in the way the women he wanted to get up close and naked with usually were. Nope. She was trouble in the maneuvering-him-around-like-a-pawn-on-a-chessboard way. "That's why she's not here."

Tom didn't say anything, but his gaze shifted to the kitchen doorway. Frankie followed the older man's lead. Lucy stood there, her hair pulled back into a high ponytail that she must have worn to sleep because it was beyond jacked up, with chunks of hair that looked like hair bubbles popping up around her head.

"What did I set up?" she asked, her voice still thick with sleep.

She was wearing that damned tank top and pair of shorts that should not look sexual at all, but on her, with the massive rack she had? Yeah, he was officially up now.

Shifting in his chair, Frankie dropped his gaze back to his cereal.

"Nothing, Muffin," Tom said, brushing over the question she'd walked in on as he made his way to the coffeepot and poured some of the brew into a muffin-shaped mug. "How did you sleep?"

"Like the dead," she said, seemingly looking everywhere but at Frankie.

Yeah, Frankie could definitely not claim a good night's sleep. He'd spent most of the night thinking about Lucy. At three in the morning, he decided that he didn't give a shit how much he was proving the point that all he did was follow his dick and jerked off while thinking about the sway of her heavy tits under the tank top she was still wearing.

And when in the hell had he turned into the kind of asshole who was overthinking everything? He liked things simple. House burning down? Put the fire out. Hot chick giving him the look? Bang her in the bar bathroom.

His life had been simple, right up until it wasn't. Fucking A.

This is what happened when there was an attempted

therapy intervention first thing in the morning.

Lucy, studiously ignoring the fact that he was sitting at the table, shuffled into the kitchen with Gussie trotting in on her heels, his eyes bugging out and his tongue hanging from his mouth. When she didn't drop any flakes on the floor as she poured her cereal, the dog gave a little huff of disappointment and made a beeline for the doggie bowls by the back door.

"So, what's the plan?" he asked, unable to look away from her.

Who'd known he was such a glutton for punishment? First the no sex—and wow had he spent a lot of time looking for loopholes in that little pledge he'd made to himself—and now spending almost every moment of the next week with a woman who could make him harder than the pole at the firehouse. Shit. He really did not need to make that comparison right now, because all he could picture was Lucy sliding down that pole in a Marilyn Monroe–type dress that would fly straight out. Good God. He was turning into an upskirt perv. Maybe he should take Tom up on his offer to talk this shit out before he joined some online I'm-a-loser chat group.

Of course, staring at Lucy right now wasn't helping. She kept her back to him, which gave him the perfect view of how her ass looked in those sleep shorts. Like the view from the front, it was definitely more than a handful and it made his mouth go dry with wanting.

Oblivious to the direction of his thoughts, Lucy answered the question he'd forgotten he'd asked as she poured almond milk into her bowl. "We have to get down to the high school and pick up our reunion packets."

The sheer level of totally not thrilled in her tone broke through the lusty haze of his thoughts. "You make it sound like we're going to our own hanging."

She turned to face the kitchen table, still not looking

directly at him, gripping her cereal bowl hard enough that her knuckles were white. "That's because I've met Constance Harmon."

"Do I want to know?" Rhetorical question because he hated that Constance bitch on pure loyalty grounds.

Lucy's gaze flicked over to him and then back down. "You'll find out soon enough. I don't want to spoil the surprise."

Then, with only the slightest of pauses by the empty chair at the table, she hustled out of the kitchen with her bowl of cornflakes.

"Now, that was interesting," Tom said from his spot by the dishwasher as he stared at the empty space in the doorway where Lucy had been only moments before.

Yeah, that was one way of putting it. Frankie was suddenly very anxious to meet this Constance chick. With four sisters, he'd learned a long time ago how to fight like a girl, and he was more than ready to rack up some points in Lucy's honor.

• • •

Lucy set her now-empty cereal bowl on the desk and looked around at the untouched memorial that was her childhood bedroom. Everything was exactly as it was the day she'd left after college graduation for Waterbury—including the debate trophies lining the top of her headboard. Yeah, some people had notches in theirs, she had little metal gavels. A set of quick raps at the door followed by the insistent scraping of doggie nails against the wood tugged the corners of her mouth upward. When she opened the door, Gussie burst inside, vaulted up, and landed in the middle of her bed. The little guy went straight to work, messing up the made bed to create a little nest of pillows and fluffed-up comforter.

Her dad, though, stopped just inside the doorway.

"Something you want to tell me, Muffin?"

Besides to stop calling her that? "Not really, Dad."

Nodding, he walked into the room and picked up her empty bowl. He didn't have to do that, but she'd given up years ago on telling him that she could, would, and did pick up after herself. The man couldn't stand having anything out of place.

"You know," he said, looking down at the empty bowl. "It would be a nice gesture for Frankie if you put on a robe before coming down to the kitchen tomorrow morning."

What was everyone's problem with her cat pajamas? "Why's that?"

"Frankie seemed a little distracted by your outfit." Her dad looked up from the bowl and gave her a small, understanding smile. "I know it might seem silly to us, but he's trying to work some things out that obviously he's buried deep for quite some time."

"And how does my being in my comfy PJ's at breakfast play into that?"

"Because I don't think he was seeing them that way."

"Trust me. We talked about my PJ's last night. He's definitely not into them *or* me. You can rest easy, Dad. No one is going to be hitting on your little girl on your watch." She winked at him.

"Well, he is making some major changes in his life, and whether you realize it or not, he does very much see you that way. He alone is responsible for his behavior, and what you choose to wear is about you and not him, but I don't think you're immune to him, either. You both are playing with fire if your plan is to keep things strictly platonic."

As if that was even an option. She was Lucy Kavanagh, controller of images and righter of publicity gone bad. However, she was not a leggy goddess with an impossibly tiny waist and shampoo-commercial hair. While she was pretty damn happy with herself for the most part, she wasn't the kind of woman who caught Frankie Hartigan's eye—nor did she want to be one of a numberless horde.

"Dad, I love you," she said with a chuckle. "But I think this is a case of when you're a sex therapist you see everything as sexual in nature."

Her dad gave her *that* look, she knew the one. It meant a seriously awkward and bad dad joke was incoming.

"Sooo," he said, drawing the one-syllable word out, "you're saying I have a sex hammer that makes everything look like a nail."

She squeezed her eyes closed in her best effort to block that mental image and let out a groan. Damn. She really should have seen that one coming. "Oh my God, Dad. Why do you *say* things like that?"

"Because no matter how old you get, making you embarrass-laugh is one of my jobs as a dad."

"Good to know." And weirdly enough, comforting to hear. "But for the record, you're wrong. Frankie doesn't see me like that."

He put his therapist face back on, a deep *V* wrinkle forming between his eyes. "An interesting assumption on your part."

A twinge of oh-shit made her lungs tight. "What does that mean?"

He tapped his fingertips against her empty cereal bowl and lifted an eyebrow. "That for as much as you like to give me a hard time for never changing things…" He paused, giving her one of those piercing looks that he normally reserved for his clients or Gussie. "You don't seem to like to change things, either—especially not your thinking. And the result is you leading with insults and defensiveness instead of an open mind. You gotta take a risk someday, or you'll ultimately just prove your worst assumptions right."

That hit uncomfortably close to the dark place where she shoved her self-doubts and questions, but she just double-locked the door because her dad was wrong. She knew what she was about, that's all. She knew who she was, what she wanted, and what she definitely didn't need in her life. "Isn't there a rule against analyzing your own kid?"

"Just making an observation, Muffin." He gave her a quick peck on the cheek and headed for the door, followed by Gussie who'd jumped down from the bed at the first sign of her dad leaving her bedroom. "I'll let you get ready. Remember to have fun today."

She was going to do her best to try. All she had to do was avoid Constance Harmon as much as possible and not think too hard about what her dad said, because she was most definitely not playing with fire when it came to Frankie Hartigan. That was just crazy talk.

Her phone buzzed on the bedside table just as she started getting dressed.

Gina: *Are you dead?*

Lucy: *Not yet.*

Fallon: *Is Frankie dead yet?*

Lucy: *No.*

Tess: *How's cutie boy Gussie?*

Gina: *The dog? Really? That's what you're going with when she's halfway across the country with a hot firefighter????*

Tess: *He does look so cute in pics.*

Fallon: *Gross. That firefighter is my brother.*

> Gina: *We'll let you know when it's safe to rejoin the group text, then.*

> Lucy: *Gussie is fine.*

She shared a pic of the dog she'd taken before her ill-planned trip to Frankie's room last night. She'd barely hit send before the hearts started exploding on her screen and the text alert notifications told her that all of her girls had hearted the photo.

She pulled on her shirt, a cute green V-neck T-shirt that was about as soft as soft got, and her skirt while the three little dots announcing someone was typing appeared and disappeared on her screen. No doubt her girls were having a side discussion about the whole reunion trip with Frankie right now. God help her if they ever got in a room with her dad. There'd be no resisting that interfering foursome. Her phone buzzed.

> Gina: *Any news to share or juicy gossip?*

Yep. They were definitely having a sidebar conversation.

> Lucy: *We just got here last night. Had some car trouble.*

> Gina: *Is that what the kids are calling it these days?*

> Fallon: *Again. My BROTHER.*

> Tess: *Who said it was okay for you to read again? :)*

> Lucy: *So funny. Let's remember who we're talking about.*

> Gina: *Exactly. We're talking about you, ya badass.*

Despite the fact that they were just giving her shit

and looking for dirt—that most definitely was not going to appear—Lucy couldn't help but giggle at their texting shenanigans. Delusional or not, hearing from her girls was exactly what she needed to gird up for the day ahead.

Lucy: *Well this badass has to go pick up her reunion registration packet.*

Tess: *Go forth and be awesome!*

Lucy: *xoxo*

Okay, so she was grinning like a fool by the time she swiped on the extra coat of red lipstick that should just be called Confidence Booster and walked out of her room. Badass, huh? Yeah, she just had to remember that she was a different woman than the one who'd left Antioch.

But she couldn't help wondering how everyone was going to react when they saw Frankie on her arm. Probably not the way she imagined.

Chapter Nine

Wolfie, the Antioch High School mascot, looked down at Lucy with its perennially off kilter, possibly drunk, definitely homicidal toothy grin from the wall behind the bleachers in the gymnasium. Somehow it seemed appropriate that the place where she'd gotten tormented the most during her formative years was watched over by the painting of a deranged gray wolf.

"Oh my God! Muffin Kavanagh, is that you? And look at you in that skirt! I could never wear that retro style like you do."

Anyone not well versed in passive-aggressive grenades may not have heard the pin being pulled and would have just been left wondering why their internal organs had exploded after the sugary insult. Judging by the almost flirty look on Frankie's face as he gave Constance Harmon the slow up-and-down, he'd missed it. Not a surprise. He was a dude, after all. And if the insult wasn't delivered via Daisy Cutter, then it didn't register.

That was the reason for the annoyance squeezing her

lungs, because it sure wasn't the fact that Sir Flirts A Lot was giving Constance the hey-baby look. Sure, he was just *pretending* he was Lucy's date, but that didn't mean he had to do a shitty job of it. She was, after all, standing right here.

And to think her dad had stopped in her room to deliver that playing-with-fire warning.

"You are so right, it takes a woman with some luscious curves to do it justice," Frankie said as he curled his left arm around Lucy's waist and offered his right to shake Constance's hand. "I'm Frankie Hartigan. You must be the Constance I've heard so much about."

Her heart started hammering in her chest as she realized Frankie Hartigan had just stuck up for her. She would *not* swoon at his feet.

Constance blinked for a few seconds, still not sure if she'd been insulted or not—she had—and shook Frankie's hand. "All of it good, I hope."

"It was all something," he said, letting go of the other woman's hand.

It hung in the air for a second, and Lucy could practically see the dots being connected in Constance's head. Yep. She definitely realized she'd just been insulted. Twice. Lucy managed to cover her laugh with a cough but couldn't stop herself from smiling.

Well played, Frankie Hartigan.

The other woman turned her attention back to Lucy. All of the fake warmth was gone from her bright blue eyes. Yeah, that was the Constance Lucy knew and loathed.

"We're just here for our welcome packet," she managed to get out as Frankie pulled her closer so she fit against his side as if she was meant to.

She knew she wasn't, but that didn't stop her body from semi-melting into his. She was a big woman and Frankie was a big guy, but he didn't overshadow her size or make her feel like some stereotypical tiny little waif of a thing—really, why was that the go-to for societal expectations of what a woman should want? However, it was pretty damn hot to curl up against someone who looked like he could take all of her and enjoy every last inch of her curves.

"Of course, let me get that packet for you." Constance flipped through several envelopes before pulling one out. "Here we are." She handed it to Lucy. "Now, there's everything you need in there, such as the reunion picnic time, and some things I'm sure you don't, such as the reunion decathlon challenge."

Lucy's amusement died a cold, hard death. Of course Constance would think she'd want the information about the eating thing and not the fun thing.

"What's the decathlon challenge?" Frankie asked.

Constance turned her attention back to Frankie, flipping her blond hair over her shoulder as she did so and giving him a flirty smile. Either Constance had already forgotten the digs he'd made at her expense, or she'd figured he was hot enough to get away with being an asshole. Either option was possible, but Lucy was leaning toward the second one.

"Oh, it's a bunch of challenges like a scavenger hunt, carnival stuff, and an obstacle course, with the couple who gets the most points being declared the reunion king and queen." She pressed the palms of her hands to the table and leaned forward, the move pressing her breasts together for their best advantage. "My husband and I won it at the five- and ten-year reunions. We're the favorites for this year, too."

"That sounds like fun to me," Frankie said.

Constance lowered her voice to just above a whisper. "I'm not supposed to do this because the rules require at least one member of the team be an Antioch graduate, but I'm sure we could make an exception for you to go it alone."

Frankie turned to Lucy and tucked a stray hair behind

her ear, his touch lingering just long enough to make her breath hitch. "Do not make me do this by myself. You kick ass at this stuff."

Before she could call him on that bullshit, Constance—eyes wide with surprise—opened her mouth. "Of course she does," she said with fake sweetness.

Oh hell no. That wasn't about to stand.

"Yeah," Lucy said, thinking back to her twice-weekly dance cardio class and the tai chi that helped her focus. "I do."

"Just imagine how surprised you'll be when we win it," Frankie said with a big grin.

Constance's smile was anything but friendly. "Well then, good luck to Team Muffin Kavanagh."

"I agree, she's very tasty, but that doesn't have a damn thing to do with this," Frankie said. "You might want to warn your hubby now not to make space on the trophy case."

Constance looked from her to Frankie and back again, obviously unable to work out why someone like him would be with someone like her. "There's no trophy," Lucy said.

"Good." He dropped a quick kiss on Lucy's temple. "Bragging rights are even better."

And while Constance was still staring slack-jawed at them and Lucy was trying to wrap her brain around what in the hell was going on, Frankie swung Lucy around and steered her away from the registration table and toward the exit. They made it out the door and to the corner of the school parking lot before Lucy yanked Frankie to a stop.

"What are you thinking?" she asked, forcing herself to keep from yelling. "The last thing I want is to actually do this stupid decathlon."

If there was one thing every picked-on kid ever learned in high school, it was not to wave a red flag in front of the bullies' faces, which was exactly what he'd done. There was a difference between standing up for herself and antagonizing the woman who'd been a total bitch to her for four years straight.

"Why?" He slid on his sunglasses and grinned down at her. "It sounds fun, and it's not like you aren't competitive."

"I am not." She wasn't. There was a difference between wanting to win everything and wanting to win when you were right.

"Really?" He chuckled. "Miss Always Has To Have The Last Word is a passive player? I'm not buying that for a minute."

He had her there. Damn it. "Fine. I like to win."

"So, let's go show that bitch queen how it's done." Frankie took the welcome packet from her hands and pulled out a piece of paper with the words Antioch High Decathlon written across the top. "Let's go figure out where the 1843 cornerstone is." When she didn't move, he turned on the charm, lowering his sunglasses so she couldn't miss the amusement in his blue eyes. "Come on. Play with me."

"Have you ever see me run?! It is not a pretty sight."

His gaze zeroed in on her boobs. "Looking forward to it."

She sighed. "I'm only doing this under protest."

He pushed his sunglasses back up. "Whatever it takes to help you sleep at night."

Oh, she knew what it took to really help her sleep after last night's epic sexually frustrated tossing and turning. However, since riding Frankie wasn't on the list of activities for the Antioch High School reunion decathlon, she was going to have to make due with her hand and her imagination. In last night's fantasy, they'd been back at the B and B. He'd walked out in just the towel, dropped it, gotten on his knees, and feasted between her thighs. She'd come so hard all over her fingers that not making noise had not been an option.

"You look guilty," Frankie said with a smirk, as if he knew exactly where her mind was.

Ignoring his statement and the heat it brought to her cheeks, she said, "I know where the cornerstone is."

She took off across the street and toward downtown at a brisk pace. Sure, it was July, but a little power walking in the heat was better than that cocky look in Frankie's eyes right now. She just had to make sure they found every item on the scavenger hunt as fast as possible so they could get back to her dad's house and she could hide in her room.

Jeesh. What was it about going back home again that turned a person into who they were at twelve?

Lucy was not a nice person. How did she know this? Because she was enjoying herself way too much as she watched Frankie try to charm the location of the next item, a golden wolf's tooth, out of Henrietta Campher.

For her part, Henrietta was having none of it.

Henrietta had run the Wolfsbane Antiques and Collectibles on Main Street since the La Brea Tar Pits were trapping saber-toothed tigers, and she'd heard every tall tale and sales pitch that had come with folks selling off Grandma's spoon collection that had been used by one famous person or another. So the more times Frankie complimented the steel of the woman's spine or the way her hair had maintained such a striking shade of red—his favorite color—the more she rolled her eyes at him from behind her thick glasses.

"Now tell me again how you got saddled with this goliath?" Henrietta asked Lucy.

The look of shocked disbelief on Frankie's face almost made the fact that they'd been busting their asses for the past four hours on the scavenger hunt from hell worth it.

"His name is Frankie Hartigan, Mrs. Campher," Lucy said from her spot by the stuffed squirrel dressed up to look like a pirate. "He's a firefighter back in Waterbury."

From her spot behind the counter, Henrietta sipped from the straw stuck through the opening of her can of Diet Dr. Pepper before responding, "I'm not asking for a résumé, I want your meet-cute. Isn't that what they call it in the movies?"

Just the idea of Henrietta sitting down and watching rom-coms on Netflix was blowing Lucy's mind, making it difficult to remember their cover story. All she could think about was how embarrassed she'd be if she got outed for bringing a fake date to her high school reunion to Mrs. Campher of all people. It would be epically bad.

"This is a great story," Frankie said, jumping in to fill the dead air. "My brother, who unfortunately did not see the light and join the fire department but instead became a cop, met a woman."

"I don't care about your brother. I care about her." She hooked her thumb toward Lucy.

"I'm getting to that," Frankie said.

Ignoring the man, Henrietta turned to Lucy. "Does he do everything this slow? I mean, some things are nice at a leisurely pace—walks, jazz, and making love, for instance—but storytelling ain't one of them."

Lucy would have answered, but there was no way she could do so without letting go of the laugh building up inside her, especially when she spotted the offended and confused expression on Frankie's face. The poor guy had probably never been shot down so completely in his life.

"An asshole was hitting on her." The words came out of his mouth in a rush as if he hadn't been planning on saying them.

Henrietta's eyes went wide with interest, and she turned

her attention to Frankie. "Go on."

"He was telling her she wasn't the hottest thing on the planet just the way she was."

No. No. No. This wasn't good. This was the truth. It wasn't the funny story about him spotting her crossing the street that they'd worked out. This was real-life humiliation used as story-time fodder.

She wanted to open her mouth and say something—anything—to shut Frankie up, but she was frozen like she was stuck in some kind of living dream where she couldn't move. This was hell. This was like being in high school all over again before she'd gained the brass balls to take on the world with her chin high.

Damn. It wasn't that you couldn't go home again, it was that you *shouldn't* because it was like returning to a time when you were your most awkward self all over again.

"So," Henrietta said. "This man was an idiot *and* an asshole."

Frankie grinned at the older woman, crossed over to the counter, and leaned on his forearms. The move wasn't lost on the older woman, who snuck a look at the way his biceps peeked out from his T-shirt sleeves.

If he noticed, he didn't play it up. Instead, he dropped his voice to a conspiratorial whisper. "I went over to Lucy and said I was sorry I was late for our date. Then I helped the asshole see the need to vacate the premises."

"Did you punch him in the face?" Henrietta asked with a bloodthirsty expression.

Frankie shrugged his broad shoulders. "Didn't need to." He crossed over to Lucy and wound his arm around her waist, pulling her in close. "And that's how I ended up as the lucky guy dating Lucy Kavanagh."

Finding jeans that fit her ass and the dip of her waist was a problem. What wasn't a problem? Finding the right words for almost any situation. There was a reason why she'd gone into crisis communication: she didn't panic, and she always knew what to say.

But standing in the middle of the antique and collectibles shop next to a Queen Anne dressing table and a cabinet of paste jewelry from the 1920s, she couldn't string a sentence together. Why? Because Frankie Hartigan was doing the unthinkable—he was taking one of those really shitty moments that was repeated too often in her life and tweaking it so instead of being at the butt of the joke, she was the center of the story's action in a good way. She had no idea what to do with that.

Henrietta didn't seem to be similarly affected as she gave Frankie a considering look. "Top drawer under the stuffed cock."

Of course that's where it was. Lucy walked over to the rooster that had fallen under the taxidermist's knife. It was a Brahma and stood almost three feet tall, with pure white feathers accented by a smattering of black plumage that went down to its feet. It stood next to a sign that said *Cock of the Walk* on top of an old library card catalog cabinet. She opened the little drawer with a tiny picture of Wolfie clipped to the front and pulled out one of the gold wolf teeth found inside.

The pop of a new can of Diet Dr. Pepper being open sounded, drawing Lucy's attention back to where Henrietta and Frankie stood on opposite sides of the counter, looking like two people who'd spent the last two decades gossiping over drinks.

Henriette moved her bendy straw from the empty Diet Dr. Pepper to the new can. "How long have you been dating?"

"Not long." Frankie looked over at Lucy and grinned, obviously so pleased that he'd figured out how to charm Henrietta that he practically reeked of self-satisfaction.

That massive ego of his should annoy her. Instead it just made her giggle—something she covered with a short, fake coughing fit. *Remember, this is all fake. Nothing to feel here. Just move along.*

After waiting for Lucy to stop cough-laughing, Henrietta asked Frankie, "What are your intentions?"

"Mrs. Campher!" The exclamation escaped her lips before her brain even had a second to register what she was saying. And people paid her the big bucks to always think about the message before it went out. So much for being able to apply that skill to her own circumstances.

"What?" Henrietta shrugged. "I'm near death. I don't have time to beat around the bush."

The woman was full of it. She'd outlive them all.

"My intentions?" Frankie said, seemingly unruffled by the older woman's nosy question. "Nothing but trouble."

Pure orneriness glittered in Henrietta's eyes. "The kind that leaves a girl sighing or the kind that leaves her crying?"

Frankie gave Henrietta a wolfish smile and deepened his voice so his next words came out all sexy and low. "The kind that leaves her screaming for more."

And for the first time in her entire life, Lucy watched as Henrietta smiled. As if the shock of that wasn't enough, the old woman let loose with a creaky laugh that ended with a wheezing fit.

"Are you okay? Do you need us to go get your son?" Lucy asked, hustling over to the counter.

"I'm fine," she said, waving off Frankie as he was about the round the counter and come to the older woman's side. "Don't fuss over me."

Frankie stopped, but he didn't look happy about it. "Thanks for your help, Mrs. C."

"Bah." She rolled her eyes. "Enjoy that man of yours, young lady."

"Yes, ma'am." Really, what else could she say? Henrietta was incorrigible. Sometimes the better part of valor really was admitting defeat.

At least this once.

...

Frankie was standing in the magma-hot July sun, sweating his ass off in a public park at a little after four in the afternoon. It wasn't sexy. It sure as hell wasn't comfortable. It was, however, a fact of life, and there wasn't a damn thing he could do about it.

Why was this happening? Because he decided to show off, like an asshole.

Yeah, he was in enough pain to admit it to himself if not out loud—because that was going to happen exactly never. A smarter man would have read the directions stating that the bowl needed to be held at exactly six feet, eight inches off the ground at ten past four in some sort of Indiana Jones trick to find the final item on the scavenger hunt, and he would have gone and put it on the stand provided just for that purpose. However, Frankie was the kind of moron that decided to hold it aloft. Why? Because Lucy was watching. So yeah, he was a jackass.

"I'm dying," he said as another bead of sweat took its sweet time sliding down his spine while his shoulder muscles started to scream at him. "How much longer?"

Lucy kept her attention focused on the clock app on her phone. "Don't wimp out on me now, Hartigan. It's almost time."

"You're not the one holding a fifty-pound concrete bowl above your head." His ego was bigger than his brain.

"Come on, don't tell me a big guy like you can't take it." She looked up at him and smirked—yes, smirked. No sexy smile. No come-hither curl of her lips. Smirked. And damn if it didn't turn him on enough to give him that extra burst of adrenaline to hoist the bowl a little higher.

She continued, "Anyway, you were the one who declared it was no big deal."

Yeah, tell that to his biceps, which were lodging a criminal complaint for stupidity because to really add fuel to the fire, he hadn't waited until the last minute to lift the big-ass bowl. There was no way he could put it down now without admitting total defeat, and he never did that. So, he bitched. "I signed on for a scavenger hunt, not to be a human sundial."

"But you look so good doing it." She gave him a slow up-and-down.

Now *that* he was used to. He'd been getting double takes since forever. It wasn't a brag. It was the truth. But it felt different coming from Lucy. Better. Hard-won. "Story of my life."

"So how come you haven't been in one of those hot firefighters calendars?" she asked, looking back down at her phone as the seconds flowed like molasses in January on the frozen tundra.

"Didn't want to pick up a second job to cover the cost of security because of all the extra stalkers." And because it was creepy as hell. He liked people. He did not like being an object.

"You mean you don't have stalkers already?" she asked with a snarky little giggle.

This woman. She didn't let him get away with any shit. She gave as good as she got. Of course, realizing this while he was holding up a concrete bowl in the hot July sun getting the arm workout from hell didn't mean he was going to admit to her that he liked her scary, ball-busting ways.

"Ladies love me." He winked at her.

She snort-laughed. "That sounds like the title of your

autobiography, *Ladies Love Me: The Story of a Former Sex Fiend*."

Oh yeah. There was that. Good for a lay, but not good enough to take home to Mom. That wasn't exactly how Shannon put it, but it was close enough.

He adjusted his grip on the bowl without lowering it. "It wasn't always sex."

"Oh yeah, what was it?" Her question was as brash and to the point as usual, but there was more than a hint of concern and empathy in her eyes.

"It's different for every woman," he said, trying to put it into words for the first time. "Sometimes it's the smell of her perfume or the way she struts through a room. It's the little things that you don't notice right away, like the way someone adjusts her walking speed to stay on pace with someone else instead of speeding ahead. Other times, it's the little things you have to earn—a secret she's never told before, or way she lets go and laughs without worrying about what it might sound like to someone else."

"Holy shit, Frankie." Lucy stared at him, her eyes wide with shock. "You're a romantic."

Whoa. That was not where he'd been going with that. He was an appreciator of women, all women, not some dweeb who wrote bad, sappy poems and spent nights in watching chick flicks and did stupid shit like profess his love in front of the entire world. That was not him.

"Did I mention the sex?" He puffed out his chest, a move he realized too late just made keeping the heavy-ass concrete bowl in the right position above his head even harder. "That part is really fucking good, great, the best."

"Calm your gonads, I'm not going to let your secret out." She didn't even bother to hide the fact that she was laughing at him as she glanced down at her phone, then back at the spot on the shady ground where the sun spilled through the cutout in the bowl. "And that's it."

"Thank God." He sat the bowl back down on its low pedestal.

Really, it was a pretty brilliant way to end the scavenger hunt. The final item, programs from the class's graduation, were hidden in different spots around the park. Each of those spots could only be found following a path illuminated by the sun through the hole in the bowl at a certain point in time. He marked off the time 4:10 p.m. on the clue sheet left by the concrete bowl so others trying later in the week would know that the program hidden in that location had been claimed. So far only one other time had been marked off the list. Not bad odds for placing high in the competition.

For her part, Lucy was marching north in accordance with the written directions for the last clue on the scavenger hunt.

"Ten, eleven, twelve," she counted out loud with each step forward. "Thirteen."

That brought her to a rose bush with about a million red blooms. Frankie watched as she pondered the situation, too distracted by how the breeze toyed with the hem of her bright blue skirt and showed off a couple of more inches of sexy, thick thighs to think about where someone could have hidden the program. Lucy obviously wasn't as distracted, because it took all of ten seconds of concentration before she bent down and retrieved a rolled-up graduation program from a box hidden underneath the rose bush.

She held it up above her head, using both hands as if the piece of paper was as heavy as the fifty-pound concrete bird bath bowl. "Victory!"

"Good thing you're not competitive." He strode over to where she stood in the shade of the trees bordering the walking path and the rose bushes.

She gave him a cocky grin and fanned herself with the

program. "It's one of my best qualities."

"Now, that's a long list," he said, stopping next to her in the shade so there was only an arm's length of space between them.

She turned to face him, tossing her long brown hair over one shoulder and rolling her eyes at him. "Henrietta's not around to hear you."

"Doesn't make the truth any less so."

And it didn't.

Without considering if it was a good idea, he stepped in so close that if there'd been any sun shining through the thick tree branches it would have had to fight to get between them. The urge to touch the silky strands of her hair hit him hard enough that he had to shove his hands in his pockets to keep from doing it.

The woman was pretty damn amazing—not that he needed to confirm that, but yeah, thinking that had him checking her out using his peripheral vision. It was a mistake, but what a sweet one to make. What she did to that shirt tucked into her swirly skirt was fucking phenomenal.

"Frankie Hartigan," she said, shaking her head and letting out a soft chuckle. "You can't breathe without flirting."

"Good thing you're so much fun to flirt with."

"That's not what most people say," she said with a sigh and sank back against a tree trunk, some of that gleeful, smart-ass attitude of hers dimming in her eyes.

Pivoting until he stood face-to-face with her, still not touching her no matter how much he wanted to—and damn did he want to—he needed to set the record straight. "Then you spend too much time around assholes."

"No argument there." Her agreement came out breathy, and her cheeks had taken on a pink tinge.

"Present company excluded." He meant it as a light little tease, but it came out too rough for that because it was taking every ounce of self-control he had not to put his hands on her generous hips, which were the perfect size for his big hands, and kiss her until she forgot all those other men and could only think of him.

"Of course." She looked up at him from beneath her long eyelashes and let out a shaky breath. "We should go."

"Why?" Leaving was the last thing he wanted. Lucy Kavanagh was a woman who needed kissing and more—God knew he was more than man enough for the job.

He was playing with fire. Good thing he had years of the best training for being around flames without getting burned. Still, considering that the kiss he was millimeters from delivering was only the beginning of all he wanted to do with Lucy Kavanagh, he could feel the flames licking his fingers.

They were close but not nearly close enough. Somewhere way in the back of his head he heard the warning not to follow his dick, but the rush of attraction was much louder. Yes, Shannon and the other women of Waterbury were right about him, and he didn't have the strength right now to deny the truth of it. He just wanted to give in with Lucy.

Seemingly as caught in the moment as he was, she didn't make a move to put any space between them. "You know why."

He did, and he was a giant fucking dumbass for even coming up with the idea of going cold turkey on sex and then spending a week with Lucy Kavanagh. He'd been a jackass to think this would be a week free of temptation. The woman was temptation personified, from her red mouth to her whiplash-inducing curves to her ball-busting sense of humor. He was in so much trouble—and he fucking loved it.

Still…she was right. He couldn't shake the feeling that if he didn't get the big head straight before he got his dick involved it'd be an epic-level disaster. Of course, knowing that didn't make pulling away any easier.

But he did, one achingly slow millimeter at a time, before he could give in to the electric draw between them. Gone was the scent of her wrapping around him, the warmth that came from being so near her, and the tangible sense of anticipation that always hit when he was within touching distance. He fucking hated it.

Man, was he screwed—and not in the way he normally was.

"I guess we should go turn in the scavenger hunt items," he said instead of begging her to come with him to a secluded spot along the trail where he could drop to his knees and explore everything that was underneath that skirt of hers.

Lucy—the woman who had a comment for just about everything—only nodded.

They stared at each other for another moment heavy with promise, then she slipped past him and started heading back toward the high school. It was a short walk, and Constance was walking out as they were walking in.

"Back already?" She pressed one hand to her chest in mock concern. The woman really was a piece of work. "I totally understand. It was really hard this year. It took Dave and me forever to find everything, and for a second I even thought we were going to have to go back and finish up tomorrow, but of course that didn't happen. We just turned ours in. We were the first."

"Looks like we'll have to settle for second place," he said. "At least for this event."

There was a beat of silence in which he could have sworn he heard Lucy's mental answer of "fuck yes" because she was thinking it so hard. Then he held up the bag with all of the loot they'd collected.

Constance let out a little "huh" that almost sounded like respect. "Congratulations." Then she sashayed off toward a bright blue BMW.

"Thanks," Lucy said, watching the other woman drive off and wondering if maybe she'd misjudged her. "I was close to doing all the things I tell my clients not to do."

He laughed. "No worries. Come on, let's go claim second place and then plot how we're going to do that hag in over cheeseburgers. I'm starving."

"Only if I get to shower first."

That, of course, only put the mental image of a naked Lucy in his mind, her peach nipples slick with soap. How often had he pictured some variation of that since he'd caught sight of her fabulous tit that had broken free from her tank top at the B and B the other morning? Only nearly every waking moment. It was the last thing he needed to be thinking about—at least when there wasn't a damn thing he could do about it—but he couldn't seem to stop.

"Sure," he said, not sure what he was agreeing to, but knowing he needed to say something before her quick mind put together that he'd gone into the perv zone.

"Great." She took the bag of found scavenger hunt items from him, the graze of her fingertips setting off an electric pulse that shot straight to his dick. "Let me go turn this in and then it's bubbles and burgers."

Thank God she didn't seem to expect him to respond since she simply turned and strode into the high school gym, because he wasn't sure he had enough blood still going to his brain to form words. It was a situation that was beginning to feel normal with each day he spent with Lucy.

This week just might kill him, but what a way to go.

Chapter Ten

Charbroiled was an Antioch institution. Thick, juicy cheeseburgers on toasted sesame seed buns slathered with a tangy sauce only three people in town knew the recipe for—and they weren't talking. Then there were the shakes made from homemade ice cream and topped with whipped cream so fluffy and light it was like tasting a cloud. Needless to say, everyone in town—including Lucy—was a fan.

"Who in their right mind wouldn't be?" Frankie asked as he demolished the last of his double cheeseburger. "That was so damn good."

The sound he made then was enough to make her reach for her half-finished cherry limeade because it had suddenly gotten a few degrees hotter in the restaurant. "I want to hear what happened next."

Frankie grinned at her, and she gulped down the rest of her tart drink as an act of desperate self-preservation to cool herself off because after spending the day with him—and gawking at him as he held up the birdbath bowl for close to forever in the park—she was in serious need of a reminder that he was off-limits. *Not interested. Out of my league.*

Lucky for her, there were lots of reminders. First, he was a first-round draft pick of a player when it came to women, and that way lay nothing but heartache and disaster. Second, he'd declared himself a no-sex zone, so pushing him into something he was trying hard to resist—the act, not her—was very much not a cool thing to do. Third, even if he wasn't into temporary celibacy, he was a six-foot-six-inch, sexy-as-hell, work-of-art level, ginger firefighter with large hands so perfectly sized, she couldn't help but wonder if the rest of him was as well. Oh and fourth, totally not into her.

"Oh, this is when it gets good," he said, totally oblivious to the path her thoughts had gone down.

Before their food had been delivered, he'd been telling her about his run-in with a pompous asshole who parked his Jaguar in front of a fire hydrant. Frankie and his crew had to break the passenger's and driver's windows so they could thread the hose through the car and fight a warehouse fire. The car's owner was totally irate and had taken his complaint to the top brass at the Waterbury Fire Department. When the food had arrived, though, all conversation had ceased as they both dug in. The only sounds they'd made had been groans of appreciation.

"Well, he came marching out of the strip club covered in enough glitter to make it look like he was glowing and started screaming at the probie, as if the kid was in charge of a damn thing."

"A misperception you disabused him of." Because—she was realizing—that's what Frankie did. Just like with her and the asshole telling her she should have ordered a salad, he stepped in and did his knight-on-a-white-horse thing.

"I told him I'd be happy to bring any complaint he had directly to the captain."

Her bullshit detector went into overdrive. "In those

words?"

"Not even close." He gave her a cocky grin.

She shook her head. The man would be a nightmare as a crisis communication client. Hell, he'd give Zach Blackburn a run for his money on the pain in the ass scale.

"And that's how you ended up on a forced vacation?"

"That was my assumption when the captain called me into his office, but no, it was just a simple human resources requirement to not let so much vacation time build up." He swiped a crinkle fry through the pool of ketchup on his plate and popped it in his mouth. "It's such a stupid regulation."

For someone like him, she could see that. What better job for a guy with a rescue complex than a firefighter who rushes into burning buildings to save people and rescues cats stuck in trees? Other than his job, his family, and a few close friends, he didn't seem to have a lot of activities going on—beyond the one he was currently shunning.

He was a workaholic with a rescue complex.

Guess who was the kitten out on a limb this time? That realization—along with her dad's advice earlier to open herself up to the fact that she could, possibly, *maybe* be (on occasion) wrong about people—made her prickle.

"And you thought what a better way to spend a vacation than in Antioch, Missouri, with me as your safety date?"

One of his eyebrows shot up. "Safety date?"

"Yeah, the one you don't have to worry about making you fall off the no-sex wagon." Okay, that came out a little harsher than she meant it to, but she was salty. No one wanted to be the pity date, especially not the woman who some men thought should be eating a salad with no dressing or shredded cheese or anything that tasted remotely like it had touched an unsaturated fat at any point in its existence.

He stiffened and looked at her with annoyance. "That was the initial plan, but it hasn't worked out that way."

She sat up straighter in her chair and gave him the icy look that froze her badly behaving clients in their tracks.

"Look, I know you're not into me, and I'm okay with that. I'm not fishing for compliments. I know I don't turn most men on," she said.

"You are the most frustrating woman…" He groaned and stared at her long and hard. Like he was wrestling with something. He finally nodded, making some decision, and continued, "Good, because I'm not giving them out," he said in a low voice with enough gravel in his tone to put her on alert. "Consider this a list of complaints." He began counting off with his fingers as he went through each point. "You've made it so a good night's sleep is an unobtainable goal, because I can't close my eyes without seeing your ass and wondering how it would move when I buried myself balls deep in you."

Her cheeks flamed. That was not what she was expecting. Not at all.

"When I almost ran Scarlett off the road in Illinois?" he went on, holding up a second finger. "That was because I was imagining the sound you'd make when I grazed my teeth over the tip of your nipple and then sucked on it hard enough to make you beg for more."

And there went her panties. Call the fire department. Oh wait, she had someone with a hose right across the table.

His words were so unexpected, she was having trouble breathing. She couldn't tell if it was embarrassment that he felt the need to lie to make her feel better or imagining him doing all those things to her. It was a toss-up at the moment.

He stared at her with a look she'd never seen him have before. Oh, she'd seen flirty Frankie. This wasn't him. This was something different altogether. Hotter. More intense. The air around them sparked and sizzled.

He lifted a third finger. "I have had more inconvenient

and unplanned hard-ons in the past five days than a grown man should admit to. And after I woke up in that B and B and saw you sleeping in the bed next to me, with your tank top not even having a hope in hell of containing your boobs? That's when I started revising my definition of what sex is, because thinking about how good you must taste is all I can think about when I've got my hand wrapped around my dick. There is nothing more that I want to do right now than find out just how much my imagination sucks, because I bet you taste better when you come than anything else in the world. And there's not a damn thing I can do about it."

It was probably just because they were together twenty-four seven. It was a vacation-from-reality reaction on his part, that was why he couldn't do anything about it. Besides, he was an admitted man-whore, and she was basically the only single woman he'd met all week.

Still…it was hot in here.

Check that.

It was scorching. Her whole body had that oh-my-God-yes tingly thing going on. Just from his words. Was that possible? She hadn't thought so until that moment.

It was so disconcerting that her next question flew out before she had a chance to consider it. "You saw my boobs?"

One ginger eyebrow went up. "After everything I just said, me seeing your fan-fucking-tastic rack is what you're caught on?"

"Yes," she said as she shook her head no.

He shoved his fingers through his hair. "Thank God I didn't tell you the rest of it."

She gulped, her heart beating so fast it had to be approaching light speed. "There's more?"

This was how he flirted? She resisted the urge to fan herself and pull at her collar like some kind of cartoon. No wonder the women of Waterbury couldn't resist him. The man was lethal to the better-decision-making process.

"Would you like to hear all about it?" he asked, his voice low and rough as if he was trying not to sound so damn sexy and failing miserably.

Of course, that's when the waitress stopped by their table and asked if there was anything else she could get them and—judging by the fact that the waitress stood so her back was to Lucy—by "them" she meant only Frankie and by "anything" she meant a blow job.

The dismissal of even the idea that Lucy could be with someone like Frankie by the waitress was enough to take an ice pick of reality to her hot air balloon of sexually frustrated anticipation. This was reality.

"Just the check," Lucy said to the waitress's back.

The waitress glanced back over her shoulder with a shocked expression as if she'd genuinely forgotten Lucy was there. It wasn't the first time Lucy had gotten this reaction after speaking. It was as if being fat put a target on her and gave her an invisibility cloak at the same time. If she wasn't so used to it, it would have pissed her off. As it was, it just made her tired.

"Don't even think you're paying for this," Frankie said, ignoring the waitress. "I asked you out, I get the check."

Nope. That took this whole thing too far into the pity date territory she was determined to avoid at all costs, and she was still too flustered from Frankie's outburst to agree to that. "You know why that's not gonna happen."

"There's a lot that's not gonna happen."

And double ouch. Sure, she knew it was just an attraction-by-proximity thing with him, but the swiftness of his declaration made her wince anyway. "With the number one being you paying for lunch."

The waitress let out a huff and smacked the bill down on the table. "Once y'all figure it out, you can pay up front."

Then she sashayed away from their table without a single look back.

"I think you pissed her off," Lucy said, stating the obvious because her brain was too fried and her body's reaction to the man across from her too strong to think of anything witty.

And the constant belly-tightening awareness of him made no sense. She knew she and Frankie couldn't be a thing. Taking a deep breath, she went over the list. One, she wasn't his type. Two, he wasn't hers. Three, he was on the sex bench. Four, he was only flirting with her because that's what he did, not because he meant it. Five, they'd have to go back home eventually, and being one more on the long list of Frankie Hartigan's women did absolutely nothing for her.

Okay, it did something for her, but only in a late-night-fantasy way, definitely not in a real-world, light-of-day way. No way did she want to turn this pity date week into a pity fuck, too.

Flustered and annoyed with herself, she grabbed the bill before he could and hustled over to the cashier by the door. Chicken? Her? Totally.

Frankie didn't press her on her fast getaway from Charbroiled. He changed the subject and kept her laughing and made her heart beat faster with a little touch here or a look there all the way back to her dad's house. They'd no more than walked in the door—Frankie having to pivot to avoid a flying ballistic missile otherwise known as Gussie, who seemed to be as interested in what Frankie had behind his zipper as she was—when she spotted the note. It was three sentences on a yellow Post-it stuck to the mirror next to the coatrack.

Muffin,

Leading group session and then meeting Alvarez for drinks. Don't wait up. Be good.

Dad

Be good? Like she needed to be told that. She was a grown woman. Her gaze drifted over to Frankie, who was holding Gussie in his arms but at a distance, sort of like a non-kid person held a toddler with a stinky diaper. Her pulse ticked up. Shit. Maybe she *did* need a reminder if watching him avoid getting a Gussie tongue bath as the French Bulldog whined in frustration was getting her worked up.

"What are we going to do with ourselves?" he asked, putting down Gussie, who immediately began running in excited circles around him.

She had ideas. She had *lots* of ideas. None of which would be put into action.

"Up for a movie?" he asked.

"Sure." She could totally sit next to Frankie Hartigan in the dark and pretend to pay attention to a movie plot instead of how sexy he looked with a few days beard scruff, or how even the idea of his thick fingers touching her made her need to squeeze her thighs together to relieve the ache that had been building since they'd left Waterbury.

She was a grown-ass woman.

Of course she could do that.

Really.

Maybe.

Okay, this was going to be hell.

• • •

It took about ten minutes into the movie before Frankie realized he was the world's biggest dumbass.

They'd sat down on the couch, Gussie collapsed in his doggie bed across the room, and he flipped on the first movie on Netflix that didn't sound like complete crap and turned the lights out to better get the movie experience—that's when things went south.

The choice of movie didn't help. It was supposed to be a comedy. What he hadn't realized was that it was a sex comedy about two friends who decided to add benefits to the mix. There was nothing like being alone in the dark watching two people decide whether or not they could fuck without making things complicated to pretty much guarantee that he wasn't going to be able to stop imagining how a similar conversation would go with Lucy.

In his mind, it always ended the same—both of them naked—but the where and the what they were doing changed. Sometimes she was bent over the back of the couch, her ass high up in the air. Sometimes she was straddling him as he sat on the couch, his hands gripping her round hips. Sometimes she was on her back with her legs resting against his chest and her ankles on his shoulders as he pistoned his hips forward and back, going as deep as possible into her hot, wet warmth.

Fuck.

He'd lost his damn mind.

Leave your dick out of it, Hartigan. You are on a break!

At the other end of the love seat, Lucy let out a snort of disbelief. "This never works out."

It took Frankie a second to realize she was talking about the action that was happening on the screen, not in his head. "What do you mean?"

She turned to face him. "Sex always changes everything."

"That's not true. I have had lots of no-strings-attached sex, and it never changed anything." It was *not* having sex that impacted his relationships with women.

Oh sure, they remained friendly, but later when their clothes were on the women always treated him differently, as if he'd served his purpose.

The light from the television may have been the only light in the room, but reading Lucy's no-shit expression didn't take any effort.

"And that's why you're now in a no-orgasm zone," she said.

Okay, he was trying to figure things out, he wasn't punishing himself with a fate worse than getting stuck working a desk job downtown at the Waterbury Fire Department HQ. "I am not banished from orgasms."

She chuckled. "As long as it's..." She cleared her throat and gave him a teasing look. "Hands-on, huh?"

"Very funny." He scooted a few inches closer, letting his arm fall across the back of the couch so that his fingertips almost brushed the curve of her shoulder. He shouldn't have. He should have stayed where he was, but he was an idiot. A very turned-on idiot who had to shift to make sure he kept that information to himself. "There are a lot of activities in between holding hands and fucking."

"Suppose it depends on what your definition of sex is."

"It's P in the V." Okay not really, but he liked it when she got worked up. Her cheeks got all flushed, and she got a fiery spark in her eyes. Okay, *and* she always took in a deep breath before she let loose on him that lifted her tremendous tits so he was gifted with a spectacular view of her cleavage.

She rolled her eyes. "Could there be any more of a straight male definition of sex than that?"

No deep breath. Damn. He needed to work harder at it.

"Fine." He leaned closer. "Sex equals penetration from a penis either to the vagina or the anus."

There was a beat of silence—even the people on the movie stopped yammering about whether fucking a friend was a good idea or not—and then she took a deep breath. Her breasts strained against the cotton of her V-neck tank top.

Score!

"That is totally wrong," she said, looking at him like he was the last firefighter to get on the truck. "A man's dick might be fun, but it isn't necessary for sex."

Was he an immature asshole for arguing such a dumb position just to get a peek down her shirt? Yes. But he could live with that. What sucked was having to keep arguing such a dumb position so she wouldn't see right through him.

She arched an eyebrow and gave him a you-are-so-full-of-shit look. "So, hand jobs don't count as sex?"

"No." And now the image of her fingers wrapped around his cock had him adjusting himself as discreetly as possible, because talk was all and good but they weren't going to get naked. Did thoughts get any more depressing?

"And oral?" she asked, shifting her position and causing her skirt to raise a few inches on her thighs. The space where her creamy flesh pressed together drew his gaze, hypnotizing him.

It took everything he had not to close his eyes and revel in the mental picture of diving between her legs. "No."

She cocked her head to one side and considered him. He wasn't going to like what was going to come out of her mouth next. Correction. He was going to like it. A lot. And he shouldn't. Not at all.

"And sliding your cock up and down a wet slit," she said as she leaned closer, the move brushing her bare shoulder against his fingertips and shooting a bolt of electricity straight to his balls. "Does that count as sex as long as there's no penetration?"

Sweet fucking mercy.

He was going to die—right here, right now—with pre-come on the tip of his raging hard-on.

"No." The word came out rough and desperate, sort of like how he felt at the moment.

Yep. He was going to die and then go straight to hell for uttering such idiotic lies. Some might say he was going to H. E. double hockey sticks because of the dirty thoughts he was having about what exactly he wanted to do to and with Lucy, but he had a feeling God would forgive him. Frankie was only human, after all, and she could tempt a saint, which he very definitely was not. He was just an asshole who decided to go on a sex break to prove something—he couldn't remember at the moment what—to himself and get his big head straight.

"And what," she asked, pausing long enough to tug her plump bottom lip between her teeth, "is it that the lesbians of the world are having without a man's dick?"

Yep. He was going to hell for lying. "Oral."

"Oh my God," she said with an astonished laugh, pressing her hand against his chest and shoving. He, of course, didn't go anywhere, and she didn't drop her hand. "For a man who's seen more vagina than some gynecologists, your ignorance is astounding."

"Careful, you might dent my ego." Not possible, since it was made out of titanium, but his zipper was definitely in trouble.

"Your definition of sex is asinine."

"Why?" He agreed, but the way Lucy's brain worked was a total turn-on, and he liked getting a peek at that almost as much as checking out her tits.

This was a new one for him. He didn't usually spend this much time *talking* to the women he spent time with, and their discussions didn't have a lot to do with their definition of sex so much as the demand for what to do sexually.

The thing was, he was having fun, even with the zipper biting into his hard dick.

Lucy dropped her hand from his chest to his thigh as they sat there facing each other on the love seat in her dad's darkened living room while the movie played on, forgotten on the big-screen TV. Moving away from her was the last thing he wanted to do, but he shifted farther back anyway as the last thing he wanted was to make her uncomfortable because she'd accidentally touched his junk.

Every nerve was attuned to Lucy as she seemed to think out her response. The way she fiddled with her hair with her free hand. The way she wet her bottom lip with her tongue. The way her breathing hitched and her pulse picked up at the base of her throat each time her gaze moved from his face to her hand on his thigh and back again.

"Because all of those things mean making yourself vulnerable to another human being, and that's the importance of sex," she said, her voice soft but confident. "The orgasms are great, but what makes sex amazing is the personal connection."

It wasn't that she lost him with that argument so much it seemed old-fashioned for her to say.

"Isn't that a stereotype?" he asked. "The good old days called, and they want their catchphrase back. You know the one: men use love to get sex, and women use sex to get love."

She shook her head. "Don't try to deflect because you know that's not what I'm saying at all. Love and intimacy are not the same things, and lust is definitely something different altogether. *How* you have sex, or define it, is not important. The emotional connection you have, however you're having sex, is what makes it go from good to amazing—and that includes everything from holding hands to kissing to orgasms galore."

He'd had a lot of sex in his life, with a lot of different women, and in a lot of different ways, but that emotional connection BS? He wasn't getting it. Sex was fun. It was easy. It felt good. All of the rest of it was just shit that marketers used to sell greeting cards and expensive jewelry—even if it did sound good coming from her.

"When was the last time you had sex?" Yeah, it was a rude question to ask in most contexts, but in this conversation? It seemed prudent to find out. Okay, he needed to know because… He had no frickin' clue why, but he did.

"Going by your definition?" she asked, her tone teasing as if she knew he'd just been talking shit before. "Six months."

"Holy shit." The words came out in a rush. "That's a long time."

She screwed up her mouth and narrowed her eyes at him. "Thanks for reminding me, you jerk."

Shit. He was usually smoother with women than this. Lucy threw him so far off his game, like he was suddenly the guy who showed up for an Ice Knights hockey game in a baseball jersey. "That's not what I meant."

She chuckled. "Yes it is, and it's longer than I like."

"So, what do you do?" Really, this woman should be getting laid regularly. She was smart, funny, and hot. There had to be something he could do to help her put herself out there more.

"I masturbate," she said with a shrug.

Okay, that was not what he meant, but now he had another unforgettable image implanted in his brain.

"But it's not the same," she said, pulling her hand away from his thigh with a little sigh. "Sex, orgasms, hooking up, whatever you want to call it can be better when you're with someone else, and are fucking amazing when you actually give a shit about that person."

He hated the loss of her touch. He hated the sad acceptance lurking in her eyes as if she had at least partially resigned herself to those orgasms with others being few and far between.

"I care about the women I've been with." It was true. He liked them. It wasn't love, but he never told them it would be.

"Yeah." She looked him dead in the eyes. "But did you ever give any of them the chance to care about the real you?"

How in the hell was he supposed to answer that? Even the idea of unpacking everything that went along with that question made his gut clench. This was why he liked his job. He was a man of action, not someone who was going to sit on his ass and think about things until the end of time.

So, he got up and walked away from Lucy and did what he'd do at a fire scene. He took a big-picture look and assessed the situation—then he got ready to make his move.

Chapter Eleven

Frankie thought he was so clever, but Lucy saw right through him. He might like to make people think that he was all surface and old-fashioned ideas, but he'd given himself away. She didn't believe he actually agreed with what he'd said earlier about the definition of sex for a second. How? Because she spent every working moment surrounded by real-life egomaniacs, sharks, and assholes. She could spot such a foul specimen at one hundred paces. He wasn't that. He just liked pressing her buttons.

The truth was, Frankie Hartigan was a softie—all six feet, six inches of him. Well, maybe not *all* of him. Even by the glow of the TV screen there was no missing the hard lines of him as he stood just inside the doorway.

She was about to tell him just that—not the part about noticing his impressive endowments, but the fact that he was full of shit—when he started toward her like a man on a mission. With those long legs of his, he was next to her before she unwound what was happening. Then, he took her by surprise, leaning down and cupping her face with his hands before putting those talented lips of his to work. After that? There wasn't a whole lot of anything going on above her eyebrows, because every other part of her had taken command of the ship.

She opened her mouth on a sigh—okay, a moan—and his tongue swept inside, sending electric jolts throughout her body that tightened her nipples into hard peaks that pressed against the unlined lace of her bra. He teased and tempted with every stroke of his tongue against hers, every press of his lips. The old song was wrong. A kiss wasn't just a kiss—at least not when Frankie Hartigan did it. It was so intense that it was like being at the center of a hurricane with the world swirling around them.

She didn't recline on the love seat so much as she melted back into the cushions. Frankie followed her down, his weight solid against her. His position anchored her to him and this moment, if not reality, because there was no way this type of thing should be happening, not between them, not in the real world. Except that didn't make it right, because she wasn't about to let him break his word to himself, nor did she want to be with him because she was conveniently the only one handy.

She broke the kiss with a desperate groan against the column of his throat. "Frankie, we can't."

"You don't want to?" he asked, drawing back.

"It's not that, it's…" She couldn't find the words, not when he was looking down at her as if she was the only woman in the world, the only one he really wanted. She almost believed him.

"You're trying to save me from myself?" He pressed against her, his hard length fitting against her so perfectly. "Lucy, I'm already lost, but I feel found any time I'm with you."

They were just words, pretty words, but she wanted to

believe. That should scare her, but just as the reality started to scrape against the edges of her consciousness, one hand glided down to her hip and he ground his hard length against her.

"But don't worry, this is just a kiss between friends, right?"

If she'd had words in her head at that moment, she would have answered the desperate need in his tone. Instead, she gave into it and swiveled her hips against him in a desperate search for relief from the throbbing need between her legs. This wasn't right. He was on the sexual bench, and she was trying to escalate a scorching kiss to something that would leave them both naked and happy. However, it wasn't to be, because she wasn't going to take advantage of him like that.

Laying her head back against the love seat's arm rest, she kept her eyes shut tight as she tried to regain her breath.

"That was…" She tried to come up with something, but her brain needed a total reboot at this point.

"Yeah," he answered.

Breathing hard, mental facilities on emergency power, and so turned on she worried about spontaneous combustion, she cracked her eyelids open and halfheartedly prayed for the strength to slide out from underneath him. Seeing his face from this position, close enough that she could drown in the want she saw in his blue eyes, sent a shiver of anticipation through her. Averting her gaze in an effort not to raise her head the few inches needed to start the kiss up again, she looked down the length of their bodies.

Most of his body weight was supported by how he was propped up on his left forearm as he lay on the couch, keeping him above her and not on her. His right hand rested against the rise of her hip—and whoa. His hands were big, and strong, and she just wanted to experience all the fabulous things he could do with them. She bit down on her bottom lip, needing the pain to surface to keep from giving in to the amazing feeling of having his hands on her body.

"Frankie," she said, too turned on to know what to say after that beyond the fact that she needed to say something to put a stop to this.

He brushed his thumb over her hip, following the paisley print on her skirt, as he looked down at her face from his position above her. "Whatever you're thinking, don't."

"We shouldn't." It wasn't fair to him. It wasn't right. He deserved better than that. Better than a convenient fuck.

"You say that a lot for a woman who kisses me like she wants me."

Wants him? It seemed like such pedestrian words for how she was feeling right now—needy to the point of being desperate for the brush of his lips or the stroke of his touch.

"I do," she said, her voice breathy. Was it wrong to use him to relieve her aching need if he was using her, too? Yes, it was, the rational part of her brain inserted. "But I don't want to push you into doing something you don't really want to do."

"You don't think I want to touch you?" He emphasized just how much he seemed to want to by lowering his hips forward so his hard cock rubbed against her core, tugging her skirt higher. "Or kiss you?" His mouth was on the column of her neck as he kissed and nipped his way up to her ear. "Or make you come repeatedly until your whole body is wrung out?" He followed that not by rocking against her, but by going completely still. "You can imagine that, can't you? Clenching around me as the whole world breaks apart over and over and over again?"

She nodded because her ability to form words had disappeared. Again. This was all too much and not enough, and bad decisions were about to be made—the absolute best kind of bad decisions.

"Good, because I know I've imagined it. I've wanted it. I still do." His fingers glided down from her hip to the hem of her skirt, an intense, hungry look on his face. "So I'm asking you to let me come off the bench with you."

She cupped his face and turned his head so he had to look right at her. There could be no mistakes in this. "Are you sure?"

"My idea to stop having sex until I got my head straight was about as stupid as that bullshit definition of sex that I used earlier to get a rise out of you."

"I knew you were full of it about that." She added pot-stirrer to total flirt under her mental list of Frankie's attributes.

"Couldn't help it. You're fucking hot when you're riled up." He toyed with the hem of her skirt and dipped his head low for another kiss that was as mind melting as it was quick. "And speaking of hot, I want to slide my hand underneath here and feel how slick you are right now because you are so wet, aren't you?"

"Yes." It was moaned more than spoken, but it was so very, very true.

"Spread your legs."

She did without even thinking about it. That time was so far past. All she could do was feel and want. Tomorrow, she'd probably be embarrassed about this, once she had time to think about how all of Frankie's words were probably born of a collective pent-up desperation, not an individual desire for her. Tonight, however, she was going to give in to the lust streaming through her and find relief for the ache building in her core.

"Fuck, I love the feel of you." His hand spanned the expanse of her thigh as he slid his palm upward under her skirt until his thumb grazed the damp center of her panties.

She arched her hips, needing more than just the soft brush of his touch, and he let out a strangled groan. It wasn't enough. She needed to feel more, to feel him. Instead, he was circling her clit with his thumb over her panties. Unwinding her hands from around his neck, she reached under her skirt to get rid of the damn things.

He stopped with his thumb the moment her hands went under her skirt. "Be patient."

"I don't want to be." Her, whine? In this situation? Oh fuck yes. She was half a breath away from begging.

"What do you want?" he asked, his voice as rough as his touch was gentle.

Everything. Now. "To come."

"Now? This second?" He nipped her bottom lip, drawing it taut before kissing it better. "Or do you want to go slow." He circled her panty-covered clit with a butterfly-soft touch. "Build it up." He picked up the pace but kept his touch agonizingly light. "Stoke the flames until you can't take it for another moment and you come so hard you can't see."

God. When he put it like that, what choice did she have? Especially when he was looking at her with barely checked control and heat. It was almost as if he really did want *her* and not just any woman. It was in that moment she decided that Frankie Hartigan deserved every single bit of his reputation as the best sex in Waterbury, and she hadn't even seen his dick. But oh, she would.

She brought her hand out from under her skirt, cupped his jaw, the bristles of his day's growth of beard tickling her palm, and kissed him.

It was so much sensation, the feel of his lips on her mouth, the sweep of his tongue across her lips before he deepened the kiss. Then he moved his thumb again in agonizing, slow turns about her clit, stopping every time she got close. That's when he'd talk as he kissed his way across her exposed cleavage. Over and over the cycle repeated. He'd bring her right to the edge, so close the tingling sensations were shooting up her thighs, and then he'd pull back. The world could have exploded outside of the living room and she wouldn't have been able to notice.

Everything had narrowed until it was just the two of them—both still fully dressed—on the love seat, his hand up her skirt, his thumb rubbing her through her wet panties as she went higher and higher and—

He stopped. "So close, wasn't that?"

"You're killing me." And she just might kill him.

His all-too-knowing chuckle tickled her skin as they lay on the couch, totally wrapped up in each other. "But you're so wet now. You've soaked through all that lace and cotton. You want to come so bad, don't you?"

"Please." Oh yes, she was begging and she didn't care.

He started again, deliberate circles that made her entire body ache for release. "What do you think about when you touch yourself?"

"Lately?" She arched her hips, trying to increase the pressure of his touch. "You."

He rewarded her by pressing harder against her clit, not enough to come, but enough to make her body rejoice.

He shifted so he was lower on the couch and dipped his head to kiss along the *V*-neckline of her tank top before moving down to her nipple pressing against the thin material. Offering up a silent thank-you to the universe that she thought to put on the one sexy bra she'd packed after her shower. It was crap for actual support, and the straps bit down into her shoulders, but it was made of the prettiest unlined lace, which meant the heat of his mouth and the rough feel of his teeth went straight through the thin cotton of her tank top and the lace of her bra to her sensitive nipple. She shivered against the onslaught. It was absolute, blissful torture, and she wanted more—something Frankie must have sensed, because the evil man stopped. The wet cotton and lace only seemed to highlight the absence of his touch more.

He just grinned up at her when she glared at him. "And what am I doing with you in this fantasy?"

Too many images assailed her at the same time to try to pick one. "Everything."

"You're gonna have to be more specific." He punctuated his demand by blowing against the stiff peak of her nipple poking against her tank top.

Of course, that's all it took for one of her many fantasies about being with Frankie to rush to the forefront.

She swallowed her embarrassment at admitting she fantasized about him. It would be worth it if he'd just make her come now. "I'm riding you. My hands are on your shoulders. Your hands are on my hips, your grip is tight, and I'm rocking against you."

She could picture it. His muscular chest, the sprinkling of red hair that formed into a happy trail. The feel of his fingers digging into her flesh with just the right amount of pressure to urge her on. Tension built in her body in response to Frankie's touch and the movie playing in her head. She raised her hips, needing more and needing it now.

Her eyes closed as his thumb moved against her clit again, and she was there, right fucking there, on the edge of exploding. She was so expecting him to stop touching her the closer that she got that she just fell into the fantasy and let go of everything else.

"I want to see that," he said, slipping two thick fingers inside her. He pumped them in and out while pressing against her clit. "I want to see those tits of yours bounce and feel you wet and slick against my cock."

"Oh my God, Frankie," she cried out, unable to stop herself.

It was like having an orgasm in slow motion or watching a wave go out, knowing it was going to crash back down on the shore with double the force. Her whole body vibrated all the way down to her toes. It moved upward slowly, inching up to her ankles, then her calves, and her knees.

By the time it got to her thighs, she was holding on to Frankie like he was the only thing keeping her from taking off like a rocket. But she did anyway, the orgasm hitting her hard and wrecking her as she came, riding what seemed like a never-ending wave of pleasure.

She refused to let the heat now clinging to her cheeks lessen the moment. She'd deal with that in a minute.

. . .

Feeling Lucy come all over his fingers and watching her blissed-out expression as she came down from her orgasm was the best and worst thing Frankie had ever experienced.

The best because Lucy wasn't wrong. Being with someone when it was about more than just getting off was different—and better. The worst because he couldn't just observe and respond like he usually would. This was about more than just getting his rocks off—and he had to convince her of that, which meant she was the only one coming tonight.

"Don't think," she said, her voice husky as she reached for the button of his shorts, "this is done."

Ignoring just how bad he did not want to move, he did anyway. They were going to do this, and they were going to do it right, meaning he wasn't going to fast-fuck her on her dad's couch like they were back in high school.

Confusion wiped out the last of the lingering satisfaction in her expression as she watched him pull back until he was once again standing a few steps away from her on the couch. Hurt flashed in her eyes for a millisecond before she shut it down. His chest tightened at her expression. *Fuck*. He was fucking it all up.

After sitting up, she smoothed her skirt down, turned so she was facing the TV, and reached for the remote.

"I stand corrected," she said, her voice carefully neutral. "This is done."

For a man who always knew the right thing to say to a woman, he had no clue how to express what was going on inside his head about her, about *them*. He'd run into the burning house without a plan, and now he could feel the flames licking at his back. It was a rookie mistake.

"Lucy," he started, but she stalled him by holding up her hand.

"It was a thing—an awesome thing, but a thing. I understand. Close proximity and all that. We don't have to talk about it. No big deal."

She was wrong. This was a very big deal. He took a step toward her, hoping like hell that the right words would come out of his mouth when he opened it. But he didn't get the chance.

Lucy stood up and clicked the power button on the remote. "In fact, I'm going to head off to bed." Then she strode in the opposite direction from him, tossing a single word over her shoulder. "Goodnight."

Fuck-nutters.

That had gone exactly not how he'd wanted—except for the Lucy's orgasm part, that had been fucking phenomenal. However, he'd flubbed it hard-core after that.

But they had the entire day together tomorrow.

All he had to do was figure out how to convince her that this wasn't about proximity. It was about a helluva lot more than that.

Chapter Twelve

Frankie was off for a run by the time Lucy made it down to the kitchen for breakfast the next morning. Gussie and her dad were waiting for her though and, judging by the fact that the big coffee pot on the counter was down to one cup, they'd been there for a while.

This didn't bode well.

Who was it that said a person could never go home again? They were wrong, because you *could* do it, but that didn't mean a person *should*. It was sort of like the too-tight jeans in every woman's closet they refused to get rid of—she might be able to button them, but that didn't mean she wouldn't regret wearing them. Maybe that's why Lucy mostly wore empire waist dresses like she was now.

"Waiting for me?" she asked, snagging a cup down from the cupboard and filling it with the last of the coffee.

Her dad folded the morning paper and set it down by his breakfast plate, empty except for a dollop of syrup. "Seemed like a good idea after last night."

Playing dumb was the last resort of someone who had no

clue what else to do, which pretty much described her before her first cup of coffee, since her dad never had Mountain Dew in his fridge. "Why's that?"

"I came home earlier than expected and quickly went upstairs. Not that either of you noticed," her dad said. "He seems nice enough."

Oh yes. Here it was. The Midwestern passive-aggressive advice framed as help when it was actually an invisible switchblade knife to the kidneys. She took her mug and sat down across from her dad, steeling herself for what was going to come next.

"But," he went on, "I don't think he's interested in being just friends, so if that's all you want then you should probably tell him."

Okay, that was not what she'd been expecting—especially not after last night, which had been all about letting off some sexual steam and nothing more. Not with him. Not when it came to her. Still, she was so tossed off-balance by the sincerity in her dad's voice that she just sat and blinked at him while he took a sip of his coffee.

He set the mug down and let out a deep breath. "It's not nice to lead someone on."

Her dad spoke from experience. After the divorce, her mom had married a Greek tycoon, yes, an actual real-life one. After that, neither of them had seen much of her—unless Lucy's new stepdaddy had picked up a new mistress. These women had never lasted long, but while they did, her mom always came back to Antioch to visit her sweet baby and see dear friends, her mom had always said. In reality, she'd come for the ego-buffing that only Lucy's dad could offer.

She'd tell him in a low, confidential voice about how horrible everything was while pressing her hand—bright with diamond rings—against his upper thigh. Lucy had walked in on them like this, once, twice, too many times to count. And it had always ended the same, with her dad believing this time was different.

It never was. Her mom always left.

Bless his heart, her dad had loved her mom. He'd told Lucy one night that he'd fallen for her mom the moment he first saw her and didn't stop until the tycoon's lawyer showed up on their front door to inform them of her death. Accidental drowning when she'd fallen from the tycoon's yacht.

Lucy had been sixteen, and even on the day of the funeral, she didn't cry. She never had. What was the point? Tears weren't going to fill that empty ache of abandonment.

"I know you'll do the right thing, Muffin."

Leading someone on was the last thing Lucy would do, even if she looked like her underwear model mom instead of her dad's favorite high-calorie treat.

She cleared the emotion out of her throat and found her voice, finally. "Frankie is just a friend."

"Does he know that?" her dad asked as he bent to the side and scratched Gussie behind the ears.

"Have you seen him?" What was her dad putting in his coffee these days? "We're not exactly in the same dating league."

He cocked his head to one side. "Why not?"

"Dad, I love you, but I don't want to have this conversation."

They'd had it too many times. She'd come home crying after another day of people being shitty to her—the taunts, the cruel practical jokes, the just general meanness of people for no other reason than that she was an easy target. Her dad would hug her and promise it would get better. It did, but not until she'd figured out the best defense is a great offense.

She wasn't born brassy, mouthy, balls-to-the-wall tough. It had been how she'd survived.

She must have been silent for too long, because her dad

got up from his seat and walked around to her side of the table.

"You know I love you."

"I know, Daddy. I love you too." Damn, and there was that clogged throat again, this time with the uncomfortable sensation of unwelcome tears in her eyes. Blinking the wetness away, she stood up and hugged her dad just like she used to on those bad days—the ones when the kids in her middle school had asked her if she'd eaten her mom and that's why she was gone. "Do you think she ever realized what she was missing?"

Her dad gave her an extra squeeze, then took a step back, lifting her chin so she had to look him in the eyes.

"If she didn't, then she was a fool."

In twenty years, that was as close to a bad word as she'd ever heard her father say about her mother. Her chin was just starting to quiver when Gussie went nuts, scampering across the kitchen floor like a bullet shot from a .44. She and her dad turned just in time to see Gussie launch himself at Frankie, who protected himself by catching the flying French Bulldog and holding him out at arm's reach.

"Am I interrupting?" he asked as the dog wriggled in his grip.

The dog was distracting, but not enough for her not to take in the sight before her. He stood in the kitchen doorway, running shorts riding low on his hips and a sweat-soaked T-shirt clinging to his washboard abs.

"No," her dad said. "Just a little father-daughter bonding."

Frankie squatted and released the dog, then stood before Gussie could make a run at his face. "Well, I'm just going to head upstairs to shower and then I'm good to go to kick Constance's butt today."

Now wouldn't that be nice. She wasn't above a little revenge in the form of idiotic picnic games.

"Sounds like a plan," she said.

He opened his mouth as if to say something else but must have changed his mind, because instead of saying something he gave her a look she felt down to her toes. Then he turned and walked down the hall.

She shouldn't have leaned a few inches to the side to watch him walk away. She shouldn't have…but she did.

"Just friends, huh?" her dad asked with a chuckle.

She hustled over to the kitchen table, where her coffee loaded down with a Mountain Dew's worth of sugar waited. "Yeah, Dad. Just friends."

The kind who gave each other knee-knocking orgasms and drove cross-country to act as fake dates at a high school reunion. What could possibly go wrong?

• • •

Everything went straight to shit the moment Frankie picked up the potato sack from the pile at Constance's feet.

"You've got to be kidding me," he said, holding up the narrow bag chest high. "I can barely fit one of my legs in here, let alone one of mine and one of Lucy's."

Constance made a tsk-tsk sound. "Well, we can't have different sizes for different teams, that would just be preferential treatment and we like things to be fair. That's the size that fits the majority of people, so that's the one we went with."

Yeah, it would fit the majority of people who were twig-sized and short. The bag covered his knee and that was it.

"You know, there's two words for someone like you, Constance."

She stiffened and crossed her arms in front of her chest. "What's that?"

Leaning in close enough that the cloying scent of her

flower perfume just about cut off his oxygen, he said, "Second place."

Then he turned and started toward where Lucy stood across the Antioch Park by the potato sack race starting line. The sound of Constance's outraged gasp put a smile on his face that he couldn't have hidden even if he wanted to.

When he stopped by Lucy, she took one glance at him and shook her head.

"What have you been up to?" she asked, looking like one of his fantasies come to life in a red top and a red skirt that swirled around her thighs at even the hint of a breeze.

"Psyching out the competition."

It must have worked, because they managed to make the stupid narrow bag work and ended up coming in first place. The fact that the bag was such a tight fit actually worked in their favor because they could concentrate on speed rather than trying to hold up the potato sack. Of course, the downside to that was that he didn't have an excuse to put his hand anywhere near the hem of Lucy's skirt.

He didn't get the opportunity during the next game, either. That was blind building, which meant he was blindfolded and tasked with building a replica of Antioch High School out of popsicle sticks with Lucy's verbal directions being his only guide. They probably would have done okay, but ended up coming in at second place behind Constance and her pencil-pushing husband, Bryce.

It was Frankie's fault. He kept getting distracted by Lucy's voice.

And by distracted he meant turned on. It was damn hard to listen to her and not picture those cherry red lips of hers forming each word. What could he say, he was a walking, talking billboard for pent-up sexual frustration after being around her for the past few days. Add in what they'd done last night, and he was a lost cause.

However, all he had to do was to hold out until tonight, and then he was going to turn on the potent Hartigan charm that had been getting him laid since forever. She wanted him. He wanted her. There was no reason why this couldn't work. It was just what both of them needed.

Really, as far as the relationship tools he had in his arsenal, good sex was pretty much the best thing he had going for him.

"Oh, too bad about how things are turning out," Constance said after sidling up to him as he stood in the lemonade line. "There's just one more event this afternoon, and Bryce and I have it locked up."

"The obstacle course?" He glanced over to the other side of the park, where that event had been set up.

There were tires contestants had to hop through, a section where they'd have to army crawl under ropes, a water balloon firing squad, and more. Lucy had taken one look and dashed home to change so she wouldn't have to deal with all of that in a skirt.

"There's a climbing wall," Constance said, pointing to the wooden structure at the end of the course. "It's a tough one."

There was nothing in her tone that was a callback to her bitchy greeting the other day, but he couldn't shake the feeling that there was an underlying animus. "What is your problem with Lucy?"

She smoothed her palms over her blond hair, held back in a ponytail, and looked around as if to make sure no one overheard him. "I don't know what you mean."

"You have to admit this attitude of yours is extreme for someone who's not fifteen and a hormonal wreck. Hell, it's extreme even for that."

Something flickered in the woman's blue eyes, something that looked a lot like the kind of old hurt that had been picked at for so long it was just layer after layer of scar tissue. "Let's just say she brought it on herself, coming into school with those expensive clothes and fancy jewelry her mama bought her when most folks barely had enough money to put food in the fridge after the Pacifica Company plant shut down."

Bingo. Insecurities didn't skip over the pretty people. "So you were jealous?"

"No." She narrowed her eyes at him, her entire body practically sparking with fury. "I was pissed."

"Seems like you still are." And that was the understatement of the year.

Constance marched off right as he spotted Lucy making a beeline straight for him. Gone was that sexy skirt, replaced with a pair of cropped yoga pants and long, flowing sleeveless shirt.

"Cavorting with the enemy?" she asked once she got to him.

He handed her a lemonade. "Just trying to work some shit out."

"Well, do it from the starting line. We've got to win this one if we're going to stay in the race. Good thing I do the Waterbury charity color run obstacle course every year. Now let's go do this."

And they did. It wasn't easy, that was for sure, but Lucy was in great shape. The woman would kill it on the fire department obstacle training course.

He and Lucy were celebrating with drinks in a corner booth at the only bar in downtown Antioch before heading back to the house to get ready for the Antioch town carnival tonight. Then, there was one more day of activities and the reunion dance, which was set up to be a repeat of Lucy's senior prom, complete with the Under the Sea theme.

"Who did you go to your prom with?" he asked, handing her a beer.

"I didn't." She gave him a look that just about screamed *duh*. "I was the fat girl and designated class punching bag, no one was going to ask me."

"Not everyone could have been like Constance." Just the idea of it had him grinding his teeth.

However, he'd seen her today talking with people at the park, giving old friends hugs. Surely all of those people couldn't have been complete assholes.

She seemed to think about it for a second, taking another drink. "You're right. Really it was just Constance and her friends that were total jerks"

"Did you wear a lot of expensive stuff to school?" he asked, thinking back to the conversation he'd had with Lucy's archnemesis.

"Oh, you mean the mommy guilt gifts?" She chuckled, the rough-edged sound not even hinting at amusement. "Yeah, my mom left us for a rich tycoon when I was a kid. But she'd visit whenever they were on the outs and she'd feel guilty, remembering the daughter she'd left. So she bought all these ridiculous clothes. They weren't really me, but she'd convinced my dad that if I just dressed in a certain way— basically the way she did—that I'd have more friends."

"It didn't work out that way."

She shook her head and sighed. "Not even close."

"Constance mentioned the clothes." He had no clue why he was getting involved in all of this. It would be easier just to chalk up Constance as a class-A bitch and move on, but he couldn't let it go. It was a sore spot for Lucy, one he could tell she couldn't stop poking at—and she wouldn't until she worked it all out, and that was as bad for her as it was for Constance to hold on to a stupid high school grudge. "She said you thought you were better than everyone else in high school."

"She couldn't have been more wrong. I thought

everyone—and I mean everyone—was better than me. My insecurity was legendary."

"You don't seem like that now." If anything, she was the kind of tell-it-like-it-is, stand-up-to-anyone woman who could kick someone's ass without chipping a red-tipped nail. God knew, she loved giving him shit all the time.

She raised her bottle and clinked it against his. "It's amazing what a thick, defensive layer of fuck-you can hide." Taking a short pause, she eyeballed him. "Now are you just avoiding talking about last night, or are you really into years-old gossip?"

That was his Lucy, getting straight to it. Really, she'd held out longer than he'd expected, considering how direct she usually was. Of course, that didn't mean he was ready to lay all of his cards out on the table.

"You want to talk about last night?" he asked, taking a drink of the super hoppy local IPA.

"I know I said we shouldn't, but it's a woman's prerogative to change her mind." She took a deep breath, a *V* of worry creasing the space in the middle of her forehead. "I don't want to be the person to make you break your word to yourself."

"About being on the sex bench?"

She nodded. "Yeah."

"It's okay, I'm back in the game." Oh, was he ever.

That little break had shown him one very important thing. It wasn't what he was doing that was the problem, it was who he was doing it with. The time he'd spent with Lucy was different than with other women because of his need to compartmentalize coming back to bite him on the ass. He'd put Lucy in the friend zone, but she wouldn't stay there. Their whatever-it-should-be-called was about more than just physical satisfaction. Hell, up to this point it had been all about physical denial. She made him laugh. She made him think. She made him wonder how in the hell he hadn't figured all of that out before their little what-is-sex conversation last night.

The truth of the matter was, she was right. Sex was different when you cared about the other person in more than just the general humanitarian sense.

"Don't make a joke of this," she said. "Consent is important, and I don't want to put you in a position where you don't think you can say no because you're a nice guy, or because you're just really horny and I'm willing."

Fucking A. Lucy had no clue what she did to him. He dropped his hand to her knee, skimming it upward. Thanks to their booth's location, no one could see what he was doing—which was basically nothing because she'd switched from a skirt to yoga pants. However, it was enough to remind her of exactly what had happened last time he'd had his palm on her thigh.

"You're not pushing me." He slid his hand higher until his fingertips brushed her center, making her eyes flutter. "I'm fucking desperate to be between your thighs again—not anyone's thighs but yours. And I will be, if you'll have me." He withdrew his hand, picked up his beer bottle, and hoped like hell she didn't notice how badly he was white-knuckling his control right at the moment. "But not until tonight."

Lucy laid the back of her head against the booth and closed her eyes. "You've got to be kidding me."

Yeah, that was the desperation raging through his body, too. But he had to stick to the plan he'd cooked up last night. Build it up. Draw it out. Make her want him as much as he wanted her.

In other words, hope like hell he could convince her that he just might be more than a good lay.

"How many times do I have to tell you that patience makes it hotter?"

Going slow, as he was learning, was all about savoring,

building anticipation, making the want a need. Fuck. Their entire trip so far had been foreplay, and he wasn't about to blow it in the home stretch.

And whatever happened with Lucy, it wasn't just a let's-fuck-in-the-bar-bathroom kind of thing. It was more. It could be more. He didn't know. All he knew was that this was different, and he couldn't wait for tonight.

...

Lucy shut her bedroom door and put her thumbs to work.

Lucy: *SOS*

Gina: *That sounds promising.*

Lucy: *In what world does SOS sound promising?*

Gina: *The one where you're off gallivanting around with Frankie Hartigan.*

Shaking her head, she crossed the room to her closet so she could find a sundress that would help her stay cool at the carnival tonight. These weekend long events were the social event of the year in Antioch and other small towns across the state. Families timed their family get-togethers around them so the out-of-towners wouldn't complain there was nothing to do. Locals looked forward to them as a well-earned way to let off steam and check out potential dating partners. The county carnival was such a big deal that the reunion schedule for the night was left totally open so everyone could go—including her and Frankie, which, much to her chagrin, was why she was spending more time looking at her dress options and texting the reinforcements.

Lucy: *Gallivanting? With Frankie? You are a hopeless romantic.*

Gina: *Hello? Wedding planner here. Of course I am. So what's up? Did you kiss him?*

She hesitated, her thumbs hovering just over the keys, her heart beating fast as she remembered that kiss and what came after.

Lucy: *Yes.*

Gina: *And?*

Lucy: *More.*

Gina: *Hell, I was just looking to see if it was good. U had sex with Frankie Hartigan???*

Lucy: *Not yet.*

But really that's exactly where they were heading—a prospect that was both terrifying and electric.

Gina: *Get you some!*

Lucy: *This is a bad idea.*

Gina: *Why? You have a thing against orgasms?*

She flopped down onto the bed and let out an exasperated huff. Not that she was annoyed with Gina. Nope, the target of her ire was herself.

Lucy: *No, because it's Frankie.*

Gina: *Exactly. If the Waterbury chick whisper network is to be believed, you will have many, many orgasms.*

Lucy: *That's the problem.*

Gina: *???*

Lucy: *Because, despite what some people may think, I have options and I don't need a pity fuck from Frankie, who has probably banged every other woman in town.*

Gina: *1. Hell yes you have options. 2. Who said anything about a pity fuck? 3. No slut shaming.*

Lucy: *He just came on this trip as a weird favor for unknown reasons. And no shaming meant. He can fuck as many women as he wants, I just don't want to be just another faceless number.*

And really, that's what it came down to. She wanted to be wanted for her, not because she was convenient.

Gina: *So you like him?*

Lucy: *Of course I do. He's very likable.*

She let out a groan and closed her eyes. It wasn't fair. She snapped her eyes open at the ping alert of a new text.

Gina: *No, you really like him.*

Lucy: *Liking him would be a very bad idea.*

And a moot point because it was too late.

Gina: *Stop being so cautious and live a little. There's nothing wrong with liking someone.*

There was when the likelihood of ending up hurt was less than a sliver away from 100 percent.

Gina: *You're awesome. You know it. Stop focusing*

so much on maintaining that tough-chick facade and let yourself have fun without worrying about what it all means.

Lucy: *Are you saying I'm overanalyzing things?*

Gina: *Only since probably birth.*

Her bestie wasn't wrong. It took work to always be on alert for a nasty look or a snide comment so she could be prepared to strike back. It was a survival skill that had translated into the job she loved. The skills she'd learned walking the halls of Antioch High School made it so she was always ready with the perfect answer for whatever crisis one of her clients found themselves in. Of course, it was really hard to turn that off—especially when it came to protecting her own vulnerable soft spots.

Lucy: *Thanks for the chat. Gotta run.*

Gina: *No worries. Gotta go, too! It's cannoli time. xoxo*

Sitting back up, Lucy let all of it roll through her head, then stopped herself. Gina was right. She did overanalyze. But not tonight. She seized on the thought with both hands. Tonight she'd just roll with it.

Chapter Thirteen

The sun was setting, and downtown Antioch was packed with people for the annual summer carnival, but Lucy just kept searching the crowd for one man in particular. They'd gotten here fifteen minutes ago, and he'd disappeared almost immediately.

She scanned Main Street, looking down toward the big public parking lot that had been transformed into ride central with a neon Ferris wheel looming over the Tilt-A-Whirl and teacups. The street from the park to the parking lot was shut down to traffic and lined with booths offering everything from predictions of the future to games of skill. Sure, there were a lot of people, but finding a giant redhead shouldn't be that hard.

"Looking for me?"

A surprised gasp escaped, and she whirled around. "Where have you been?"

Frankie held his hand above his head to show off a long row of tickets that dangled almost all the way to the ground.

"You've got to be kidding." She was here for local beer

and people-watching. That was it.

Frankie just grinned at her like a kid on Christmas morning. "Who comes to a carnival and doesn't try to knock over the milk jugs with a baseball or ride the Ferris wheel?"

"This woman," she said.

There was nothing fun for a woman like her in going to the guess your weight booth or having the carnival worker give that little oh-boy-here-we-go huff before shoving the safety bar into her stomach and fastening the latch.

"Okay, I won't make you actually have fun at the carnival," he said, wrapping an arm around her waist and pulling her tight against him in a way that sent her pulse into overdrive. "You can watch me win you an oversized stuffed llama. You know you're desperate to have one to put in your office back home, so it can stare disapprovingly at your clients when they come to you for help after fucking up."

"I don't need any backup in that department. I scare my clients enough as it is." It was true. She'd had football players who could bench press a car go apologetic after she'd read them the riot act.

"Then Luke the Llama can lighten things up." He stuffed the tickets into the pocket of his jeans and jerked his chin toward the line of skill game booths lining Main Street. "Come on."

She hesitated, looking around at everyone, knowing that there would be stares, maybe a comment or two from concern-trolls about whether having those deep-fried Oreos was a good idea for someone like her. Her skin crawled with the ugly anticipation of it.

Really, it was amazing. In her office, she never had a moment of doubt, because when it came to spinning a crisis, no one did it better than she did. But back home in Antioch? That nervous and insecure fifteen-year-old she'd thought she'd ditched all those years ago came rushing to the forefront—and she hated it. Really. Hated. It.

"Okay, let's do this," she said.

And they did. There was the game where they had to throw the baseball to knock over the milk jugs (which they both decided were weighed down with anvils), a magnetic fishing game (where she won and declined a goldfish), and a test-your-strength hammer (Frankie's ego grew three sizes when the metal puck went flying up the pole and slammed into the bell). And the whole time, they laughed and talked about dumb things, like which *Bob's Burgers* character was the best (Louise, always Louise).

In a way, hanging out with Frankie was like hanging out with her girls. For the past few years, she, Gina, and Tess had a standing girls' night at Paint and Sip, where they'd drink wine, catch up on one another's lives, and paint something ridiculous—nothing could top the woolly mammoth in a hot tub. Those nights involved a lot of wine, a ton of gossip, and relaxed giggles.

Running around the carnival with Frankie while trying to beat the rigged games was like that, with the addition of extreme sexual tension.

Like right now, when she couldn't help but notice how nice his ass looked in the shorts he was wearing and the way his dark T-shirt showed off just how broad his shoulders were as he stood in front of the Shoot the Duck booth. A shoulders girl? Her? She never had been before, but then again, she'd never spent this much time with someone like Frankie Hartigan before. It was definitely a blessing and a curse. That little talk they'd had over beers at the bar hadn't been far from her mind since lunch. His whole "patience makes it hotter" philosophy was going to kill her.

He turned away from the lineup of paint splattered ducks, a paintball air rifle in his hand, and shook his head. "I'm from Waterbury, not the sticks of Antioch. When in the hell would

I have ever shot off a gun?"

The way he said it with just a hint of teasing and the dip of his gaze to the lowish neckline of her shirt let her know just how full of shit he was. He thought he'd get her to take this game, so he could stand behind her and watch her ass instead of her gameplay like he had at the other booths. Yeah. That wasn't going to happen.

"It's easy," she said, not making a move to take the air rifle from him. "You just point and shoot. Sort of like how a hose would work."

One side of his mouth kicked up into a sexy grin. "I am familiar with those."

Of course he took it there. She rolled her eyes at him but managed to keep the giggle his comment elicited under wraps. "A fire hose, not your personal one, you pig."

"Don't knock the animal who gives us the glory known as bacon." He held up the air rifle. "Now, how do I do this? Are you sure you wouldn't do better at this one?"

"Oh, for the love of Sunday mornings," she grumbled.

Sure, she sounded frustrated—and she was, but not the way some may have thought. When she grabbed a step stool that raised her up to his height, plunked it down behind Frankie, and then took her place behind him, her entire body was humming. She had to step close to him, so much so that her breasts pressed against his back, so she could reach around him and put her arms in line with his as he held the air rifle.

"See that little thing that sticks up from the barrel?" she asked, her lips practically touching the shell of his ear.

He took in a ragged breath. "Yeah."

"Line that up with your target." She waited a few beats. It was about time he was the one suffering with the whole patience-makes-it-hotter thing. "Let out a breath." She blew against his ear, just to demonstrate proper technique, of course. "And pull the trigger."

Just as he was about to fire, she licked his earlobe. The man jumped. The shot cracked. The paintball pellet exploded out of the barrel and splattered against the giant stuffed llama hanging in the corner of the booth.

Quicker than she could let out a breath, he turned around and curled an arm around her waist so she didn't fall off the stool. They were face-to-face like this, and she could take in every detail of him up close from the dusting of freckles across his nose to the small, faded scar on his chin to the heady promise in his eyes that he would get her back for that in the most patient way possible.

Her pulse went haywire as anticipation skittered across her skin until her entire body felt like a live wire.

"You did that on purpose," he said, his voice low and his mouth almost close enough to kiss.

"Yeah." Okay, that's what she meant to say, but it came out as more of a sigh. What could she say, getting the full force of Frankie's attention when you were pressed against him in the most intimate way possible with clothes on was a lot for a woman to process.

She could barely hear the tinny sounds of the carnival music or the crowd filtering past. Everything had been muted as she stood there on that stool, with Frankie's arm around her, filled with the certain knowledge that a kiss—and not just any kiss, but a brain-wiping, oh-my-God-don't-ever-let-it-end kiss—was coming.

"I said, here's your prize," the older man wearing an Antioch First Baptist T-shirt who was working the booth practically shouted at them from all of two feet away. "There's no way I can give it away to someone who actually earned it now."

The rest of the world came screaming back into existence. There were more people in the world than just her and Frankie. Huh. That was a little bit of a surprise until she got her brain back online.

She stepped down from the stool, slipping out of Frankie's grasp, and picked it up. "Sorry about that."

The booth man, who like everyone else working the carnival was a local, accepted the stool and handed her the llama in return, amusement glittering in his eyes. "Not to worry, I was young and full of sass at one point in time during my life, too."

She and Frankie were laughing and arguing about which one of them was sassier while walking between the Tilt-A-Whirl and The Hammer toward the Ferris wheel when they were stopped by an unmistakable voice.

"I didn't realize they made stuffed animals that big," Constance said, her words slurred. "It's almost as big as you are, Muffin Top."

Lucy and Frankie turned. Constance, per usual, looked absolutely perfect, from her casual yet cute outfit to the waves of her blond hair—right up until a closer look exposed the pained tightness around her mouth, the sheen of perspiration making her forehead dewy, and the glassy look in her blue eyes. Perfect Constance was drunk as hell—and back to her high school mean-girl self.

Next to her, Bryce blanched and shot them an apologetic look. "I think it's time to head home, honey."

Constance didn't even acknowledge what her husband had said. Instead, she looked up at Frankie. "I don't know what's wrong with you, but it's gotta be big if you're with her. Why else would someone like you be with someone who looks like that?"

A punch in the gut wasn't the right metaphor for how Lucy felt at that moment. Run over by a train? That was closer, but still not quite right. Whatever it was, the pain of it shocked her into silence.

Next to her, Frankie wasn't suffering from the same

affliction. "You fucking bit—"

She put her hand on Frankie's arm to shush him. There wasn't any point. Bryce was dragging Constance away, his head close to hers as he said whatever it was that kept the other woman's feet moving.

Lucy just stood there, shell-shocked, the hateful words on repeat in her head.

There must be something wrong with him.

It took a second, but her anger started pummeling her in hot waves of fury. Of course there had to be something wrong with Frankie if he was with her, because people sure seemed to think there was something wrong with *her*. Her degree, her professional success, her friends, none of it mattered to some people who would only see her as the fat chick to ignore or to passive-aggressively correct. She wasn't a person. She was a walking, talking morality lesson of what happens when a woman lets herself go, when she fails to meet society's expectations.

By the time Constance and Bryce were out of visible range, her gut was a sloshing mess of angry bile and humiliation.

"I'm not really in the mood for the Ferris wheel anymore," she said, squeezing the llama too tight for a cheap carnival stuffed animal, but it was better than tracking the witch down and strangling her. "I need to cool off."

Most people would have downplayed the bullshit of what had just happened by saying it was just the ramblings of a drunk—or they would have looked at her with pity. Not Frankie. He laid his hand at the base of her spine, offering the comfort she so desperately needed at the moment.

"Does this town have a pool?" he asked. "I wouldn't mind a little cool-off myself."

"Oh, there's a pool all right, but I've got a better place in mind."

Emerson Lake wasn't really a lake so much as it was an

oversized pond a mile down a dirt road in the woods with a floating dock in the middle. When she was growing up, all the cool kids at school had hung out at Woodson Lake, which was bigger and had a beach. Lucy and her small group of friends—none of whom had come back for the reunion—had taken over Emerson Lake and made it their own.

The bubbling anger had cooled to a simmer by the time Frankie parked his car in the makeshift parking spots between two copses of trees. Once she'd slipped off her shoes and put her toes in the water, her vision wasn't tinted with red. It was close to what she needed, but not quite there. She needed more. She needed water up to her chin, she needed to float free, she needed to be able to let go.

"Turn around," she said, reaching behind her for the zipper of her dress.

Of course, that just had him turning so that he faced her straight on as they stood on the edge of the lake. "Why?"

"Because I'm taking my clothes off." The sound of her zipper going down seemed way louder than the gentle lap of the water against the shore.

But talk was cheap. She wouldn't let Constance's drunken verbal vomit hurt her anymore, and she wouldn't be fooled by Frankie's sweet nothings. Just go with it? She should have known better. This was why she led with insults. Being always on the defensive meant not getting sucker-punched by the assholes of the world who knew nothing about her but felt perfectly fit to judge her anyway. She knew who she was. She was the woman who'd made something of herself, and fuck all those people who couldn't stand that.

Fuck. Them.

"And I don't get to look?" Frankie said it with a joking tone, but even in the moonlight there was no hiding the serious set of his jaw.

"No matter what happened the other night, it's different

when you can see the whole package, and I'm done with people who can't accept me for who I am for one day."

She'd been through it before. Occasionally there had even been comments. She'd walked out on those assholes while they were holding their dry dicks in their hands. That didn't mean it didn't hurt, though—that didn't mean it didn't still hurt today.

"And you don't think I'll like what I see?" Frankie's voice rose with frustration. "Have you been listening at all to what I've been saying to you for the past few days?"

Yeah, the past few days when he hadn't been having any sex at all for the first time in forever. And it wasn't like they hadn't known each other before. He'd had the opportunity to approach her before and hadn't until he'd turned off his sex tap. Hurt and anger and self-doubt and all the old insecurities brought to the forefront by coming home again pummeled against her ribs, made her lungs tight, and clogged her throat with emotion. They'd been at the same BBQs and parties for months, celebrating Ford's engagement to Gina, but he'd never given Lucy a second look—at least not one of *those* looks. And now he couldn't get enough of seeing her?

"You want to see?" she asked, her voice strained with pent-up emotion.

Tension came off him in waves as he spoke slowly and with absolute conviction. "Yeah, I do."

Okay. If that was what he wanted, that was exactly what he was going to get.

Frankie spoke all the right words, but he couldn't help himself. He was a natural-born flirt. He had probably been born looking like the redheaded son of Apollo. He didn't know what it was like to grow up in the shadow of a woman whose posters had been on adolescent boys' walls. He didn't see the disappointment in his mother's eyes when he reached for another cookie. He'd never been given clothes that were purposefully a size too small, supposedly to encourage him to shed just a few stubborn pounds. He hadn't been the cause of a rift between his parents that had ruined a marriage because he was an embarrassment to his mother.

That had been her.

All her.

And suddenly, everything just seemed too much. The "good for you"s her co-workers would offer when she'd mention she was heading out early to hit the gym. Or the way conversations always seemed to end up on their favorite "easy" exercises and healthy recipes whenever she was around. Or how someone would ask her if she'd lost a few pounds because she looked good today, as though that were a compliment. But most of all, she was tired of the pitying looks.

Why would Frankie be any different?

If he wanted to see all of her, fine. And when he showed pity in his eyes, at least once and for all she'd be able to get her hormones off of this roller coaster ride to eventual heartache.

Because the one thing she knew more than anything else: Frankie's rejection was going to hurt worst of all. Better to just get it over with. And if there was one thing Muffin Kavanagh knew best, a good offense was always the best defense.

"Okay, fine then." She released her hold on her dress and shoved it down over her hips so it fell down her legs and landed in a heap in the wet grass. "This is what you get when you have a naked Lucy Kavanagh." She reached behind her back to her bra clasp. "There are rolls." The bra hooks gave way, and she shook it off, letting it drop where it may. "There are stretch marks." She slid her thumbs into the waistband of her high-waisted panties meant to hold her not-perfect stomach in and pushed them with more force than necessary to her ankles. She kicked them off with enough power that they went flying through the night like a red cotton bullet and landed on a bush near where Frankie had parked. "There are curves where there should be dips." She held her arms out wide. "There is all of this, and I'm not apologizing for it—not to you and not to anyone."

Was she sounding a little bit like a woman on the edge of losing it? Hell yes, she was, and she didn't care. This was it. This was her.

The longer Frankie just stood there staring at her, the expression on his face unreadable for once, the louder the doubt demons screamed in her ears. She could last it out, though. She was a strong woman made of stern stuff and—the first tears burned the backs of her eyes. No. She would not. She would not allow herself to cry. She would not. Grinding her teeth together in an effort to clamp down on her emotions, she watched Frankie do nothing but stand there and stare.

At her size-twenty body.

Naked.

Without saying a damn thing.

Her nose twitched, and she had to blink back the tears. She may not be able to stop them, but she sure wasn't going to let him see her cry. God, this was worse than she imagined. She felt raw and exposed and vulnerable—everything she fought every damn day not to be.

"Yeah," she said, her voice raw. "That's what I thought."

Without waiting on a response that wasn't about to happen, she strode into the lake, waiting until she was waist deep before she dove under the water and began swimming toward the floating dock and away from such a stupid fantasy as being more than just a pity fuck for Frankie Hartigan.

Chapter Fourteen

Frankie had no idea what had just happened. Wait. He took that back. He knew what had happened, but was clueless about how he'd become the asshole in all of this.

What in the ever-loving hell was going on?

Once actual thought had burst through the haze of WTF, he started to strip down. It didn't take long, since he wasn't slowed down by having to deliver an angry tirade directed at a person who was so turned on by seeing Lucy's naked body that they couldn't think straight, let alone form words.

By the time he was bare-ass naked, the woman in question had made it out to the floating dock. She pulled herself up onto it, and Frankie's brain went into shutdown mode again.

The moonlight caught every inch of her skin, wet and tempting from her swim. He might have been—okay, totally was—mesmerized, but she couldn't even be bothered to look back toward the shore. Instead, she went straight to the metal box in the middle of the wooden square and pulled out a blanket. With a few efficient moves, she had it spread out on the dock and sat down, facing away from him as if he didn't even exist.

Oh no. That was not going to happen.

Lucy Kavanagh wasn't going to tell him that he couldn't possibly want her when every part of him—including the part pointing right at her—wanted her very, very badly.

That need, hot and urgent, spurred him forward into the water. On any other night, the squishy ground and God-knew-what that had brushed against his leg in the murky depths of the lake may have stopped a city boy like him who'd only ever been in chlorinated pools. However, tonight was a different story.

His patience had run out.

He made it out to the dock in record time, if someone kept records for naked night swimming to go have an argument with a woman who made him nuttier than a handful of peanuts. Reaching up, he planted his palms on the floating dock and vaulted up onto it.

"Lucy Kavanagh, you are fucking maddening."

She jumped up from the blanket with a squawk of surprise as if she really had figured he'd just gotten an eyeful of her naked and had slunk away into the night. That just pissed him off more.

"I am not that bitch Constance, or that guy from Marino's who told you to eat a salad, or any of the other dumbasses who've been too stupid to see you as you are."

She whirled around. "Oh yeah, and what's that?"

"One of those women who men start wars over."

He heard her breath hitch in surprise. God, all he wanted in the world was to take the three steps it would take to reach her so he could touch his fill, but he wasn't going to do that. Precarious didn't begin to describe the situation, and he wasn't about to intimidate her with his size or the fact that they were both naked, staring at each other like they were the answer to each other's questions.

At least she was to his. He knew that to be a fact and he'd swear to it in court—just hopefully with more clothing on. "Lucy Kavanagh, you're the kind of woman who makes a man so desperate he'll happily lose his ever-loving mind for the chance to touch you."

She let out a sigh and all the brusque, angry tension went out of her. "I'm not a small woman."

"Maybe you've noticed," he said, straightening to his full height. "I'm not a small guy."

Her eyes dipped lower, and yeah, he reacted to the appreciation he saw in her eyes when her gaze moved back up. A small smile teased the ends of that sweet mouth of hers, the one he couldn't stop fantasizing about, much to the detriment of his sanity, and she took a step closer.

"Do you even know what to do with that?" Her voice had gone husky. "What if all the talk around Waterbury is exaggeration?"

He raised one eyebrow, which was all the response that asinine question deserved. Still, he answered anyway. "Why don't you give me a try and find out."

She took another step closer, the blanket still clutched around her body like a shield, but almost near enough to touch. It was killing him to stay still, not to push his advantage, but this had to be her call. Thank all that was good in the world, because she took another step forward, and another and another until his body was tense with anticipation. Then, she reached out and glided a fingertip across his chest, following the line of freckles that he'd hated as a kid but was so goddamn thankful for now because Lucy seemed to be fascinated by them.

"What happened to being patient?" she asked, her tone as soft as her touch.

And that's all it took to break the last thread of self-control holding him back. "This."

In the next breath, his fingers were digging into her wet hair, his mouth on hers, and nothing else mattered. It was a frenzy of touching, licking, tasting as they came together. He glided his hands over her body, loving the way she reacted to him with throaty moans and answering touches.

He couldn't get enough of her, the round curve of her full hips, the weighty heft of her breasts, which filled his hands as he plundered her mouth. Fuck, there was so much he wanted to do with this woman that he had no idea where to start. With other women he'd always known, but this wasn't a flirty seduction, this was a full-on, fully engaged four-alarm fire, and he was glad as hell to be burning.

...

Lucy had lost her ever-loving mind. If she had a mind. She wasn't sure anymore, not after she'd turned around in time to catch Frankie pull himself out of the lake and onto the floating dock.

He had been naked. Had she mentioned that?

And he was still naked.

And kissing her.

And touching her.

And turning her brain into total rambling mush wherein she was having a silent conversation with herself because there was no way she could kiss this man and not do something a little crazy at the same time.

Had she mentioned they were naked? Yeah. Good, because they were, and his long, hard, and thick cock was pressed against her belly. And his hands? They were everywhere at once, and his touch wasn't gentle or timid or unsure as if he wasn't sure he wanted to be doing this. Nope. Frankie was a grab-a-handful-like-you-mean-it kind of guy, and she was reveling in it.

When his hands slid down her back and cupped her ass, he gripped both cheeks in his big hands and gave just the right kind of squeeze that made her break their kiss with an appreciative moan.

He let go immediately, his gaze searching her face. "Too much?"

As if that was even possible. "Not even close. I'm not some delicate flower who can't take a man like you."

"Is that a challenge?" he asked, his voice a low rumble.

"It's a promise." Lame response? Yeah, but she was lucky to be stringing two words together at this point. "So why don't you show me what you've got?"

He gave her a grin that would have set her panties on fire if she'd been wearing any. "Everything you need."

He yanked the blanket over so it was wrapped over the steel box, sat down, and tugged her down to him, so she straddled his lap with one knee on each side of his hips. Somehow enough of her brain cells were still functioning to make sure she balanced her weight on her legs instead of giving him the full brunt of it.

"Oh fuck that," he practically growled, a heated look promising a million naughty things in his eyes. "I want you right"—he grabbed her hips and pulled her lower so that all of her was pressed against him, without holding any of herself back—"here so I can feel that slick, wet pussy of yours against me as I finally get to taste these beautiful nipples of yours. Now give them to me."

She didn't have to think twice. She cupped her breasts and lifted them higher as her nipples hardened to tight buds under his hot gaze. For half a second, he just stared at them, looking every bit like a man who'd finally gotten what he wanted most in the world. Then, he dipped his head and lashed his tongue across her aching nipples. Sensation shot straight down to her core and, unable to stop herself, she arched her back and undulated against him.

"You like that, do you?"

Hell yeah was the scream that went through her head, but all that came out of her mouth was another moan because he did it again and again before sucking one nipple into his warm mouth and doing things with his tongue that sent shots of electricity through her body. This wasn't foreplay. This was a religious experience.

"Someday, I'm going to fuck these and come all over them."

The mental image of his cock sliding between her breasts as she held them close together was almost too much. She didn't just want that. She *needed* it. But before she could make the demand that they do just that right now, Frankie plucked at one nipple while rolling the other between two fingers, and the snap and crackle of that robbed her of any thought. All she could do was feel.

"I can't wait to watch these tits bounce when I fuck you, when I bury my cock so deep in you that you'll still feel it tomorrow."

She fought for words, for the ability to seize back some control before she fell into the abyss of feeling that made her forget everything else but the man beneath her. "Maybe I like it slow and soft and sweet."

One eyebrow went up. "Really?"

He cupped her breast and lifted it to his mouth, watching her as he grazed his teeth across the sensitive nipple with just enough force to make her suck in a quick intake of breath as she rocked against him, needing relief from the rough heat of his attentions.

"I'm not so sure you're telling the truth about that." His breath against her flesh was like a wave of fire against her wet nipple, which was aching for more attention. "Are you, Lucy?"

His hands glided down her body, over the more-than-a-handful curves to her hips, where he lifted her up and away from him without even a hitch in his breath. The agony of being away from him nearly made her cry out.

"If you want me to fuck you, you need to be honest. That's the only way I can give you what you want." His gaze traveled across her exposed flesh, and by the time he was eye to eye with her again, lust had turned his blue eyes dark and his jaw had hardened as if the effort to not just throw her down and bury himself inside her was costing him. "But you have to say the words."

Jesus. The man got bossy any time her panties got wet. Okay, part of what got her panties wet was him getting bossy, but she wasn't about to admit to that.

"I don't want nice and sweet." Okay, she wasn't *planning* to admit it, but her mouth had other ideas.

He settled her down on his lap again, positioning her so that there was no missing the thick steel of him against her, so close and yet so far away from where she wanted him most.

Letting out a harsh groan mixed with mumbled words that sounded a lot like "fuck me," he glided his hands up her back, following the line of her spine. "What do you want?"

"I want you to fuck me like you mean it."

And there it was, proof that being naked with Frankie Hartigan was pretty much truth serum, because it wasn't enough that she wanted him to want her, she wanted him to want her so badly that it was like he'd been waiting years just for her. That it wasn't just fucking. They were doing something more, something that took feeling good to feeling absolutely amazing—something that mattered. His gaze snapped back to her face, a sharpness in his eyes that made her think he hadn't missed her meaning.

"I've been wanting to do that since you parked that ridiculous car of yours in my garage."

Tension stretched taut between them as the narrative of just what this night meant began to morph into more. The realization made her pulse hiccup, and that old familiar ribbon of doubt that tied her insides into knots threaded its way through her.

"That must have made for some uncomfortable driving." Defensive joking? Her? Oh yeah, that was exactly what she was doing.

"You have no idea." Then he reached up and fisted her hair, pulling her head back and stealing the words from her mouth. "Now I want you to get off me, lay that gorgeous body of yours on the blanket, and spread your legs wide."

In an act of physical grace she didn't know she was capable of, she swung herself around and did exactly what he'd said. Following orders wasn't normally her thing, but the idea of not doing what Frankie asked didn't even occur to her.

"Fuck me," he said as he looked at her spread out before him. "I cannot believe I'm lucky enough to be the man who gets to fuck you. If you don't want that, you better tell me now, because it's all I can think about."

Good to know she wasn't the only one. And while it was kind of awesome to be looked at like she was the Venus de Milo come to life, she wasn't sure how much more of his studied gaze she could take. She planted her feet on the blanket and lifted her hips, offering herself to him in all but words. He bit out a curse and got on his knees between her legs. He slipped his hands around her ass and lifted her higher before finally lowering his mouth to her aching core.

He didn't just lick or taste or curl his tongue around her clit. He feasted. He did things with his tongue and lips that she couldn't describe beyond the fact that it turned her entire body into a supercharged live conductor of sexual need. There was nothing else in the world but Frankie's hands palming her ass, keeping her in place even when the sensation got to be too much, his mouth doing magical and probably illegal things to her sex, and the building sensation tightening her belly and making her lungs tight. This was it. This was the edge that he was going to push her off of, and she was so happy to go flying into space because she knew without even a slight hint of a doubt that when she did, Frankie would be there to catch her.

And she did come, her orgasm making her vibrate from her calves all the way up to her core until it built into one final body-arching climax that exploded in Technicolor vibrancy. It washed away all of the ugly that she'd endured during the week and left only a satisfied, blissed-out peace in its wake. It took a million eons, but she eventually surfaced from that post-orgasm coma and cracked her eyelids open. What she saw demolished that sleepy sensation and brought back that hungry, needy feeling in half a heartbeat.

Frankie sat back on his heels at her feet, looking down at her with his hand wrapped around his cock, slowly stroking it up and down, the bellend of it slick with pre-come. It was too much for a woman to see and not beg for more.

"Frankie." That his name crossed her lips sounding more like a plea than a demand didn't bother her in the least. Not now. Not while he was staring at her like that. "I need you inside me now."

"I wish I could." He grimaced. "Trust me, you have no idea how much I wish I could."

"So what's stopping you?"

"No condom."

Holy. Shit. On. A. Stick. It would be comical if it wasn't so heartbreakingly frustrating. She was on edge, reaching for relief. She wasn't about to let a thin piece of latex keep her from the one person who could give her exactly what she wanted, what she *needed*. So she decided to break her no condom, no nookie rule.

"I'm on the pill," she said. "My tests are all good."

"Are you sure you're okay with this?" he asked, more concern than entreaty in his voice. "I promise, I've tested clean for everything."

Words were her stock in trade, the kind that turned shit situations into public relations dreams, but this wasn't the occasion for it. This was a moment for action. So she rolled onto her knees, wrapped her hand around the base of his cock, and licked him from root to tip. Then, while maintaining eye contact, she slipped her fingers between her legs and rubbed her clit while sucking him deep in her mouth. Staying like this was a temptation, one she'd give in to another day.

"This is good, but I'm not going to be satisfied until you're filling me up and making me beg for more of your cock," she said. "Does that answer your question?"

His only answer was to yank her up from the ground, spin her around, and press his hand between her shoulder blades so she bent over and braced herself by putting her hands on the storage box. She widened her stance, looking over her shoulder at the man who had done this to her. He looked wild, staring at her with an intensity that nearly made her come just on that alone. She lifted her hips, sending him a universal invitation to bury himself balls deep, but he didn't come to her. Instead, Mr. Patience just stood there like a stubborn giant in the moonlight watching her.

"Frankie," she said, her voice a desperate whisper. "Please."

• • •

Frankie was ready to fall to his knees with relief when she said yes, but his cock had other ideas. It usually did. And now, looking down at her sweet ass, so full and round as she looked over her shoulder at him, something shifted in him.

He'd like to say it was a gentlemanly determination to go slow, give her everything she needed. It wasn't.

What shifted in him was whatever tie he had to civilization. The *mine* that roared through him at that moment was so strong, so visceral, that he couldn't even begin to lie to himself about being a modern man. This need, this sense of being a part of her was too real to be anything other than primal.

"Frankie," she said, the plea in her voice going straight to his balls. "Please."

Who was he to deny her? As if he could deny her anything.

Pulse pounding, he knelt down, lined up with her wet folds, and slid home for the first time in his life without a condom.

Fucking A. Sensation jolted him down to his toes as he sank deeper and deeper into her welcoming warmth. It was like nothing else he'd ever experienced. Correction. *She* was like no woman he'd ever known. The instinct and need to pull back out so he could plunge inside her again had a bead of sweat rolling down his neck, but he wasn't ready to give her up yet. Hell, he wasn't sure he ever would be.

However, Lucy—being Lucy—took matters into her own hands, pumping herself forward and back against his dick, controlling the pace and the depth as he reveled in the sweet torture of it all.

"You feel so fucking good," he managed to get out before she stole his breath again with a figure eight move with her hips.

"I could ride this cock all night. I'm gonna come so hard on you."

Her unrestrained honesty flipped a switch inside him, reminding him this wasn't just about how his dick was feeling. This was something more, something he couldn't put into words yet. So he tightened his grip on the soft flesh of her hips, bringing her back hard against him. And when she let out an answering moan of approval, he did it again and again until she was meeting him stroke for stroke, giving him everything. It nearly broke him seeing how beautiful she was at that moment, her lust unfurled like a flag and flown for all to see. Then, when he thought he couldn't take another moment of delicious friction, she started begging in nonsensical words that conveyed more than any well-worded pleas could.

Closing his eyes, he fought against the climax building at the base of his spine and plunged inside her over and over, leaning forward to change the angle and deepen the stroke, until she let out a scream of pleasure and came on his cock, milking it as wave after wave of pleasure wracked her body. It was all he could do to take measure of the moment before the string snipped and he lost the last thread of control, coming inside her so hard he lost himself in the sensation as she called his name.

By the time he'd come back to himself, he and Lucy were somehow sitting on the blanket. He had his back to the metal storage box, and she was sitting between his legs, the back of her head resting against his shoulder as he held her tight.

"I don't care how old I live to be," he said, dipping his head down and kissing his way up the long line of her neck. "I'm never forgetting that."

She laughed, the carefree sound carrying over the water. "Good, because I'd hate to be the only one who remembered."

"Next time, we're going to be somewhere that I can keep you all night so I can roll over and wake you up in the best way possible."

"Next time, huh?" she asked, relaxing against him as they snuggled closer and looked up at the stars. "Isn't that rather presumptuous of you?"

"Nope." Not if he had anything to say about it. This was only the first of many times.

She pushed up from resting against him and twisted so

they faced each other, a teasing grin curling her lips. "Your ego is even bigger than your—"

"Cock," he interrupted.

She threw back her head and let out a throaty laugh. "I was going to say car, but yeah, it's bigger than that, too."

He answered that bit of impertinence with a kiss, and she settled back against him. They sat in companionable silence, watching the stars twinkle above. Frankie wasn't a stranger to post-coital cuddling. Usually his brain was spinning out ways for him to leave sooner rather than later. This time, though, he just wanted to let the world go on by. So when Lucy started to make a move to pull away, he tugged her tighter instead and wracked his brain for something to talk about to get her to stay longer.

"No matter what your dad says," he started, not sure where those words were going, but the need to keep her here like this under the stars where it seemed like the rest of the world was just a dream was too strong. "I'm not afraid of real risk."

She looked at him, the ends of her dark hair tickling his chest. "You talked to my dad about your 'thing'?"

"You mean my stupid idea to stop having sex?" Because holding her like this right now, he was convinced he'd never had a worse idea than to put an obstacle between them.

"When did it become a dumb idea?" she asked.

"The minute you got in my car." Yeah, that was about the reality of it.

She kissed the spot on his chest where he could feel his heart beating and then rested her cheek against that same spot. "What did you talk about?"

"Well, he talked. I just kept telling him I wasn't going to talk."

"And that shut him up, did it?" She chuckled against his bare chest, the puffs of hilarity tickling his skin.

"No. He's kind of like you that way." Okay, he was *a lot* like her that way. "He said I was afraid of real risk, of emotional risk."

"But you're not?"

"No." He wasn't an idiot. There were things in his life that scared the shit out of him—most humiliating among them was his bone-deep fear of clowns and talking squirrels. "I just don't want to do to someone I love what my dad did to my mom."

The breath left his chest. He'd never said those words out loud. To anyone. It was the dark secret he'd carried for so long, he didn't realize how heavy it had become until he offered it to Lucy. He felt a little dizzy with the lightness invading his body, but maybe that's just because he'd forgotten to breathe. He took a deep breath and focused on the woman in his arms.

Lucy, always a woman in motion even when she was sitting, went still. "What are you talking about? They are the happiest couple I know."

From the outside, that's exactly what they looked like. Frank and Kate, married for decades with a raucous, close-knit family who didn't know the truth. Didn't understand what kind of man they sat down with every weekend for family lunch. But he did, and the one thing that scared him more than clowns or talking squirrels or talking squirrel clowns was the chance that he could turn out like the man he was named after.

"That's what I thought, too," he said, keeping his face turned up toward the stars, but he wasn't seeing them anymore. "In high school, I went down to the firehouse and caught my dad kissing one of the secretaries from headquarters."

They'd been pressed together. His dad had his back to the wall and the other woman, Becky he'd thought her name was, had been glued to his dad from toes to lips, clinging to his old man like he was the oxygen she'd needed to breathe.

Just the mental image of it all these years later hit him like a gut punch by Godzilla that left him gasping for breath again.

"What did you do?" Lucy asked, her voice soft, comforting.

He'd raged. He'd cursed. He'd wanted to take his dad's head off. But he didn't. Once the red cleared, he thought of his mom, his brothers, his sisters. What would they do if his dad left? It would break their hearts. And if there was one thing he'd never let happen, it was to let them hurt. He'd distracted Finian with a bullshit mission to get something from the corner store before his brother caught sight of Dad sucking face with Becky. Then, he'd confronted his old man.

"I told him that if it stopped, I'd never tell." Oh, his dad had told him some bullshit line that it wasn't what it looked like, but Frankie was old enough by then to know what he had seen.

"And did he?" Lucy asked.

"Yes." He'd watched his dad like a hawk after that, always mindful, never letting the others know what was going on, never letting on that there was a problem.

The silence stretched between them as the old nightmare ghosts flooded up to the surface, along with the guilt of keeping such a secret from his family. Part of him had wanted—still wanted—to tell them everything, unburden himself, but he couldn't. It was bad enough that his dad thought so little of his family that he could do something like that. There was no way he could do the same. So if that meant he shielded them from the ugly and ate the bile that rose each time he saw his mom look at his dad as if the sun rose and set on his smile? He'd take it. If it meant they got to live the lives they wanted, he'd take it.

"Are you sure it was a thing, or could it have been a weird moment?"

How many times had he asked himself the same,

especially when there was never even a hint of a repeat or shady behavior on his dad's part? "Even back then I knew the difference between a kiss and an I-want-to-fuck-you-against-a-wall make-out session."

"Wow," she said, sounding anything but impressed. "I never would have thought it."

"Neither has anyone in my family." He wrapped his arms tighter around her and pulled her close so the top of her head fit under his chin. "You're the only one I've ever told."

"So why didn't you tell the others?"

"I didn't want to see my mom hurt." The news that Frank Hartigan Sr. had kissed another woman would be a shiv to his mom's heart.

Lucy kissed his chest, right above where his heart beat against his ribs. "A protector to the core, aren't you?"

"I'm loyal. I know right from wrong." He paused, listening to the frogs or crickets or whatever other woodland animal his city ass couldn't define sing their song. "And I promised myself on that day that I'd never do to someone what my dad had done to my mom."

"You don't want to be alone, but you don't want to hurt anyone, either. Ever think of just trusting yourself rather than have a no-girlfriend rule?"

Yeah, he hadn't really thought of it before, but that made sense. "I wouldn't call it a rule, just more of a guideline until I met someone who really would be the beginning and end for me."

Someone who made him laugh all the time and drove him nuts some of the time. Someone who challenged him and didn't fall for his bullshit. Someone who got him to share his secrets while sitting naked on a floating dock because spilling his guts was the only thing he could think of to steal just another couple of minutes like this with her. Someone he actually liked.

"Frankie Hartigan, you really are the last of the romantics," she said, her words carrying just enough bitterness to soak through the sweetness.

"You don't believe in a one and only?"

She let out a huff of disbelief against his chest. "Growing up like I did, the child of divorce with a mother who came back and, shall we say, found solace with my father whenever her new husband had another mistress? True love doesn't seem realistic."

Ouch. That would definitely sting, but still... "That's pretty damn cynical."

"Okay, truth?"

"Yeah." Why should he be the only one with his ass literally and metaphorically hanging out?

She tugged at the blanket's corner, pulling it up and wrapping it around her, not as if she was cold, but as if she was trying to hide. She pushed away from him, stood up, and began pacing across the blanket spread out on the floating dock as if the words needed motion to get out. "I want that happily ever after someday, but I'm skeptical," she said, her voice barely above a whisper.

Reaching out to put his arms around her shoulders and scooting closer to her just seemed as natural as breathing. "You just need the right person to show you it's possible." Okay, maybe being around her and still on the comedown from a killer orgasm had made him a little more touchy-feely than normal.

"Are you applying for the job?" She gasped and looked at him with a look of pure, abject horror. "I didn't mean that. I know this, whatever it is, is only fun. You haven't led me on. I know you don't want more."

The words rushed out of her so fast they nearly tripped over each other as a huge swath of red made its way northward from her more-than-impressive rack. Because he was a human with eyeballs and she was a gorgeous naked woman in front of him, his gaze dipped down to her nipples, then lower across her belly and to those round hips that made his fingers itch with the urge to grab hold of all that softness and worship it. Damn, even after spilling his guts and while she was in the middle of an embarrassed ramble he wanted to toss her down and fuck her silly.

"What if I am looking for the job?" he asked. "Do you have an application on hand that I can fill out?"

She snorted and rolled her eyes at him. "Very funny."

Sure, he'd said it as a joke to lighten the mood and ease her embarrassment, but something about the idea settled somewhere deep inside of him and took root.

Lucy, her cheeks still pink, gave him a sassy wink. "Last one in has to fold up the blanket and put it away in the storage locker."

All he had to do was look at the blue-and-green checked material for a mental flash of what they'd just done on it to make his balls tingle in anticipation. "Do you think we should leave it after…"

His words died in the face of her hearty laugh. Seriously. The woman was practically bent in half as she giggled her ass off at him. Finally, when she could take a breath, she gave him a you-dumbass look and shook her head.

"The lake is part of my family's land," she said. "I'll come out in the boat before we leave and get rid of the damning evidence by tossing it in the washing machine at home." His shock must have shown, because she started laughing again. "You don't think I'm the kind of woman who goes skinny-dipping in public, do you? Come on, I have a professional reputation to uphold. Imagine me trying to scare the crap out of one of the Ice Knights players who'd fucked up when there were naked pics of me on the internet. That's a big oh hell no."

Of course, she hadn't left anything to chance. Not his Lucy. "You really are something."

"Yep," she said, taking three quick steps that brought her right to the edge of the platform. "And you really are the last one on the dock."

Then, with a shit-eating grin, she jumped into the dark water, surfacing a few feet away, and started swimming to shore. Of course, Lucy being Lucy, she rolled over on her back to wave at him before flipping over again and taking off. And all Frankie could do was watch because the sight of her mouthwatering ass shown off to perfection in the moonlight made his brain blank out and his dick get hard.

If he had Lucy Kavanagh's boyfriend application at that moment, he would have been filling it out. In triplicate. Immediately.

But he couldn't help wondering if she'd even still want to see him when they got back to Harbor City. What if she saw that failure in him, too? The one Shannon had pointed out—not with glee but pity—that he wasn't a guy who could deliver happily ever afters.

Chapter Fifteen

One thing was for sure. Being sober did not make Constance less of a complete and total bitch. Today, however, Lucy was not going to let the über-hag get to her. It was amazing what a few brain-blowing orgasms could do for a woman's state of mind.

She ignored the other woman when she waltzed over and stood next to Lucy a few feet from the front of the stage, where the next event for the reunion decathlon was about to start.

"Interesting," Constance said. "I figured you would have been the natural choice for this."

Without meaning to, Lucy curled her hands into fists before she realized it and had to take a few deep breaths so she could unclench her hands. Instead of responding, she focused on Frankie as he tied a plastic bib around his neck and sat down in front of the homemade berry pie for the pie-eating contest. She caught his eye, and he winked at her, making her insides do that ooey-gooey thing that sent all of her happy endorphins straight to her clit.

That little buzz of pleasure gave her the strength to turn to the woman determined to make her life hell like it was high school all over again and deliver a super sugary smile in place of a knuckle sandwich. "Frankie has many talents, including eating pie. Lots of pie. With gusto. Plus, there's always a big bang at the end."

It took a second, but Constance got it. Or at least Lucy thought she had, considering the way her face got all mottled and how she let out a huff of disgust before stomping away. The woman wasn't even trying to go the frenemy route. She'd moved on to a full-frontal assault. Lovely.

Yeah, getting laid well really did have a positive effect on her mood.

She must have still been riding the high of finally giving it back to her tormentor—and the fact that Frankie came in first in the pie-eating contest, no shocker there—to agree to take on the next challenge. Really, it was the only reason she could think of as to why she had her forehead pressed to the end of a bat and was spinning around and around as the crowd of reunion attendees counted to ten. Once she heard that, though, she popped up into a standing position and started running toward Frankie, who was standing about ninety feet away—the length from third base to home plate. Or at least she meant to run. Her legs were a wobbly mess, and the world was shifting as if she was on a boat and it was going down hard and fast.

"Come on, Lucy!" Frankie hollered at her. "You can do it."

"Lu-cy! Lu-cy!" the people around them chanted as they clapped and cheered her on.

Holding her arms out as if that could stop the ground from weaving this way and that, she stumbled and bumbled her way toward the blurry redheaded giant urging her forward. Thank God he was a big target, because otherwise she wasn't sure she would've made it. But she did.

She nearly knocked Frankie off his feet with the force of her clumsy impact, but she made it. Best of all, she beat Bryce, who had stopped three feet in front of Constance and was upchucking all the pie he'd gobbled in an attempt to win that contest.

By the time the next to last contest of decathlon, a game of cornhole, ended, she and Frankie were tied with Constance and Bryce in points. It was all going to come down to the big finale to be held during the dance tonight.

"So, are you ready to go home and get psyched up to win?" Frankie asked as they made their way to his car.

She thought about it. When the invitation to her reunion had arrived in the mail, the only goal she had was to show all of the people who had given her a hard time in high school that they didn't matter to her anymore. Of course just by thinking that, she was pretty much confirming, to herself at least, that they did.

But the past few days of participating in the decathlon had shown her something.

She'd gotten to talk—actually talk—with a lot of the people she'd graduated with. They weren't the same people now that they'd been then, any more than she was. Everyone had changed and grown. She wasn't unique in that aspect. And with that realization, something a lot like contentment settled into that spot and shoved out a lot of the old bitterness.

"You know, it doesn't really matter," she said, stopping at his car while he unlocked and opened the door for her. "I thought it would, but what matters is my life back home in Waterbury, not showing up people I went to high school with for the sake of my ego."

"I hope I can still help you have fun tonight," he said, a sexy rumble in his tone.

She got into the passenger seat. "Does that mean you're

going to sing karaoke for the final event instead of me?"

"Hell no," he said with a grin. "But I'll help you have plenty of fun later."

Now that, she didn't doubt for a minute.

• • •

Frankie hadn't gone to a prom after his freshman year—not because he didn't have plenty of date options, but because the nuns of St. Mary's had banned him from the big dance his senior year after an unfortunate experiment in what would happen if someone in a snorkel mask got sprayed down with a fire extinguisher in the middle of the cafeteria. He and Finian might have gotten away with it, too, if they hadn't picked their younger and way-too-rule-following brother Ford to test out their hypothesis—without Ford knowing.

Now Frankie was standing in the Kavanaghs' living room in a suit and holding a corsage made from a trio of bright red ranunculus flowers. He'd never heard of them before, but earlier when he stopped in at Wolfsbane Antiques and Collectibles to ask Henrietta where he could get a corsage for Lucy, the grumpy old biddy had snarled when he said he wanted to get a rose corsage.

"That woman, she deserves something a little more special than the default flower for people who've never had an original thought in their head, don't you think?"

As much as he hated to admit it, Henrietta had been right.

She'd sighed and had shaken her head. "Men are so easily stumped. And that is why I never said yes to Henry, no matter how many times he asked. Well, that and the fact that our names were practically identical. Could you imagine?" She'd pulled out an iPad with the largest screen possible. "Let's check the Google, shall we?"

Like the idiot he'd been feeling right about then, he'd nodded and kept his mouth closed.

"So how would you describe our girl Lucy?"

He hadn't even had to think about it. "Pretty. Funny. Smart. Amazing."

The older woman had typed away on her screen, her fingers moving faster than he'd expected from a woman Henrietta's age. Then she must have hit on something, because her fingers had stopped moving and she'd dragged her finger down the screen. When he'd tried to peek, she'd shot him an annoyed glare.

"Don't suppose I can add sexy-as-all-get-out to that list?" she'd asked.

He'd laughed. Not because what she'd said was funny—it was really fucking true—but because hearing it from someone who had probably spent the last million decades surrounded by antiques hit him right on the funny bone.

"Oh hell yes."

"Damn skippy," she'd said, grinning back at him, and then she'd glanced back down at her screen. "And are you dazzled by her charms?"

He'd given the older woman his best wouldn't-you-like-to-know sexy smirk. "Without a doubt."

"Then here it is, the ranunculus." She'd put her iPad down on the counter between them, faceup so he'd been able to see the bright red flower with tightly wound petals that formed a big bloom. "It says they are sexy and sassy. Plus it gets bonus points for its meaning." She'd tapped the text under the picture of the flower.

MEANING: I'M DAZZLED BY YOUR CHARMS.

Yeah, that just about summed it up. "Mrs. Campher, you are a goddess among women."

Her snowy eyebrows went up in the universal sign for no shit, sonny. "And don't I know it."

And that's how he'd ended up standing in the living room feeling like he'd become a cast member in some time travel movie where he'd gone back and gotten stuck in a younger version of himself. He hadn't had this much anticipation about seeing a woman since Alice Evers had slipped off her bra and shown him the first real-life boobs he'd ever gotten to see. In that moment on the bus on the way back from a school field trip to Harbor City's Natural History Museum, it was like getting a glimpse of a whole new world that he'd never known about before. It had knocked him six ways to Saturday and changed his whole perspectives on things.

That moment was nothing, however, compared to seeing Lucy walking into the living room in a tomato red dress that would have been simple in its design if it wasn't for the woman in it. The sleeveless dress had a deep *V*-neck that showed off the beyond generous curve of her breasts. The fit followed the lines of her body down to her waist, where it flared out into a skirt that ended right at her knees, showcasing those fucking amazing legs that had been wrapped around his head out on that floating dock.

"Wow." Yeah, not his most brilliant line ever, but he'd never meant it more.

Lucy did a little spin, sending her skirt a few inches up in the air and making him forget how to breathe. She glanced down at the ranunculus tied together with a silver ribbon and let out a small gasp.

"Did you get flowers?" Her eyes went wide with pleasure. "Why did you do that?"

"Just to see that expression on your face."

She stopped mid-step toward him, her hand going to her chest. He could practically read her emotions like she had a news ticker on her forehead. It went something like *oh shit*. She'd been more than plain last night. Commitment wasn't realistic. Skeptical, that's how she'd put it. He'd been right there with her for most of his adult life. Then he'd sat down at a table in Marino's across from a woman who busted his balls while sharing her french fries and making him laugh his ass off.

Not surprisingly, because Lucy was never thrown off her game for more than a second or two, she broke the moment.

"Frankie," she said, making his name sound like a plea and a promise, then punctuated it with a little chuckle. "You're going to ruin me for other men."

He was really beginning to hope so. Not that he was going to say that out loud and freak her out, but yeah, it was there. The idea that maybe there was more to this had definitely taken root.

Continuing his innate sense of when to cause absolute, joyous chaos, Gussie picked that moment to come sprinting into the living room on one of those unexplainable canine runs. The dog barreled right toward Frankie in what had become his signature move—leaping into the air and aiming straight for his balls.

Jealous because you don't have any?

Frankie made a raised-leg-twisting move to protect the family jewels while lifting the corsage up in the air. After Lucy's reaction, there was no way he was sacrificing the red blooms at the altar of a fat-tongued, pint-sized demon dog.

"Gussie, no," she hollered, rushing over to him and snagging the dog in midair as it bounced off him like he was a human bounce house. "You are such a naughty boy."

"He's just protecting his sister," Tom said as he walked into the living room.

Tom looked between her and Frankie before nailing him to the wall with a look that really did make him feel like he was picking up a date for the high school prom. Good thing Tom was carrying a phone instead of a shotgun. The man might be a sex therapist, but Frankie couldn't shake the feeling that that didn't mean he was okay with his daughter doing the deed.

"I just want to get a couple of pictures before you two leave," Tom said.

"Dad, it's not really prom," Lucy said, holding onto Gussie, who was still trying desperately to wriggle free, no doubt to continue Mission: Nose To The Crotch. "It's not even a real date."

Frankie tensed at that pronouncement before he could regulate his reaction.

Tom aimed his dead-eyed stare at Frankie. "Uh-huh."

Agreeing with the man's obvious doubts might be what Frankie wanted to do at that moment, but Lucy's dad knew the score even if she didn't. So, Tom continued to give him the stink eye as he snapped pics with his phone, telegraphing a don't-fuck-with-my-daughter message with every extra-hard tap on his phone.

Frankie may have missed a few proms before, but he was getting the whole experience now, and unless he fucked up royally, that would include getting laid, too—but not in the back of a car.

• • •

"Hey Muffin, can I have a quick word before you go?"

The perma-grin she'd been wearing since she walked into the living room and had seen Frankie standing there with a corsage faded away. Muffin. She fucking hated that nickname. It hurt a little each time her dad said it.

"Sure." She looked at Frankie, who was hot as hell in jeans and plain devastating in a suit. "Do you mind if I stay back here for a second?"

Frankie winked and gave her hand a squeeze before scooping Gussie up from the floor and walking with the dog out onto the front porch. Once he'd cleared the door, her dad turned to her, the serious expression on his face giving her no doubts that this wasn't going to be a very fun conversation.

"I know I've said it before, but are you sure this is just friendly?" her dad asked.

"Enough." Tension tightened her shoulders until they ached. "He's just a friend, Dad, it's nothing serious. Why do you keep fixating on this?"

"Maybe it's because I've been there."

And everything she'd stuffed down, all the promises not to let someone in like her dad hit her right in the feels. Unlike those who'd only read about it in books, she'd never seen the romance in unrequited love. She'd seen it from too close up as she watched her dad interact with her mom and seen how he had to rebuild himself after her mom had left—again.

"Believe me. I'm not the kind of girl someone like him goes after for the long term. Really, I'm not sure that there is a type of girl for him for that."

Her dad gave her a considering look. "So what, this is just for fun?"

Okay, this wasn't an awkward conversation to have with her dad even if he was a sex therapist. Nope. Not at all.

"Yep, just for fun," she said as embarrassment burnt her cheeks.

And please God let that be the end of this conversation. Unfortunately for her, the big guy upstairs was busy with other things at the moment, because as she moved closer to the doorway and a quick exit, her dad cut off her escape.

"You know, when I first met your mom, it was like that." He picked up a framed picture of Lucy from the bookcase near the doorway. The shot was one of the few that were pre-divorce, showing the three of them (her and her dad holding dripping ice cream cones) at a park. "It was fun. Then things happened so fast, and I thought I could change her, make her want something more than just fun. It's hard if not impossible to change other people, but you can change yourself for the better."

The sadness in her dad's voice cut through both ventricles of her heart with an efficiency that left her breathless. Even after all these years, even after everything her mom had done to him—to them—he still loved her. And that's why this had to be just fun between her and Frankie, because if it was more then there was only misery at the end. If she'd even thought they had any hope, Frankie's story about his dad would have extinguished it.

The reality of all that sparked an anger inside her she couldn't explain, but it burned hot and bright and immediate, so she lashed out at the closest person just like she had in high school.

"Frankie and I are not you and Mom," she said, her voice dripping with resentment and fury.

Her dad's professionally neutral expression never slipped. "I know that, Muffin, but—"

"I wish you would stop calling me that." God, she hated it. Had always hated it. Weren't fathers the ones who were supposed to love their daughters no matter what?

"Muffin?" A divot of confusion made a deep *V* in his forehead. "It's short for Muffin Top."

"I'm well aware of what it means and why you call me that." She inhaled a breath to slow her racing heart and tried to block out all the times the word Muffin or Muffin Top had been used against her at school, each syllable edged with cruelty as if she didn't realize that her body shape—the one she was so beyond apologizing for, not that she ever should have in the first place, but the world did a real job on a woman it deemed undesirable—didn't fit society's ideal. She'd never gotten that cutting denouncement from her dad, but that didn't mean his choice of nicknames didn't hurt. "Still, it would really be nice if you'd stop."

"But I've called you that forever, and it describes how I feel about you so well."

And that was a Mack-truck level whack to the gut. "What?" She gasped. "Disappointed by my size just like Mom had been?"

"God no," her dad said, his voice cracking with emotion as he reached out to her, taking her hands in his own. "I started calling you Muffin Top because it's the best part of the muffin. And as time went on, I shortened it to Muffin. It was never about your size." He pulled her in for a tight hug that she felt all the way down to her bones. "Lucy," he said, his voice shaking with sincerity. "I love you no matter what you look like because you're my daughter—and the best one I could ever imagine anyone having. I'm so sorry that the nickname I started using before you could walk has sounded like a dig at your size. I'll stop using it. Now. Today. Right away."

And there went the tears, washing away all of that built-up resentment about her most hated nickname. Her friends in elementary school had heard her dad use it and picked it up, too. And it had followed her straight through high school. Hell, people in this town *still* referred to her as Muffin Kavanagh. And she was sure they used the nickname for a very different reason. That didn't mean it was her dad's fault, though.

"Dad, you don't have to."

He took a step back, keeping his hands on her shoulders, and looked her straight in the eye. "I never want to do anything to make you second-guess what an amazing woman you've become. I'm so very proud of what you've done with your life. I know I wasn't always the best father—"

"Dad," she broke in. "You were great."

And because he looked like he was about to argue the

point, she wrapped her arms around his waist and tucked her head against his neck, breathing in the woodsy-sugary scent that she always associated with him.

"What do you think of Sweet Pea? No, that's food again. What about Lulu?"

Chuckling, she took a step back and used the back of her hand to wipe away the wetness on her cheeks—thank you, world's best waterproof mascara—and gave him a smile. "How about Lucy?"

He opened his mouth, shut it, and then gave her a chagrined look. "Yeah, you're right. You're not my little girl dancing around in the kitchen anymore, are you?"

Again, a giant thanks going out to whomever invented waterproof mascara because she was about to lose it again. Here she had been dreading coming home because she couldn't help but fall back into those same patterns and face the same demons she had while being a half-bratty, half-lost fifteen-year-old and all her dad saw was the fourth-grader in pigtails jamming out while she emptied the dishwasher. Going home again wasn't without dangers—she looked at her dad, gazing at her with such love and hope that she gave in to the tears—but it wasn't without rewards also.

"I may not be dancing in the kitchen, Daddy, but I'll always be your girl."

And she would. Some things a person didn't outgrow, but the real blessing of getting older was finally learning which old hurts to hold onto and which ones to let go.

"Have fun tonight," he said, giving her a tight squeeze. "I'll see you tomorrow."

By the time she stepped out onto the front porch, her eyes were dry, her makeup repaired, and her spirit lighter than it had been in a long time.

"Everything okay?" Frankie asked as he handed Gussie over to her dad and walked her to Scarlett, where he held open the door for her.

God, how to answer that? She had a million possibilities but, looking up at Frankie as she got into the passenger seat, there was only one that seemed to fit this moment. "The only thing that could make it better is if Constance decides to stay home."

"Maybe we'll get lucky and she'll decide not to come," Frankie said with a grimace.

"It doesn't matter." And it really didn't.

That's what she'd been missing all this time, and it was past time that she realized it. The conversation with her dad, though, helped settle some of the emotional flotsam and jetsam that had been swirling around inside her for as long as she could remember.

Sure, that girl who'd walked through the halls of Antioch High School still lived inside her. However, she had grown up, learned to stand up for herself, and had prospered with a great job and amazing friends. Coming home again didn't change that. If Antioch hadn't changed while she'd been away, well, there was nothing she could do about it. But she wasn't giving up all she'd gained just because she'd crossed the city line.

"What's that smile about?" Frankie asked, pausing the motion of closing her door.

"I'm just happy."

A smile tugged at the corners of his ornery mouth. "Then I say we let the good times roll."

"Best idea ever."

"I don't know." He lowered his voice and gave her a heated look. "I kinda like the one you had last night. I'm looking forward to a repeat. I have made plans of the hotel variety."

There went her panties, because there was no way she wouldn't spend the night thinking about exactly what he had in mind and hoping like hell it was the same naked, orgasmic things making her pulse speed up. However, judging by the singe-your-eyebrows-off heat level of the kiss he gave her before shutting her door, she didn't really have to wonder. She just had to be patient. That man did love to draw things out, and she had a feeling the dance was going to be one long act of foreplay.

Who knew, maybe she could sneak him behind the football stand and have her wicked way with him.

Chapter Sixteen

The school gym had been transformed into an updated replica of the Under the Sea prom that had been held Lucy's senior year. At least, she assumed it's what it had looked like, with the mermaids and starfish decorating the walls, the blue and white balloons, and fish-shaped confetti scattered across the registration table.

"So what song are you two gonna sing?" Haven Sheraton asked as she handed Lucy her nametag. "For the last event in the decathlon, I mean."

Oh shit. She whipped her head around and stared at Frankie, who was giving her a mouth-open look of pure horror that matched hers. With all that had had gone on, it had totally left her mind.

"Sing?" she managed to get out.

"Yeah, you remember how Constance loves to sing," Haven said with a wistful sigh. "I thought she was gonna be on Broadway before all of that other stuff happened."

As the panic of it really being time to break out the karaoke started to abate, she remembered how Constance would stroll the halls of Antioch High School surrounded by her friends as she sang everything from the Broadway classics to the latest hits. Even as a teenager, she'd been confident that every dream she'd ever had would come true.

"So, it's karaoke time?" Frankie asked without the usual humor in his voice.

"Exactly," Haven said before leaning forward and lowering her volume to a mere whisper. "Good luck, a lot of us are rooting for y'all."

Lucy probably would have spent the next five minutes staring at Haven with a blank expression if it hadn't been for Frankie, who steered her away from the registration table and over to a corner outside of the gym doors. As people streamed by, she finished processing her what-the-fuck-people-are-rooting-for-us moment and realized that Frankie "Mr. Confidence" Hartigan looked like he was about to puke on his shoes.

"Oh my God." She pressed her palms to his cheeks, checking for a temperature. "Are you okay?"

"I gotta remind you of something." He glanced over at the people passing by as if they were aliens on the hunt for a new human skin suit. "I can't sing."

She let out a relieved sigh, and the worry yanking her shoulders up to her earlobes eased. "Me either, that's okay. We'll suck together."

"No." He shook his head and visibly gulped. "I. Can't. Sing."

That's when it hit her. The man who could probably talk the devil himself into giving Frankie a pass on an eternity in hell was petrified of singing in front of people. Like scared-out-of-his-mind-to-the-tenth-degree petrified. If he didn't look like it was the end of the world, she would have laughed. This was not the moment for giggles, though. This was serious. And for what? A stupid crown? Totally not worth it.

"No big deal," she said and brushed her lips across his cheek. "We'll skip the event."

He narrowed his blue eyes at her. "Then Constance will win."

A few days ago, even the idea of letting her old high school nemesis win would have been among the worst things possible. Now? Well, reality had run one helluva check on her life and had given her a new perspective. That old shit didn't matter. She had a good life, great friends, and was about to spend the night dancing with a man who made her do the happy sighs, if only for a limited time. All of that was way better than nursing old grudges and hurts.

"It's no biggie," she said. "I'd rather spend the night dancing with you."

"Are you sure?" Frankie asked, the tone in his voice telling her just how unsure he was of her answer.

"We head back to Waterbury in the morning," she said, keeping her voice as light as possible and leaving out what that meant to her and how much she was going to miss him when they got back to their real lives. "I'd rather squeeze in all the fun and memories I can tonight rather than get caught up in some stupid high-school level competition."

Whether he realized what she was holding back or not didn't matter in the next moment because that's when he kissed her, taking away whatever worries she harbored and sweetening the bittersweet reality that all of this was ending soon. And what a kiss. Damn. The man really should teach a class, with her being his star—and only—student. By the time he pulled away, she was breathless and flushed.

"We could just spend the night doing that," he said, his gaze dropping to the deep *V*-neck of her dress. "Think we can get access to the library? I've always had a thing about getting up a hot chick's skirt in the stacks."

"You're horrible," she said with a giggle.

He gave her another quick kiss. "And you love it."

Damn her mutinous body, she did. It was going to be years before she worked that fantasy out of her jilling off rotation. And since going through those gym doors looking like a woman who'd just considered having a quickie in the library wasn't on her to-do list for this week, she took a step out of kissing range. "I'll be right back."

Thank God the girl's bathroom was right across the hall. Ignoring the curious looks from the people she'd graduated with—and one woman holding up a half-filled wine glass in a congratulatory toast—she hustled into the bathroom. All it took was one look in the mirror to have her reaching for her purse. Her red lipstick had definitely traveled during that knee-knocking kiss. She was just pulling out a makeup removing sheet, a must-have for anyone who, like her, was addicted to red lipstick, when she heard a noise coming from one of the stalls.

She paused and cocked her head to the side, listening closely. There it was again. It sounded like a sniffle. No, more than that. It sounded like one of those soul-wracking swallowed sobs that only followed the worst kind of trouble. There was no way she was slinking out of here without making sure the woman hiding in the stall was all right.

"Everything okay?" she asked.

There was a moment of silence, followed by the door opening and revealing a red-eyed Constance with her trembling chin held high. "I'm fine." But her voice shook when she said it, and she was clutching tear-soaked tissue in one fisted hand as she walked out of the stall. "And if I wasn't, you would be the last person on earth who could help."

Something inside Lucy snapped at that snark, whatever residual fear of the high school mean girl fading away into nothingness. It was like having a titanic-sized burden she hadn't realized she'd been carrying for years disappearing.

"What is your problem, Constance?" she asked, curious despite it all. "I mean, I understand being a bitchy girl for no reason in high school, but don't you think it's time to grow up? Life is too damn hard to add all of this bullshit drama to it."

The other woman glared at her in the mirror. "Like you'd know about life being hard."

Was she kidding? That had to be a joke. "I think I know more than most folks."

"Really?" Constance snorted in disbelief and tore a length of brown paper towel from the dispenser and put it under the automatic water faucet. "You got to leave Antioch." She pulled the damp paper towel from under the flow of water and wrung out the excess moisture. "You got to go have a life outside of this small town." She patted the towel against the red puffiness under her eyes as she continued to glower at Lucy. "You got to be something other than that woman who peaked in high school."

Of all the whiny complaints. The woman who had made Lucy's life hell in high school was bitching about those years being the best of her life and the fact that they ended? What a crock of shit.

"You could have gone, too," she shot back. "Nothing was stopping you."

Constance balled up the paper towel, holding it in her white-knuckled, fisted hand. "Just a little thing called chemotherapy treatment, and when that didn't work, a double mastectomy at nineteen. Yeah, I had nothing but choices—of course, mine were of the cancer-treatment variety."

All the air got sucked out of the room by the mere mention of the C-word, and it made Lucy's lungs ache. Okay, she hadn't expected that—hadn't even heard a whisper about it. It wasn't an excuse for how Constance had acted in high school, but if she had the mastectomy before twenty, she must have been diagnosed when they were eighteen and still in high school. God. She must have been scared out of her mind.

"I didn't know," Lucy said. "I'm sorry."

"You think I care what you think?" Constance asked as she tossed the balled-up towel into the trash can, her gaze studiously avoiding Lucy's as her chin started to wobble.

"Yeah, I think you do," Lucy said, working to keep her voice neutral when all that was going through her head was thoughts about how someone who had been through something as life-altering as Constance had could still be such a royal bitch all these years later. "I think you care what everyone thinks, and it's killing you to see everyone back here again and realizing that you missed out on everything you wanted your life to become. I'm sorry you were sick. I'm glad you're better. Don't worry, I'm pretty damn shocked by that feeling, too. Still, who you were and what happened to you before doesn't have to impact who you are today and how you act now."

The only sound in the bathroom was the buzz of the fluorescent lights as she watched her high school nemesis's face go mottled with emotion.

"Why don't you just—" That's all Constance got out before the dam broke and tears started rushing out. Maybe it was because Lucy was the only one there, maybe it was because Constance needed something solid to hold onto in the crazy whirlwind of her life, but she rushed to Lucy, wrapping her arms around her and holding on as she sobbed. "The doctor has diagnosed my daughter as having the same aggressive breast cancer gene I have," she said, her whole body shaking. "It runs in the family. It's my fault."

And everything clicked. If the reunion had been a reminder for Lucy about all of the crap she'd lived through, it was just as horrible of a reminder for Constance. Add to that her daughter's diagnosis and…yeah, being a raging bitch may not be the best way to react to that kind of news, but it was understandable, if shitty.

"Oh God, Constance," she said, squeezing the other woman tight. "I'm so sorry."

They stood there—former high school enemies, holding onto each other in the girl's bathroom under the harsh lights. It wasn't the most bizarre hug Lucy had ever been a part of—that would be the five-way group hug between warring defensive linemen whose angry grudge match had nearly brought their team to its knees—but it was pretty close. Who would have thought it? Her and Constance? Hugging? It should have been weird, but it wasn't. It was proof that they both could move on, move forward—maybe even be friends.

"I don't know what to do," Constance said when they moved apart, and she dabbed her face with another damp paper towel. "How do I tell her that it's gonna be okay when it may not be? What if she has to give up on all her dreams like I did? What if her future is over before it even began?"

"What do the doctors say?" Lucy asked.

Constance's jaw tightened, and she set her shoulders as if she was getting ready to go into battle. "To do monthly self-exams, get checkups, and to pray."

"So let's do that."

And they did, holding hands right there in the middle of the bathroom. Lucy didn't pray often—to be honest, she didn't remember the last time she had—but this was a moment that called for it. If adding her voice to Constance's was all the comfort that she could offer, then Lucy figured God would listen. After they were done praying and finished touching up their makeup, their gazes locked in the mirror.

Constance gave her an apologetic smile. "I'm sorry for everything—for this week, for last night, and for back in school. I let my own bitterness back then and fear for my daughter now find an outlet by picking on you. It was wrong.

Can you forgive me?"

A few days earlier, Lucy's reaction may have been different, but tonight she didn't even have to think about it. "Absolutely."

Peace treaty signed with another hug, they walked out together into the deserted hall. There was a crowd gathered just inside the open double doors leading to the gym and a god-awful sound coming out. It took Lucy a second to process, but once she did she rushed inside the gym. There, sweating in the spotlight onstage, mic in hand, eyes glued to the karaoke screen like a man staring down the headlights of a runaway semi, was Frankie doing his best Danny Zuko bragging to his boys about summer loving. It was the worst singing she'd ever heard, and she loved it.

She loved him.

Oh shit. That couldn't be right. It wasn't smart, it wasn't—anything she could change, she realized with a sinking sensation. She'd fallen for the guy who'd slept his way through most of the women in Waterbury and had driven across the country to take her on a pity date.

This was bad.

It was really bad.

But she wouldn't think about that now, not while he was standing up on stage and singing—badly—for *her*. She'd deal with the rest later.

Really, it would all work itself out when they got back to Waterbury, and he went back to the women with legs for miles who never got called out by strangers for eating cheeseburgers.

Until then, she was going to pretend that the world outside of Antioch didn't exist.

• • •

There were two things universally acknowledged in the Hartigan family. One, the Ice Knights were the best hockey team in the league. Two, a drowning cat's desperate caterwauling sounded better than Frankie's singing. Standing up on the stage, hearing the hideously out-of-tune sounds coming out of his mouth blaring over the sound system, he had to agree with the family. So why was he up in front of everyone showing his ass figuratively, if not literally? For the look Lucy was giving him right now.

A happy amusement tugged at the corner of her full, lush mouth as she watched him from the doorway where she stood with Constance. Sure, there was a general shell-shocked haze to it, but there was no denying the soft appreciation on her face that bordered on something more, something that made him belt out the line about summer lovin' a little louder than necessary—much to the wincing misery of the people sitting at the tables surrounding the dance floor.

"Take pity on these poor people," he said into the mic during an instrumental break. "There's no way you're worse than me."

Thank fuck, she took him up on it. The real shock, though, was watching her hook her arm through Constance's and bring her up on stage with her. The two made it up in time for Lucy to sing the line about the boy she met over the summer and for Constance to join in on the chorus when she asked Lucy to tell her more. He was pretty damn sure there was a story behind this truce, but he couldn't say he was surprised.

Lucy had a way of making things happen.

It showed in everything she did, from her job wrangling misbehaving athletes to how she handled Gussie to the way she'd managed him. There wasn't another woman like her in the world.

He needed to send a case of beer to that asshole in

Marino's because if it hadn't been for him, Frankie may not have ever gotten to know this amazing woman.

By the time the final chorus came around, more than half of the women in the gym were singing along with Lucy and a solid quarter of the dudes were singing along with him. And after the final notes were sung, he grabbed Lucy's hand and got off that stage faster than the one time he'd exited a burning building with an armful of newborn puppies.

"I'd rather get my nuts waxed than ever do that again," he said before downing the cold beer the guy working the bar set back into the corner had given him.

Lucy, who was obviously not dealing with the aftereffects of a singing-in-public freak out, sipped her brew. "Then why did you do it?"

He could tell her that it was because he didn't have a choice, that he was forced at gunpoint onto the stage. He could tell her it was because she deserved to win that crown. He could tell her it was to get back at Constance for all of the shitty things she'd put Lucy through. All of those would have been true—well, except for the part about the gun—and he could have done that. Instead, the truth came out.

"I did it for the look on your face right now."

Her eyes lit up, and everything in the known universe shifted for him. He was a selfish fucking bastard. He hadn't made a total ass out of himself for her. He'd done it for him, because he wanted to be the guy who made her feel like she did right now. And he wanted to do it again. And again. And again. He wanted to do it until they were old and yelling at the youths to get off their lawn.

"Wow. They're going to be talking about that performance for a long time around here," said the guy who was working the master of ceremonies job, practically stepping right between Frankie and Lucy. "But you better get a move on. They need you both onstage."

The guy strutted off toward the stage in his mint green tuxedo that would give an eye sore to an eye sore. Hand-in-hand, they made their way up to the stage, where all of the other participants in the reunion decathlon were waiting. One by one, each couple was introduced, scores given, and polite claps offered as they were sent offstage until it was only him and Lucy and Constance and Bryce left.

Considering it all came down to the popular vote on who sang better during karaoke, he wasn't holding his breath. He'd given it his best shot, and if Lucy really wanted a crown, he'd go buy her one.

"And the king and queen of the Antioch High School reunion are"—the master of ceremonies paused for a recorded drum roll—"Frankie Hartigan and Lucy Kavanagh!"

As the gym erupted into cheers and clapping, he turned to Lucy, who mouthed "Oh my God" to him and was holding onto his hand like he was tethering her to earth. He didn't want to let go of her hand, but he relinquished it anyway so she could receive her crown.

Thank God he didn't have to wear one, because that was so very much not his thing. But dancing with Lucy? That really was.

Moving in an easy rhythm to a slow song, he couldn't help but draw her in close so he could feel her against him. She felt good, right in his arms. This might be Lucy's reunion dance, but he sure as hell didn't want it to end. The fact that it was going to, though, hung over him like a thirty-pound anvil.

"So, did you have a good class reunion week?" he asked before he could stop himself.

"Yeah I did," she said softly, raising herself up on her tiptoes as they swayed to brush her lips across his cheek. "Thanks to you."

"I just acted as your eye candy."

Did that sound defensive or humble? He wasn't sure

which one he meant it to sound like. The truth of it was that he was done being the good-time guy, and the worst thing would be for Lucy to think of him that way.

"Eye candy?" Lucy asked, shaking her head. "You were a lot more than that."

"And when we get home?"

Fuck. He didn't mean to ask that question—not here, at least—and judging by the guarded expression on Lucy's usually open face, she wished he hadn't, too. He wasn't sure exactly what to say next, so he just stared into her soft brown eyes. But he couldn't shake the itchy sense of impending doom he'd learned to listen to the first time he'd stepped foot into a house on fire. If a firefighter didn't listen to that sixth sense, the chances of coming out crispy went up exponentially.

"Being here this week, this isn't real life," she said, her voice so soft he had to lower his head to hear her more clearly. "It's a little cocoon."

True, but he wasn't ready to give into that just yet, tingly sense of danger or not. "And what do you think will be different back in Waterbury?"

Before she could answer, the music changed to a fast song from years ago and people streamed onto the dance floor. For a second, they just stood there, staring at each other, the full weight of future possibilities pressing down against them. Then, Lucy gave a practiced smile that she'd probably used a thousand times to defuse tense situations in her office.

"A lack of potato sack races." She grinned, then pulled him into a circle of people dancing along with the fast beat.

It was a good move—defensive without being obvious—but Frankie knew what she was doing and he wasn't having it. There was more between them than just picnic games and hot sex.

All he needed to do was persuade her that this was more than just a temporary good time.

Chapter Seventeen

An hour later, Frankie was white-knuckling Scarlett's steering wheel. There was dark, and then there was country backroads dark. He couldn't see a damn thing except the little bit of road Scarlett's headlights illuminated, a million stars, and Lucy next to him in the front seat. She was still wearing that sexy-as-all-get-out red dress that wrapped around her like a promise and a tease—oh, and a makeshift blindfold he'd made from the Antioch High School Queen sash she'd gotten along with the crown on her head.

"You know, I wouldn't do this for just anyone," she said.

The "this" being getting in his car without knowing—or being able to see—where they were going. It was a definite sign of trust from a woman so used to fighting her battles alone, one that he took as a very good sign for the trip back home tomorrow.

"It was my kick-ass singing abilities, wasn't it?" he asked, turning left onto a narrow dark driveway after passing a small wooden sign that read Laughlin Hotel.

Lucy chuckled. "You're horrible and you know it."

"True." He reached out and laid his palm on her thigh, watching out of the corner of his eye as she bit her bottom lip. "But luckily I have other talents."

"And those include driving blindfolded women around in the middle of the night?"

The words may have been flippant, but her tone was all sexy kitten and he was so down for that. Fuck. He was beyond down, he was uncomfortably up for it. For her. Always. So, he let out a sigh of relief when the boutique luxury hotel hidden away in the woods like some kind of fairy castle appeared at the end of the long driveway. It was four stories tall and built to look like a castle. Booking the tower room had made his credit card cry, but it was going to be worth it.

He parked Scarlett in one of the few available spots, cut the engine, and undid his seatbelt. Then, he leaned across and untied the sash around Lucy's eyes. "We're here."

She blinked a few times, then looked around. Two beats after her gaze found the Laughlin Hotel, she turned to him a little slack-jawed with surprise and her eyes alight with glee.

"How in the world did you get a room here?" she asked, letting out a little mewl of approval. "They are booked for years in advance."

Yep, that was exactly the reaction he was hoping for. Calling in his chips with his sister had been worth it.

"Felicia," he said and got out of the car.

Lucy was out of Scarlett before he could make it around to open her door. "More, please."

Taking her hand in his, he walked with her around to the trunk, where he'd stored an overnight bag he'd sweet-talked her into packing by saying they might want to change into something more comfortable after the dance for a trip back out to the lake.

"Well, her fiancé's family has enough money and pull to help me get in at the last minute." He popped the trunk and grabbed both of their bags before closing it. "Felicia did owe me a favor, and I called it in."

"For what?" Lucy asked as they headed toward the front door. "Saving that crazy cat of hers from a tree?"

"Hell no. If Honeypot got stuck, I'd leave the feral animal there." Okay, he wouldn't, but Felicia did have one of the meanest cats ever to cat. "I helped her pick out a dress to wear."

She pulled him to a stop outside of the hotel's massive oak doors. "You were your sister's wingwoman?"

Out of habit, he looked around to make sure no one overheard that little bit. "If you ever tell, I'll deny it."

She raised herself up on her tiptoes and wrapped her arms around his neck, bringing that luscious mouth of hers millimeters within kissing distance. If he hadn't been holding both of their overnight bags, he would have had his hands on that round ass of hers and tugged her close so he could feel every inch of her.

Just a little taste, that's all he wanted—at least until he got her up into that room.

"Like everyone doesn't already know you're a giant softie," Lucy said.

"Not all the time."

She lowered one arm and brought it between them and let her fingers graze over his dick. "And thank God for that."

It might have just killed him a little, but he managed to hold onto his control and not drag Lucy to the closest horizontal surface. Instead, they walked into the opulent hotel reception area. All Frankie had to do at check-in was show his driver's license and leave a credit card number for incidentals—and it still took too long. He needed to get Lucy into that room.

They couldn't get to the elevator fast enough for him, but as soon as the doors slid shut he dropped the bags and had her pressed against the wall. Four floors wasn't enough time to do much, but he still managed to get his hands under her skirt, skating up the outside of her thighs and over her full hips as he took her mouth, hard and with more than a little bit of a desperate edge.

Her nimble fingers were starting to work his suit pants button free when the elevator dinged and the doors opened to reveal a small foyer with two doors at the opposite end.

How he managed to tear his mouth away from hers before the door closed on them again, he had no fucking clue. All he knew was one moment he was inches away from touching the softest, wettest piece of heaven, and the next he had Lucy in his arms, holding the suitcases awkwardly in one hand, and was striding toward that lone door—which was the next obstacle to getting her naked.

Like an asshole, he'd put the room key in his suit pocket. A great plan so both hands would be free to touch her in the elevator, and a really shitty one when he wanted to keep her body plastered to his and open the door at the same time.

"If you don't put me down so you can open that door, take me inside, and fuck me until I'm hoarse, I'm never speaking to you again."

That was his Lucy. There wasn't another woman out there like her.

"Yes, ma'am."

He set her down, got the key out, slid it across the black key reader, and turned the knob of the door that wouldn't unlock. *Fuck me.* He swiped again. Nothing. Just a little red blinky light. Meanwhile, Lucy had reached up under her skirt and slipped off her panties. Hell. Just looking at the black satin ball in her hand squeezed the air out of his lungs.

She watched him, amusement curling the corners of that kissable mouth of hers upward as she reached behind her back and did some pinch-and-snap move that was followed up with her sliding the straps of her bra down her arms and somehow managing to pull it off without ever removing her dress. His gaze was drawn like a magnet to her hard nipples pressing against the soft knit of her red dress. He'd seen those nipples, knew what they looked like, with the large peach areolas framing them. That knowledge, without being able to actually see them or touch them, was making his brain a little foggy. So he swiped the key again, as if by magic it would work.

Holding her undies in one hand, she reached out and took the keycard from his grasp. "Try the other one."

Sexy *and* brilliant. Fuck yes.

He grabbed the other keycard out of the holder and swiped. The light turned green. He had the door open and both of them through it in the next half breath. Lucy wasn't done tormenting him, though; she made sure to walk just enough ahead of him—those damn panties and bra in her hand like a sweetly cruel tease—to stay out of his reach.

The room was amazing. At least, he assumed it was, judging by the look on Lucy's face when she turned toward him because he couldn't look away from her to check it out for himself. There was no better view than the one he had standing just inside the door.

"This is amazing," she said as she did a full, slow turn to look at the room again. "But why?"

"Purely for selfish reasons." He gripped the doorknob so hard he was kinda surprised it didn't bend, but he needed to stay where he was at the moment or he was going to drag her down to the carpet caveman-style and shove her skirt up so he could bury himself inside her right away.

That wasn't how tonight was going to go, though. This wasn't just fucking. This was a seduction. This was his chance to persuade her that they didn't have to end here. There was a place for them in Waterbury.

"Oh yeah?" She strolled over to the huge bed that faced the windows looking out at the vast national forest and trailed her fingers across the bedspread. "What are those?"

"I want to show you how good it could be between us."

Her jaw tensed just the slightest, but he caught it.

You not the kind of guy who delivers happily ever afters.

Shannon's words came back to haunt him at the worst possible time, but he shoved them back. If he was able to do it with anyone, it would be Lucy.

She recovered faster than he did—of course—and dropped her bra and panties on the bed and brought her fingertips up to the deep *V* neckline of her dress. "Then why don't you show me?"

The control that he'd been holding onto like a lifeline snapped, and he strode across the room to her. He cupped her face and lowered his mouth to hers, claiming her as much as he could in that moment, deepening the kiss, tasting her, teasing her, telling her without words everything he needed to say.

But it wasn't enough. He wasn't sure it ever would be with Lucy.

Without breaking the kiss, he walked her backward to the wall by the bed. He roamed her softness with his hands, loving the feel of how she fit perfectly against him, with him. Finally, he broke the kiss before he got so lost in her that he forgot what he really needed to tell her. What was really on the line.

"I have to warn you that I'm not playing here." He reached down and started to inch the hem of her dress up. "There's more between us than some itch we both want to scratch." He pulled the red material up and off of her, so he could feast his eyes on all of her.

Sucking in a deep breath, he did just that, lingering on her full tits, the gentle curve of her belly, the way her thick legs were spread just the perfect amount for him to drop to his knees so he could curl his tongue around her hard, wet clit—but not yet. First, he had to make sure she knew this was more than a good-time fuck.

"This doesn't end when we leave Antioch."

...

Lucy was about to implode or explode or spontaneously combust, she had no idea which one, but something was going to happen. There was no way she could be on the receiving end of *that* look from Frankie after *that* declaration and not be. Damn that man, it wasn't fair. How was she supposed to keep her head and heart out of this whatever-it-was between them when he pulled crap like that?

He was Frankie fucking Hartigan, player, hot firefighter, sexy ginger giant. She was Lucy Kavanagh, which was pretty damn awesome most of the time, but she was in a totally different league than he was, even if he didn't realize it at the moment because he hadn't been surrounded by Waterbury's most beautiful just waiting to throw themselves at him in a week.

"Frankie." His name sounded like a plea even to her own ears. "Let's take tonight for what it is."

"Hot, melt-your-brain sex?" he asked, skimming up her side, leaving a trail of fire in his wake as he delivered a series of soft, deadly kisses down her neck.

"Yes please."

"But you're the one who said sex was so much better if there was emotion involved." He circled a fingertip around the tip of her breast but left her sensitive nipple alone, only letting the heat of his breath tease it. "Were you bullshitting?"

God, she couldn't think. Not when they were like this. She arched her back, bringing her breasts closer to his mouth, but the evil man just chuckled and took his mouth on a detour, licking and nibbling his way down the side of her breast—so frustratingly close to where she needed him but so damn far away.

"You didn't answer my question, Lucy."

That was because she could barely put two thoughts together. "No, but—"

"Then no buts." Then his hand was on her thigh, the backs of his fingers touching her overheated flesh, and she didn't even bother to try to bite back her moan. "I like you, Lucy." His fingers went higher but stopped before brushing the tight curls covering her mound. "I more than like you."

Her core ached for his touch. Even an inadvertent brush of the back of his hand would have set her off. Breath coming in quiet, needy puffs, she spread her legs, hoping he'd take the hint. Of course, the stubborn man didn't. And when she moved to slide her own fingers through her slick folds, he encircled her wrists in one of his large hands and lifted her arms above her head.

"That's not fair," she groaned, wanting to throttle him almost as much as she wanted to fuck him.

"A man's got to use the tools at his disposal." He nuzzled his face against her neck, kissing the spot where her shoulder met her throat. "What's wrong, are you feeling desperate, Lucy? Like you need some relief?"

Oh God, that was the understatement of the eon. "Yes."

"So?" he asked, his voice a low rumble that she felt as much as she heard. "What's the harm in taking this back home?"

Oh, besides getting gutted by the broken heart that she'd eventually be nursing, because that's the way life worked? "This isn't fair."

"All's fair in love and war," he said, running his hands down from her hips to her thighs as he sank down to his knees. "Come on, take a chance on us. Take a chance on me."

She didn't miss the way his breath paused on the last word as if he was as unsure but hopeful as she was.

"You really think we could make it work?" Was she crazy for even considering it? Maybe. But even for as much as her body was urging her to say whatever he wanted to hear so they could get on with it, that wasn't what was pushing her forward. It was the strange, alien emotion that felt a lot like hope building up alongside her arousal.

He kissed the inside of her thigh, so close to her core that she nearly cried out. "Without a fucking doubt."

This was crazy. She should say no. It was the smart plan. It was exactly what she was going to do. "Yes."

It was the word that broke them both.

For as much as she wanted his mouth between her legs, it wasn't enough for the need wracking her. She needed him, hard and deep, filling her until there was no her or him, only them.

"Get on the bed."

She didn't have to ask twice. He got up, wrapped an arm around her, and fell back onto the bed, taking her with him. She landed on top of him, but the impact didn't faze him. He just cupped the back of her head and brought her face down onto his and plundered her mouth like a man starved for what only she could offer. And offer herself she did.

Swinging her leg over him, she brought herself up enough so she could reach in between them and wrap her hands around his thick cock. With a tight grip, she stroked her hand up and down his shaft, letting her thumb rub across the lip and spread the pre-come glistening there. Then, she positioned him just right and sank down onto him, the pleasure of it forcing her to break the kiss and groan out his name.

"Fuck me," he ground out the words. "You feel so good, so wet and tight."

Then she started to rock against him, and neither of them had words any more.

His hands cupped her breasts as she raised herself up and let herself slide down in one long, slow movement until he was buried deep inside her. Rotating and rocking, she lifted herself, inching upward as she clenched around his dick, trying to keep him in place but needing to feel him move. She wanted to make this last, to go slow, but she couldn't. The need inside her was already building into a tight, electric ball of want. And she gave into it. Throwing all caution to the side, she fucked him—forcefully, relentlessly—as he met her every downward thrust and groaned at her every withdrawal. Then, lifting his hand that had been holding onto her hips and guiding her up and down on his cock, he reached up and strummed her clit. Again and again he circled that most sensitive spot until she couldn't take it anymore, and she came hard and fast, sinking down onto him one final time as he came along with her.

That's when the cheering and clapping started from the other side of the wall. Had they been that loud? She looked down at Frankie, who was wearing a satisfied, cocky grin. Oh yeah, they were very much that loud.

Oh my God.

She looked at Frankie. "Does this happen to you often?"

"Only with you."

Collapsing with giggles and exhaustion, she was careful to make sure she didn't land on him as she laid down, but he just grumbled something she couldn't quite make out and pulled her close.

With her cheek pressed against his chest, she lay there and listened to the steady thrum-thrum of his heart beating. His springy chest hair tickled her nose, but she refused to give into the sneeze threatening to ruin the moment because it was a perfect moment. The kind of snapshot in time where absolutely everything seemed possible, where the idea of her and Frankie being together as a couple in Waterbury seemed plausible.

When they got back to Waterbury, they'd be out of the vacation bubble and their real lives would intrude. He'd have a bazillion women who wanted him, tall women with appropriate curves in the appropriate places, the kind who wore skinny jeans that still managed to droop, the kind who never got the wow-she-really-let-herself-go look from strangers. Would he still want her then? Would she be the one waiting, just like her dad had been? That's the way these things worked, the opposites-attract newness wore off and when it did it would be too late for her. Hell, it was too late now. She'd fallen for him, like a lemming rushing off a cliff and into a big fluffy cloud of love.

All she could do now was prep for the inevitable ending and try to enjoy what time they had together while it lasted.

. . .

Frankie could hear her thinking, it was that loud in the totally silent room.

So he gave in to the urge to wrap her tighter in his arms, but managed to keep his mouth shut. Telling her everything he was feeling now would only freak her out even more than she was already. He'd keep the news to himself that she was completely right. Sex wasn't just sex, not when it involved someone he loved. It was a dumb, cheesy thing to say, even in his head, but it didn't change the fact that it was true.

But since he wasn't planning on turning in his stubborn Irishman card today, he'd keep that to himself, instead he closed his eyes all he could picture was the future waiting for them both in Waterbury.

Chapter Eighteen

The next day, after saying goodbye to Tom and Gussie, they hit the road. For his part, Frankie had been hoping Scarlett's fuel pump would go out again for the past million miles. The car gods, however, had other plans as the miles flew by one field of crops after another until they were almost back in the Eastern Time Zone.

And with every small town they passed and interstate gas station they stopped at, he could see the truth that they were leaving some sort of alternate reality sink into Lucy a little bit more. She'd gone all silent and contemplative a half hour ago—a fact made more apparent because this part of the country seemed to get exactly zero radio stations.

He had to do something, or she'd change her mind about giving them a chance back home. It wasn't that Lucy wanted to sabotage them, but he could feel that big, bad something lingering in the air as apparent as the changing scent of a fire that warned of imminent danger. It had him drumming his fingers on the steering wheel and grasping at mental straws of ideas that could pull her back from the edge.

That's when it hit him.

"What's your biggest fantasy?"

Lucy pivoted in her seat, her beautiful face totally neutral as if she didn't know exactly what kind of fantasy he was asking about—which she totally did. "Having Wonder Woman's invisible plane."

He turned his attention back to the road and passed a tractor on the back-country highway shortcut with ease, and they were again the only ones on the lonely stretch of road. "I thought you hated flying."

"No, I hate the teeny-tiny seats," she said. "There's a difference."

"So you mean I could actually stretch my legs out and not turn into the human pretzel in Wonder Woman's plane?" Diana was an Amazonian princess, after all. Leg room had to matter to her.

Lucy nodded. "Yep."

"That's my new second favorite fantasy," he said, his thumbs tapping on the steering wheel to keep from reaching over and tracing a line across the slice of thigh visible below the hem of her skirt.

"Only number two?" she asked, her voice getting that husky edge that made his dick sit up and listen. "What's number one?"

He'd spent the past hour thinking about it and had developed something that was halfway between heaven and hell. "It involves you naked."

"I'm so shocked," she said with a laugh. "What am I doing while naked?"

"Well, you're not totally naked. You're sort of in clothes but out of them as we're driving down the highway."

Original? Not really, but with Lucy just about everything turned into a sex fantasy for him.

"Okay, I'm game. Give me some specifics."

Of course she was. The woman was fucking fierce. More than anything else, it was that attitude that turned him on most.

"Your shirt's unbuttoned."

In his peripheral vision, he saw her lift her right hand and reach for the top button of her flowy blue top. She slipped one button out of the hole, then the next one and the next until her shirt was open, revealing her amazing tits encased in a bright red bra. Red. Of course it was. Just like the woman, the color was a warning and a promise. He fucking loved it.

He gripped the steering wheel tighter and took a look down the long, straight highway. There was no one but them.

"The next thing you do in my fantasy is take out those gorgeous tits of yours."

Lucy didn't even blink. Instead, without hesitation, she tugged down on the satin material of her bra until her breasts came free. Yeah, he was driving, but there was no way he was going to miss taking a good look at her like that. It was like he'd been imagining, her half undone with a lusty look in her eyes as she bit down on her full lower lip.

His cock pressed against his thigh, aching at the sight of her. Then she upped it, pinching one hard nipple between her fingers and rolling it.

In an act of extreme sacrifice, he peeled his focus off her and back on the boring, straight line of a highway that went on for a fucking eternity. He should have kept his big mouth shut. There wasn't a pull-off site or hotel for miles.

Lucy shifted in the passenger seat, turning so that her back was to the passenger door and she was facing him, legs spread as far as possible in the car's confines. "And how about I add a little of this."

Before he could even dream up what might happen next, she one-upped his fantasy by inching the hem of her skirt up until she was showing off her red-satin-covered mound.

And if that wasn't enough to turn his knuckles white with the effort of not reaching out to touch her, he spotted the tell-tale damp spot right in the center of her panties.

If he thought he'd been hard before, he learned different at that moment, because the mutual one-upmanship of this fantasy had turned him to steel. It wasn't that she was just humoring him, giving him a little glimpse of what he wanted. No. Lucy didn't play that bullshit game. His woman always gave as good as she got, and it got her all slick and wet.

"Is this turning you on, Lucy?"

She relaxed against the door, one hand on her thigh and the other tugging on a nipple. "Even more than Wonder Woman's invisible plane."

He was going to die of frustration right here in Scarlett's driver's seat in the middle of nowhere in farm country. "At least you can do something about it. I'm driving."

"You mean something like this?" she asked as she continued to play with her tits, cupping and squeezing them, rolling the nipples to hard points.

The speed limit might have been sixty-five, but Scarlett's speed had dropped down to thirty-five as he watched Lucy torment him with such enthusiastic glee that he almost forgot that she'd taken control of his little fantasy and made it bigger, better, and almost more than he could bear.

"Or maybe," she said, her voice low and breathy. "You meant I could take it a step further."

And that's when she tried to kill him by moving the hand that had been resting on her bare thigh higher. His lungs burned from holding his breath, but as he watched her slide her fingers under the damp center of her panties, he knew there were only a maximum of two things he could do at one time and those two were watch Lucy and keep the car on the road. Breathing be damned.

Every second he had to divert his attention from the sight

of her fingers circling her clit under her panties to check the road made him want to scream with frustration. It made him want to pull over and sink his face down between her thighs and lick up all that sweetness. He was more than half tempted to do that right now, but Lucy was the master of this fantasy. It may have started as his, but she was in charge now, and if she wanted him to pull over, she would have told him.

"Tell me how that feels," he demanded. He may not be able to touch her right now, but he could give her his voice, his dirty thoughts to crank up the intensity a little more, just like she liked it. "How slick is that pussy right now?"

"So wet." Her hand started to move faster and faster under her red panties. "So ready." Her eyes drooped shut as she let the back of her head fall against the passenger door window. "So soft."

"You're killing me." And she was. The image of her playing with herself in the front seat of his car, her shirt hanging open and her tits just begging to be teased and licked, was going to be with him forever.

"Just keep half an eye on the road so you don't kill the both of us, because I'm almost there."

He did. Well, maybe a quarter of an eye, because there was no way he could really look away as she came on her fingers fast and hard. It was the best/worst thing he'd ever seen. The best because there was nothing sexier than watching Lucy have an orgasm. The worst because his cock had never been so desperate for attention in his entire life. He was a good driver and an expert at jacking off, but there was no way he could do the two at the same time without killing them both.

"Gotta tell you," Lucy said, a satisfied grin curling up the sides of her sexy-as-sin mouth. "*My* second-place fantasy—after the invisible plane—is good, too, but that felt fantastic."

Her fantasy? She'd claimed his fantasy but still had one of her own? He shouldn't ask. He wasn't sure he could live through another show like that one. Yeah, asking was definitely not a good idea—but where was the fun in that?

"What's your fantasy?" he asked.

Something wicked and way more fun than should be legal flashed in her eyes. "How about I show you?"

...

Lucy grabbed the seat, needing something to hold onto when the car jerked to the left at her question. There was no missing the hard-on pressing against Frankie's shorts, and her mouth watered for it.

She knew what he was doing, using sex to soothe her worries. Good thing she didn't mind, not when it was this much fun.

"Of course, I don't know that you can handle my fantasy," she said, scooting a little closer as she slipped the shoulder seatbelt strap down so she would be able to lean over. "You're already driving pretty erratically."

"I walk into burning buildings," he said, the low rumble of his voice making her clench her thighs. "I can take whatever you've got."

"You sure?"

He turned the full power of those sexy-as-hell blue eyes of his on her. "Fuck. Yes."

"Okay, in my fantasy I'm sitting like this in the passenger seat of your car and my thighs are slick from my orgasm."

"I like where this is going so far."

"And I slide my finger like this." Her finger glided up her toward her core, wetting the tip with her satisfaction. "And let you taste." She lifted her arm and brought her finger, glistening with her satisfaction, and held it in front of his mouth.

Keeping his hands on the wheel with a grip so tight she

was beginning to wonder if there would be indents when he finally let go, he sucked her finger into his mouth.

Holy shoe heaven. Who knew having someone do that could feel so damn good, and why had no one told her before? Her moan of appreciation escaped before she could stop it. Then, she pulled her hand back and dropped it to his leg. She had plans.

"Next in my fantasy, I tell you to hold onto the wheel."

For once, there wasn't a smart-ass remark or a flirty rejoinder. Instead, his jaw tightened, and he kept his focus 100 percent on the road as if sneaking even one peek at her right now would send them sailing off the highway into the fields bracketing it.

"Whatever happens," she said, tracing a direct line up to his zipper, "don't let go."

She unzipped his shorts and pulled his hard cock out, which was so much easier in her imagination than in reality. Thank God his legs were miles long and his body set a good distance from the steering wheel. Yeah, there was definitely some awkward scooting and weird angles, but it was totally worth it when she took him into her mouth and he let out a harsh hiss of a curse. She sucked him in and worked her tongue around his girth, lowering until her lips met her hand wrapped around the base. Goaded on by the half-groaned orders to "take him all" and to do it "just like that," she took him in until he hit the back of her throat—and then she swallowed.

"Damn, Lucy, do that again."

She did, and then she moved up and down his dick, teasing and tasting him until he said her name in a strained tone that had her sealing her lips around him seconds before he came.

When she sat up again, she noticed the speedometer was down to ten miles an hour. Giggling to herself, she brushed her skirt down and buttoned up her shirt as he got himself squared away. And when the scenery started going by fast enough that she couldn't pick out individual stalks of whatever the green stuff growing was, she flipped down the visor and got her lipstick from her purse, feeling every bit like a badass who'd just conquered the world.

"Our fantasies really go together," she said as she uncapped her favorite shade of red.

"Hell yes, they do. Just like us." Frankie nodded in agreement as he zipped around a slow-moving sedan that thank God hadn't been around them a few minutes ago. "You are a real wild one. I can't wait to find out what other wild things you want to do."

She almost went outside of her lip line with that quip, her pulse picking up speed and her body temperature rising. How many times had she heard something close to that? The first time had been in high school, and it had been repeated again and again in college. The thing about fucking fat girls, the saying went, was that you were always guaranteed a good time for half the work because they were just so damned grateful for the attention that they'd let you do whatever you wanted, any way you wanted, and you didn't even have to worry about getting the chubs off.

"*You're wild.*"

Is that what he meant? She took a deep breath and let it out before she finished putting on her lipstick while trying to work it out. Nothing that Frankie had done so far had come anywhere near that kind of thinking. Surely, he wasn't one of the assholes who'd brag to his friends about what he got the big girl to do. She snuck a peek at him. The permagrin on his face wasn't tinged with snark or nastiness. It was just happy. He turned, catching her undercover glance, and winked.

"I can't wait to get you in my bed at home," he said. "That sucker is custom-made and so big you can get lost in it."

Her pulse picked up again, but for a different reason. She was being ridiculous. Frankie wasn't like those other assholes. Still, she couldn't ignore that part of her that acted as an alarm system, the one warning her that things were going to be different once their real lives got involved.

"How are we going to make this work back in Waterbury?"

His mouth flattened into a line. "Same way we did in Antioch. Why?"

Damage control. It's what she did for a living. There was nothing wrong with applying the lessons she'd learned from years as a crisis PR maven—and, get real, what she'd seen growing up—to her personal life. The last thing she wanted was to make the people in her life she cared about have to pick sides between her and Frankie when the whole thing ended. If her parents' marriage had taught her anything, it was that opposites didn't make for forever.

Lust with Frankie she could deal with. Love? That was begging for trouble.

"Are you over there already planning our breakup?" he asked, the words coming out sharp and pointed.

Yes. No. Maybe. Just preparing for it. "It's not that—"

"Good," he said without looking her way.

Lucy stared at his stubborn profile, set like granite, for a few seconds and then turned her attention to the highway in front of them and the approaching interstate on-ramp that would get them back to Waterbury within a matter of hours. Unless the fuel pump went out again. They could get lucky that way.

"You aren't having any doubts about it we can make this work outside of the Antioch bubble?" she asked.

"Not a single one."

Good. That was good. Right? Yes, totally…except there was no missing the way his entire body was tense, the way he hadn't looked at her when he'd responded, or the way he'd started drumming his thumbs on the steering wheel again.

None were the sign of a man confident in his declaration.

But she'd keep her mouth shut, take the good times while she still could, because she knew better than anyone that they never lasted.

Chapter Nineteen

Usually after a long trip home, there was nothing better than starfishing on her own bed in her own apartment, doing only what she wanted to do on her own. Yeah, she had a pattern after a long period of peopling, and it was pretty much not peopling for as long as humanly possible—or when she had to get up and go into the office again, whichever came first.

This time, though? Her bed felt too big. It was weird. It felt totally normal-sized before she left, and now that there wasn't a six-foot, six-inch hot ginger firefighter next to her—there was just too much space.

He hadn't been in her bed since six this morning. That's when he'd gotten called back into work, his forced vacation cut short, because another firefighter had gotten injured during training exercises and they needed coverage. While he hadn't been excited to leave, there was no denying that the man was jonesing to get back to the job he loved. How could she tell? The fact that he got dressed and was out the door in five minutes flat.

Of course, he only made it as far as the hallway of her

condo building before he rushed back in and kissed her like a man possessed for about ten minutes, got her all hot and bothered, and then told her she needed to be patient, he'd be back in twenty-four hours. The man was evil, totally and completely.

She was contemplating her ceiling when her phone vibrated on the bedside table.

Frankie: *Miss me yet?*

Lucy: *Nope. Totally starfishing.*

The man had a big enough ego, he didn't need her to be his fluffer.

Frankie: *You got your legs spread wide and everything?*

Was it weird that she heard the teasing in his voice in her head, and it sent a shiver down her spine?

Lucy: *You're incorrigible.*

Frankie: *Pretty much.*

Lucy: *Can we grab lunch tomorrow?*

Frankie: *Breakfast? Can meet you at your place after I get off shift.*

Lucy: *See you then.*

Frankie: *G2G got a call.*

...

Frankie had six grocery bags hanging from his forearms when he got off the elevator on Lucy's floor. Sure, he could have left half of the breakfast ingredients in Scarlett and taken two trips, but multiple trips was for wimps, and he was too ready to finally see Lucy again.

After smiling at the old lady who got on the elevator when he got off, he hustled over to Lucy's door and lifted his hand to knock. The door opened before his knuckles even met the wood.

She stood there in a long gray sweatshirt with Boss Babe written across the front and a pair of yoga pants. Her hair was pulled back in a ponytail, and she was wearing those sexy red glasses of hers. Damn she looked good.

But that wasn't what made him relax.

It was that feeling of coming home to her that eased the tension in his shoulders and loosened the vice grip on his lungs.

"Hey," Lucy said, a nervous but excited smile playing on her lips.

He fucking hated that unsure smile. Without thinking twice, he dipped his head down and kissed it right off her face. When she let out a moan of appreciation, he followed up by sliding his tongue inside. It was so fucking good to touch her again, to be near her again, that he almost that forgot one of the bags he was about to drop had a dozen eggs in it.

He broke the kiss and looked down at her, loving that her smile was all smart-mouth Lucy again.

"Do you always answer your door that way?" he asked.

One of her eyebrows went up. "By kissing whoever knocked?"

"Technically, I didn't knock," he teased. "You opened it before I got a chance. I think you're a little excited to see me again."

She rolled her eyes. "That ego." Then she took two bags from his grip. "You brought groceries?"

"I'm making you breakfast." Okay, he'd gotten way more

than they needed for breakfast, but he wanted to make sure to have a little bit of everything just in case she hated one thing or another.

"I made brunch reservations," she said, leading him inside. "I'd figured you'd be tired after your shift and wouldn't want to cook."

He shut the door and followed her into her kitchen, setting the bags down on the island in the middle of the room. "When it comes to being with you, I'm never tired." He leaned down and stole another kiss. "In fact, we'd get arrested for what I plan on doing to you after breakfast if we were in public. So, would you be cool staying here?"

Standing on the other side of the island, she cocked her head to one side and did the world's worst impression of total innocence. "You have plans for me?"

"All sorts of them." He gave her a wink and then started unpacking the bags. "But first, let's make apple French toast."

Lucy helped him unpack the bread and eggs, apples and real maple syrup, the milk, the OJ, the croissants, the bacon, the turkey sausage, the hash browns, the muffins, and everything else. By the time it was all spread out on her island, they were both laughing at the sheer spectacle of it all.

"So," he said, looking at the huge spread. "I may have gotten a little too much for just the two of us."

"Ya think?" she asked with a laugh. "Please tell me you know how to cook, because I'm shit at it."

"Every firefighter knows how to cook." He zipped around the island to her side and pulled her in close before kissing her again. "It's part of what makes us so sexy."

"Prove it," she said, her tough talk undermined by the turned-on breathiness of her tone.

Oh, challenge accepted.

And that's how he ended up teaching her to make French toast. She took over the whisking of the eggs while he peeled and sliced the apples so thin they were almost see-through. Next came the vanilla and the cream that she stirred into the eggs. After that it was an assembly line of dipping the bread into the egg mixture, laying it on the electric griddle, and adding the thin apple slices on top before flipping and letting that side toast.

"You sure you got this?" he asked as he looked over her shoulder while standing close enough behind her that it was just natural for his hands to fall to her hips.

"As long as you don't distract me into burning them."

That was just the kind of comment that needed to be responded to, but not with words. Instead, he dipped his head down and started kissing his way up the column of her neck to the sensitive spot behind her earlobe. As soon as he got there, she almost dropped the spatula.

"Frankie," she said in encouraging censure. "Don't you have bacon to cook?"

"Yes, ma'am." He nipped her earlobe and gave her a light smack on the ass before moving to the stove and putting the bacon into the pan.

They ended up skipping everything else but the juice and the scrambled eggs because by the time the French toast was done and stacked on two plates, both of their stomachs were growling. They hustled out to the balcony, where they sat at the tiny little bistro table and took in the Harbor City skyline, eating in companionable silence—unless you counted Lucy's moans of pleasure when she took her first bite of the apple French toast.

It was nice, the lowkey ease of it. He'd never made breakfast with anyone who didn't share his last name before. Like everything else with Lucy, though, it just felt…right.

He was trying to figure out how to put that into words when her phone buzzed and a photo of Lucy with her dad popped up on the screen. Looking down, she screwed up her mouth and flipped over the phone. Considering how close they'd seemed in Antioch, that was weird.

"Didn't you want to take that?" he asked.

She turned her face toward Harbor City. "I'll call him back after breakfast."

Oh yeah. That set off every warning bell in his head. He'd thought Tom had liked him; hell, he'd seemed to practically give his approval for Frankie going after Lucy. Why the change? Unless he'd gotten it wrong. After all, he was the guy who'd never realized what all the women of Waterbury said about him behind his back until Shannon dropped her truth bomb.

"What is it?" He forced his fingers to loosen their grip on his fork. "He doesn't like the idea of me dating his daughter?"

"Is that what we're doing?" she asked, a teasing lilt to her voice.

"Yes." Of that he had absolutely no doubts. Now, whether he could actually trust himself not to be his old man's son, that was another thing, because for as much as he didn't want to think he could, it was hard to ignore the family ghost that had been haunting him since high school. "I'd ask you to wear my class ring, but God only knows where my mom packed that away. So, what's the deal with your dad?"

"He's just watching out for me." Still, she didn't look at him. "Doesn't want me making the same assumption that he did with my mom."

As if all of the nonverbals she was sending him weren't enough to make the back of his neck itchy with dread, the fact that she'd mentioned her mother sure was. The tightness around her eyes and the way tension filled her voice whenever she talked about her mom was more than enough to let him know that the comparison wasn't a good one.

"What assumption was that?"

"That it was possible to change other people." She let out

a tortured sigh and pivoted her gaze from the sailboats in the harbor to him. A red spot had bloomed at the base of her throat. "The truth of it is that you can only change yourself—for good or for bad."

And that's what it came down to for him. Would he be able to change what seemed pre-ordained? Could he avoid being the man who seemed so straightforward on the surface but cheated on his wife when no one was looking? For Lucy, he wanted to. Nothing else was good enough for her. He wouldn't be good enough for her. The French toast that had tasted so delicious a half hour ago turned into a lead weight in his gut.

"So what happened with your parents?"

She pushed what was left of her breakfast around on her plate with her fork. "Long story."

"I've got time." He had forever when it came to Lucy—at least he hoped he did.

She laid her fork down on her plate and dropped her hands to her lap, clutching them together as if she needed to hold onto something. "They met young, and there was this whole opposites-attract thing. He was the nerdy psychiatrist, and she was the sexy underwear model. Total freak meeting on a cross-country train trip. They started in Harbor City and by the time they got to Los Angeles, they were in love. They got married in Vegas."

She inhaled a deep breath and let in out in a slow, controlled breath.

"It was a total whirlwind—one that probably never had a chance at a happily ever after. By the time I started grade school, they were basically living different lives, with him operating his practice and her flying off to Harbor City and Paris for modeling jobs. All that separation didn't help things, nor did having a chubby kid, which was anathema to my mom's world.

"That seemed to be what really broke things up, at least according to what I overheard my mom telling her friends during one of my very rare trips to visit her in Harbor City. It's why she always kept her distance, why when I did visit we never went anywhere but her apartment, and why the only photos she had of me were always cropped so you never saw all of me beyond my face shot from an upward angle to slim me down a bit. Could you imagine having a child you were that ashamed of?"

His gut clenched as he watched her chin tremble. Then she quickly turned her face away from him and began to blink away the moisture in her eyes that she hadn't been fast enough to hide. Frankie knew it wasn't right to think ill of the dead, but Lucy's mom was a right royal bitch for ever putting that thought in an impressionable girl's head. He was up before he thought about it, standing next to her and drawing her up.

"Their divorce wasn't your fault," he said, pulling her into his arms.

She laid her head on his shoulder, and a small sigh escaped. "But I didn't help."

"People's actions and reactions are on them, not on you," he said, pulling her in close and holding her tight for all the times her mom should have but didn't. "Your dad was right. You can't change other people, only yourself."

They stayed that way long enough for it to turn from comforting to something else as her nimble fingers snuck under the hem of his shirt and started to explore his lower back. "Smart and sexy, you're a double threat, Frankie Hartigan."

"Correction," he said, picking her up and carrying her inside. "I'm a triple threat—and the fact that you failed to mention that means I need to give you a reminder course in the bedroom so you don't forget again."

And they almost made it all of the way there before they'd lost all their clothes.

...

After their breakfast, which had left her kitchen a disaster, and her day-long lesson in orgasms, flirty text exchanges were pretty much the highlight of her days at work. On the nights he wasn't on shift, the texting usually ended with Frankie knocking on her door, armed with dinner or his Netflix password. They never seemed to make it out of her apartment, but considering how quickly they usually got naked, she didn't give it much thought.

She'd had to cancel tonight, though, after Zach Blackburn, got arrested for punching out a fan—well, not one of his, obviously—and Lucy had to go earn the big bucks. Well, medium-sized bucks. Peon bucks compared to the millions Zach was bringing home if she could get him out of his latest snafu—which put her at odds with Frankie's schedule, since he was still taking a few extra shifts to cover for the guy who'd gotten injured.

Frankie: *Still on that bed with your legs wide?*

Lucy: *I wish. I'm still in the office. It's gonna be a really late and professionally frustrating Friday night. Sorry.*

Frankie: *They never should have signed that jackass.*

Lucy: *Don't you start, I need someone in my corner.*

Frankie: *I'm always there.*

Lucy: *xo*

Frankie: *See you at Gina's and Ford's party Saturday?*

Lucy: *With bells on.*

Frankie: *That gives me some new ideas to curl up with while I'm missing you.*

Lucy: *Got a lot of those?*

Frankie: *So many I had to start a list. Hope you have the next few months open.*

Lucy: *Perfect motivation to get Zach back on Harbor City's good side.*

Frankie: *Good luck with that.*

Lucy: *My six-pack of Mountain Dew just got here. Armed and ready to go do battle.*

Frankie: *Kick their asses and leave them scared.*

Lucy: *Always.*

Okay, not always, but her track record was solid.

"One of your media sources send you good news?" Zach asked from his spot in what he called the naughty chair in the corner of her office farthest away from her desk.

"No, why do you ask?" she asked, checking the messages on her phone again in hopes of a silver lining to this shit cloud.

"Because you usually only look that happy when you've fixed whatever I fucked up."

Lucy focused her attention on the tatted-up, bearded player who, despite what the tabloids said about him, was actually a big teddy bear—one with a mean right hook and an even worse temper. Okay, so maybe teddy bear was the wrong description. Maybe grizzly bear napping? Very cute until someone woke it up, then a fucking nightmare.

"Maybe, Zachary Elliot Blackburn," she said, using his

full name, which always managed to stop even her most pain-in-the-ass clients in their tracks, "if you stop being such a jackhole, you wouldn't be needing my services so much."

He stuffed almost the entire white cheddar rice cake into his mouth. "Can I just buy you season tickets instead?" he asked, the words coming out barely understandable.

"Instead?" She chuckled, guffawed, threw back her head and laughed, playing it up to really let the defenseman know how annoyed she was with his antics. "You're funny. Zach, you're paying my full fee *and* getting me season tickets, too. Be warned, I have a large group of friends, so you're gonna need to set me up with at least eight tickets."

"And people say I'm the shark," he said, shaking his head.

"Only on the ice, my friend." Her phone buzzed with an incoming message from one of the reporters at the Harbor City Post, who'd agreed to do a humanizing profile now as long as he got an exclusive at a later date that was more than a sit-down, but really gave new insights into the most hated man in town. "I own the rest of the ocean."

It wasn't until two in the morning that she put Zach's latest mess to bed and slid between the sheets so exhausted that she was asleep before her head hit the pillow. It had been easier in Antioch where their schedules had always meshed. Now they were back to her nine-to-five—in the morning or evening, depending on the size of that day's shitstorm—and he was back at the firehouse. He'd be on a twenty-four-hour shift starting at seven Sunday morning, but at least they'd have all day Saturday leading up to the engagement party BBQ.

The whole situation and its echo of her opposites-attract parents' marriage was giving her that itchy sense of feeling like the other shoe was about to drop any minute.

Saturday morning, she woke up to the sound of her phone vibrating on her bedside table. She couldn't help but grin. Someone was excited to see her again.

But the message on the screen wasn't from Frankie.

Tess: *Calling in a 911. Anderson just quit without notice and walked out. I have a bazillion deliveries scheduled today and can't be doing those and working the register at the same time. Help!!!*

Oh, that was beyond an emergency. Just the idea of super-introverted Tess having to deal with the public by doing deliveries from her florist shop had Lucy out of her bed in half a heartbeat. God bless her bestie, the woman hated dealing with people she didn't know well, and the result was a mix of cringeworthy embarrassing factoids, like the fact that an elephant's penis is six and a half feet long, or compulsions, like her need to count the number of tiles in someone's kitchen.

Lucy and Gina found Tess's quirks to be pretty fucking awesome and lovable, but people receiving bouquets for funerals or graduations rarely wanted to know the average diameter of the human eye (one inch). Tess didn't have family to fall back on or a big-ass inheritance, she needed her flower shop to be successful if she wanted to, you know, pay her rent.

Lucy: *On my way. Will take deliveries.*

Tess: *I love you so hard.*

Lucy: *You'll owe me.*

Tess: *Add it to my tab.*

While she was brushing her teeth ten minutes later, she grabbed her phone to see if Frankie had messaged. He should be off shift by now. No luck. Good thing she wasn't the kind of woman who felt the need to wait for a man to take action.

Lucy: *Bestie emergency (Tess not Gina). Acting as*

flower delivery goddess until BBQ. See you tonight!

She waited, staring at her phone. No text bubble with the three little dots appeared. He was probably asleep. It might have been a busy night. She hadn't seen any news this morning about any big fires, but that didn't necessarily mean anything.

She'd see him tonight. Everything would be just like it had been a week ago in Antioch. No reason for her heart to be doing that speed-up-and-dive-straight-down-to-her-toes thing. Everything was fine, perfectly fine. And if she kept repeating that to herself, maybe that other shoe would stay lodged wherever it was.

Chapter Twenty

Frankie sat behind Scarlett's wheel while parked in his driveway and honked the horn for a third time. He had no fucking clue what was up with Finian, but he needed to get his ass in gear already.

The passenger door flew open, and Finn slid into the passenger seat. "Asshole, relax."

Frankie was reversing down the drive before his brother had even finished fastening his seatbelt. "We were supposed to be there ten minutes ago."

"And when did you get all antsy about being on time for anything but your shift at the firehouse?" Finn asked, then smacked the heel of his hand hard against his forehead. "Oh wait. I know the answer to that, and it's as soon as you got home from your"—he held up his hand and made air quotes—"'just friends' trip to the middle of nowhere Missouri."

"Shut it, Finn."

"No fucking way, this is too much fun. So how is your"—more air quotes—"just friend, Lucy?"

Like he was going to tell him. He could barely think

about how fucking lucky he was with Lucy. Truth was, he was scared shitless of doing anything to fuck it up, so keeping everything on the down low just made more sense. If no one knew about him and Lucy, how could he fuck it up?

Stuck at a stoplight, he glared at his mirror image—well, if he had dark hair, no freckles, and was a full half inch shorter. "You know everyone thinks I'm the hotter twin."

"No worries," Finn said with a shrug. "I'm the mysterious one—everyone always wonders about me."

The light turned, and Frankie floored it. "Just because they have no clue what an annoying weirdo you are."

He drove the last few blocks to Marino's accompanied by his brother's laugh. He sounded like a hyena after it had taken sixteen hits off a helium balloon. Seriously, it was a weird-ass sound coming from someone who looked like he spent his days cutting down trees in a forest to build a log cabin from scratch. How some women found the sound attractive, Frankie had no idea. Not that he cared. Finn could have his pick of the women in Waterbury. Frankie only wanted one, and as soon as he found a parking spot in Marino's crowded lot he was going to get see her.

Normally, he tooled around a parking lot a few times to find the most protected spot for Scarlett. Tonight? He pulled into the first spot he laid eyes on and killed the engine. Ignoring the oh-really look his twin was sending him, he got out of the car and hustled across the parking lot to Marino's beer garden behind the bar, which had been reserved for Gina's and Ford's engagement party.

He spotted Lucy right away.

How could he not when she was wearing his favorite color and looking face-of-the-sun hot? Of course, it took longer to get to her than the drive from Antioch to Waterbury.

First, he had to say hello to every member of his family—and there were a million of them. Then, he had to wind through the equally huge number of Gina's family members. Even her brothers had flown in from a still-undisclosed location to surprise their sister. Finally, he got to where she stood with Gina and Tess, who gave him and Lucy a bemused look and started whispering in each other's ears.

"Hey there," he said, leaning in close because there was really no way he couldn't.

She looked up at him and smiled. "Hello yourself."

Holy hell. Every nerve in his body was attuned to her as if he was a volcano about to erupt, and if he didn't do something to relieve the pressure and soon, things were going to get really graphic in the middle of his by-the-book brother's engagement party.

"I need your help real quick," he said, grabbing her hand and pulling her toward Marino's main building. "I need to ask you a question about Gina's and Ford's wedding gift."

Yeah, that didn't pass the smell test, but he didn't care. His only concern was getting her somewhere private. They made it as far as through Marino's door and into a dark, empty hallway. Spinning her around so her back was to the wall next to the supply closet door, he put his hands on the wall on either side of her and went in for one kiss. At least that's all it was supposed to be. The minute his lips touched hers though, one kiss turned into a dozen long, drawn-out, breath-stealing, mind-melting, dick-hardening kisses that made the rest of the world disappear—and he never wanted it to end.

The insistent tap on his shoulder had other ideas. He broke the kiss, tore his gaze away from Lucy's beautiful, slightly kiss-dazed face, and got ready to tear a new one in whichever one of his brothers had the balls to interrupt.

The person standing behind him wasn't one of his brothers, though; it wasn't even a relation. Shannon the bartender, his former good-time companion.

"Sorry to interrupt," Shannon said with a friendly smile.

"No worries." Lucy started smoothing her hair in that way that women did when they were trying to get themselves back in order. "We were just saying hello."

"Huh," Shannon said, amusement plain in her tone. "Usually I just wave."

Then she stepped past Frankie now that he wasn't blocking the hall and went into the supply closet.

Lucy's cheeks were an adorable shade of pink when she looked at him and attempted to give him a censuring look. "You are forever messing up my lipstick, Frankie Hartigan."

And he didn't feel even the least bit bad about it. "Can't help it," he said, dipping his head down so his lips were practically touching the shell of her ear. "There's just something about that mouth of yours that is begging for someone to kiss it hard and good."

One of her dark eyebrows shot upward, and she gave him one of those looks that he knew meant nothing but the best kind of naked trouble. "I know other parts of me that could use a kiss, too."

Like every single inch of her? "Can we leave yet?"

She shook her head and smiled. "Not even close."

"Damn, I was afraid you were going to say that."

Normally, he loved his family and hanging out with them was one of his favorite things. However, tonight he would have pushed them out into the ocean on a raft if that meant a night alone with Lucy.

Yeah. He was pretty damn messed up over her. He'd fallen for her somewhere between Waterbury and Antioch. Hell, he'd fallen for her somewhere between his garage and the end of his driveway. For the first time in his life, he was in love, and all he wanted to do was spend time alone—and hopefully naked, but not was okay, too—with her.

Lucy raised herself on her tiptoes, necessary even in

those ridiculously sexy red heels she had on, and brushed a kiss on his cheek. "I'll be right back," she said before slipping away into the women's bathroom.

All he could do was stand there like an idiot staring at the closed door she'd gone through. Why? Because he was fucking petrified that he'd fuck it all up—and that's what made his palms clammy and his gut twist. His entire adult life had been spent protecting people—his family, the people of Waterbury, everyone who crossed his path. What good would he be if he failed to protect the one woman he never ever wanted to hurt?

"On your left," Shannon called out before walking toward him with a stack of bar towels that there was no way she could see over.

Now that was a situation he could do something about, so he did. He swiped the stack from her arms.

"Here, let me," he said. "I need to get a couple of beers anyway, so we're going in the same direction."

Shannon gave him a look like she didn't quite believe him, but in the end just strutted down the hall and into the main bar area. Frankie followed, placing the towels on the end of the bar for her.

Marino's had amazing bartenders and the worst clientele in Waterbury. Why? Because it was filled with cops, and the police department and the fire department had a centuries-deep rivalry. His brother Ford was one of the boys in blue, and Frankie would admit quietly, to himself, in a location where there was no way another human being could overhear him, that not all of the men and women on the force were horrible (that was as far as he could go and keep his firefighter card).

"So," Shannon said as she pulled two Buds from the tap. "What's going on with you and Lucy?"

"A lot, I hope." If he could manage not to fuck it up.

Of course, he had to get Lucy on board with going public

with him, too. Now that part grated on his nerves. He knew how other people saw him. Hell, he'd spent years encouraging everyone to see him as just the neighborhood fuck buddy. But with Lucy, he hoped for more. He hoped she'd see him as more than that—she'd see him as a forever kind of guy.

"So, it's finally happened, huh?" she asked, setting the beers down on the bar. "I always liked her. Plus she tips great."

"I owe it all to you, really."

"Oh yeah, how's that?"

"If we hadn't had that little chat, what's going on with me and Lucy wouldn't have happened."

"Well it took you long enough and enough women to figure it out."

"I guess I was slow."

"Aren't guys always?"

"Hey, we're not all idiots."

"Just you. And hopefully not the new owner."

"What are you talking about?"

"Mr. Marino sold the bar."

"To who?"

"No one knows. Hopefully not a total asshole."

Frankie held up his bottle. "Here's to hoping."

She clicked his bottle with her glass of water.

"So, it's finally happened, eh Hartigan?" asked an asshole on the barstool, his mouth twisted into what was probably as close as he got to having a genuine smile. "You ran through all the nice ass in this town and now you're on to second-tier talent."

Frankie was going to wear the guy's face like a glove. "Shut up."

He straightened to his full height and took a step toward the jackass, his hands curled into fists, but Shannon reached out with the fast reflexes of an experienced bartender and put a hand on Frankie's forearm.

"He's drunk and not worth it," she said.

At the moment, smashing the asshole's face seemed very worth whatever would happen next. Still, he played it out in his head as if he were about to go into a burning building instead of starting a bar fight. He'd punch this piece of shit, the other cops hanging around the bar would join the fun, and his brothers would come running because of the noise. The whole thing would end with a wrecked bar, the need for serious bail money, and Shannon out of a job for letting the whole thing go down.

Fuck.

Sometimes life really did suck rotten cop balls.

He shook out his hands and relaxed his shoulders. Shannon released a deep breath and gave him a thank-you nod.

"Hope she's as wild in bed," the jerk said with a knowing wink aimed at Frankie. "You know what they say about fat chicks—they're demons in the sheets because they have to really work it to keep a guy's attention. But hey, if you want to keep her a secret and not let your family out there in the beer garden know, I totally understand. Sometimes a man just needs to get his dick wet, even if the landing spot isn't what they really want."

Fury snapped, crackled, and exploded like someone had pumped a tanker truck full of oxygen into an enclosed blaze. "What I'm doing with Lucy is none of you or anyone else's fucking business," he said, practically nose to nose with the cop. The words flew out of his mouth loud enough for most if not all of the people in the bar to swing their heads around to see what the hell was going on at the bar.

Frankie could imagine what they were seeing, but he didn't give a fuck. All he could do was concentrate 99 percent of his effort on not killing the man too stupid to know when to shut his piehole.

"Frankie." Shannon's voice penetrated the red-tinged fog blocking out everything else, snagging his attention.

But when he looked at the bartender, she wasn't looking at him. She was looking behind him. He glanced back, and his gut collapsed in on itself.

Lucy stood at the end of the bar, her face white with fury. It wasn't aimed at the two asshole cops, though. She was looking right at him as if she was about to pick up a flamethrower and charbroil his ass into ashes.

...

Lucy couldn't breathe. Her lungs stopped functioning. Her brain went on the fritz. Her whole body was hot and cold at the same time, and the only sound she could hear was the rush of blood in her ears.

Certain words screamed louder than others in her head.

Sex.

Wild.

And she'd thought she wouldn't have to deal with that whole fat-chicks-are-crazier-in-bed bullshit with Frankie. But maybe he'd just been better at hiding it than some of the others. God knew he'd been good enough at hiding her. When had they ever gone out in public since they'd gotten back? Even here at the party, he'd made sure no one could see them when he kissed her. She'd been waiting for it to all go to shit without realizing that it already had.

Forget pity fuck. She was his secret fuck.

Frankie turned to her. "Lucy—"

She glanced around, her stomach twisting into knots at the idea that the whole bar was hanging on their every word, watching the fat chick get humiliated. It was bad enough this was happening to her at her friend's engagement party. To be the butt of an entire bar's joke would be too much.

"Which part was so wild that made it worth it even though it was me?" she asked, so pissed at herself for that nugget of hope that had somehow grown into a mountain that she was shaking. So she fell back into her most familiar defensive posture. She attacked. "Sex under the stars on the floating deck? Maybe the road head? Or there was the time at the hotel that ended with us getting calls of bravo from the room next door? Which one of those so-called crazy sexcapades made it into your big-girls-will-let-you-do-anything category? Or is it that all of the many, many women you fucked before me were just that boring in bed?"

The color went out of his face. "It's not about that."

He reached for her, but she took a step back to avoid his touch. If he made contact, she'd break down completely, and she'd be damned if she did that. Not here. Not in front of everyone. Instead, she'd battle and fight to prove they hadn't gotten to her. They never would.

"Really, then what is it about?" she asked, her voice starting to shake a little as emotion bled through. "How you were so hard up during your sex break that even someone like me started looking good?"

Frankie froze. Then a flush of angry red rushed up from his shirt collar. "What the hell, Lucy. You know that's not the case."

"And that's why we always met at my apartment then, right? That's why we never left it?"

"I didn't want to scare you off. I wanted to prove to you that I was different." He took a step forward, reaching for her.

She waved his attempt off. "Oh yeah, the no-sex pledge. How did that go for you? How long did you make it? Almost a week? Wow. You really are different now."

"That's a really shitty thing to say." His voice was carefully neutral, as if he was trying to hold onto whatever sense of control he still had of his temper. "You know it was about more than that."

Well, it was too late for her. Her fury was on a roll now. Like an avalanche, there was nothing that was going to stop it. All she wanted to do was to make him hurt as much as she did right now.

"Don't worry, Junior. You're not turning into your dad. You're so fucking scared of taking a real risk that you're spending your life surrounded by people but without making a commitment to anyone. It's fascinating, really. You're so petrified of being alone, but you can't commit, either. But you've got them all fooled, don't you? Everybody loves Frankie Hartigan, it's just important not to fall *in* love with him."

He flinched as if she'd just delivered a solid punch before straightening to his full height and narrowing his eyes as he glared at her. "You sure didn't seem to be complaining when you were coming all over my dick."

"Don't turn this around on me," she said, jamming a finger into his chest. "That's not what I'm saying."

"Sure it's not. You're just walking around with all of your emotional baggage waiting for me to fuck you over like your mom did your dad," he said, his voice harsh and low. "You said you were suspicious of actual love, but it's not that. You're scared shitless."

The truth of his words slammed into her, stealing her breath, but not for long. "Oh, that's rich coming from someone who barely said five words to me before a week and a half ago," she said, knowing she sounded like some haughty bitch who got paid to make grown men feel like children, but not giving two shits. "You don't even know me."

"That's shit," he snarled back, his control obviously ripped to shreds. "I know you better than you think because you're just like me."

She narrowed her eyes and gutted him with a glare. "You know what? There are a million men out there who have mansplained everything from my weight to my food choices to my audacity to wear clothes that show off all eleventy billion of my curves, but I've never had one who mansplained my own emotions."

"Maybe it's past time someone did," he said, his volume spiking, "because you've been lying to yourself about them for long enough that you believe your own bullshit."

That was crap. She practiced brutal self-honesty—about her size, her personality, her skills, her weaknesses, her ambitions, her accomplishments. Everything. She would never lie to herself about something so important. She wouldn't.

Oh really?

She shoved that quiet voice in her head back down and faced the man she'd been stupid enough to fall in love with. See? Brutal self-honesty.

"Fuck you, Frankie Hartigan." Her voice broke on his name, her eyes filling with tears.

. . .

And that's what broke him. Not the words. Not the things she must have been thinking about him all along. Not the pain tearing him up inside. What got to him was that he'd made her cry. He'd hurt the one woman he should have protected with everything he had.

He'd failed her.

He'd failed them.

Desperate to roll back from the edge they were rushing over, he reached out again, but she avoided his touch. "Lucy."

"Just stop." She held up a hand, warning him off as she took a step back so she was outside of arm's reach. Then she took a deep breath, letting it out in one slow exhale that seemed to bring her back from the height of her anger. "This wasn't going to work out back here in Waterbury. Everything that happened in Antioch was that false connection that happens sometimes on vacation when you are with people under unusual circumstances and you forge a bond off of that. It doesn't last. It's not real. I knew it. Deep down, I'm sure you knew it, too. There is too much history for you and skewed expectations for me. I don't have the energy for it when we both know it's not going to work out."

Jagged edges, that's all he was on the inside, and there was nothing left that he could say. She'd made up her mind. She'd made it up before they'd even left Antioch, and he'd been too fucking thickheaded to realize it. He'd thought they could be different together. So, he stood there and watched Lucy walk away because there wasn't a damn thing he could do about it.

He had no clue how long he'd stood there, staring at the door leading out to the beer garden, before his sister Fallon came storming over.

"What in the hell was that all about?" she asked, her voice low and angry. "What did you do?"

He looked at his sister and tried to find the words to explain how he'd epically fucked up—just like their dad had. All this time he'd kept his emotional distance from the women in his life, and it hadn't made a difference in how things worked out. History was forever repeating itself, with the sins of the fathers passing down to their sons.

What had he done?

"Not enough," he said.

And losing Lucy was his punishment for that.

Chapter Twenty-One

Sitting in The Pink Narwhal when it was packed to the gills for ladies' night, Lucy turned to her companion and shared a real world truth.

"You know, there are few times in a woman's life when having female friends is as important as when you're contemplating murder."

Zach Blackburn just sat there like a silent hockey Yoda and lifted one eyebrow.

Of course he did—because he was a man, and they did not know the magic answer to not-really-serious homicidal ideas post-breakup.

Could it be a breakup if we'd never really been together? Oh, that was even more depressing.

However, every woman in the world would know that the proper response to kinda-sorta plotting the demise of a man who did someone wrong was not silence, but to share in a low, conspiratorial voice, "I have a shovel." That was what women did for each other. They were ride or die. Tend and defend. They weren't silent hulks of muscle and wry glances who drank whiskey neat.

When the need for a bar buddy arose, though, her choices were vastly limited in this situation.

"But I can't call my girls because Gina is marrying into that damn Hartigan family, Fallon is already a member of it, and poor sweet Tess shouldn't be stuck in the middle trying to pick between friends."

Another lifted eyebrow—this time it was the one with the metal bar through it—and another drink of whiskey before Zach finally said something. "I'm so glad that you, as the woman who recently chewed my ass out for punching a guy who literally *hocked a loogie* in my face for costing the team a trip to the playoffs, have begun to see the beauty of a little violence."

See? A girlfriend would never have thrown Lucy's hypocrisy back in her face. Well, a really good friend would, but she'd pick the right moment after all the initial I-am-woman-watch-me-bury-him-in-an-anthill-naked feelings had abated. Tactical error on Zach's part.

"Oh boo-hoo," she grumbled. "Your asshole insulted your pride. My asshole broke my heart." She took a long drink of her third (fourth?) vodka and Mountain Dew, relishing the burn as it went down. "Although the whole spitting phlegm thing is pretty gross. And unhygienic. Why are men so nasty?"

He laughed. That was his tell. The first time she heard the soft rumble, she knew she had a tatted, pierced, growling grizzly bear with a Pooh Bear center on her hands, and she knew she could work with him.

"That is a longer conversation than I think you're going to stay conscious for if you keep going at that rate," he said.

"What?" she squawked at a loud enough volume level to turn heads and make her realize that she just may have had more than she'd thought. "I'm just keeping pace with you."

"One, as an athlete who hits the gym hard every single day, my body can take five of these in a row."

Shit. Five? Also, did he just break out the metabolism thing? With her? He had. Asshole.

"Fuck you."

He chuckled at her. "Oh, ow. If I had feelings, that would hurt." He sipped his whiskey. "Two, don't worry, we haven't had five drinks. I'm on my second and you're on your third. Yes, I could see you trying to figure it out because your lips were moving when you were counting."

Of all the signs in the world that she should go home now, being told by her most troublesome client that she was drunk in public—not that he used *exactly* those words—was pretty much the equivalent of a massive neon sign. Instead of heading out, she held up her hand and waved the bartender back over.

Before the guy could make his way over, though, he made eye contact with Zach, who did some kind of silent man-to-man mind-meld thing. The bartender turned his gaze to Lucy, shrugged, and turned in the other direction.

She shot back the rest of her drink and set the glass on the bar before turning to the man she knew was trying to help, but damn she was tired of men thinking they knew what was best for her, beginning with her dad thinking that calling his overweight daughter Muffin Top was okay right up to the now, with Frankie spouting off about how she was the best sex to those assholes who only thought fat women were good for banging because they worked more for it. Way to feed right into the stereotype. How could she stay with a guy like that? It wasn't that she was scared of putting herself out there, of ending up like her dad, mooning after someone who didn't really want them but only saw them as a soft place to land when things got rough.

Oh yeah, that doesn't sound like you're projecting on

Frankie at all.

Ignoring that little voice in her head that hadn't shut up since she'd walked out of Marino's two nights ago, she turned and glared at Zach. It was, after all, his fault that she couldn't drown out the voice with another vodka and Mountain Dew. Men. They were the worst.

"You know," she said, giving him the glare that left the majority of her clients quiet and quaking. "The Post is right. You really are an asshole."

But, of course, he wasn't just a regular client. He shrugged those big shoulders of his that only reminded her of Frankie and how he'd held that stupid birdbath bowl for close to an eternity all to help her win some stupid competition.

"Probably," Zach said, glancing at something behind her. "But I'm also off duty."

"What do you mean?"

"Reinforcements have arrived," he said before mumbling something that sounded a lot like "thank fucking God."

She pivoted on her barstool to take a look at what had caught Zach's attention. However, it wasn't a what. It was a who, three of them to be exact. Fallon was there, face clean of makeup and her hair thrown up into a messy bun, not because that was even close to fashionable but because she'd probably just got off shift in the emergency room. Gina stood next to her, wearing one of her signature pink dresses with the buttons not quite fastened correctly because more than likely she and Ford had been messing around before the friend 911 call came in. Tess, per usual, stood a little bit behind the other women with her hands clasped tight together in front of her, peeking out from behind long bangs that almost covered her eyes completely. Peopling in places where there were lots of people was definitely not Tess's thing.

Lucy turned back to Zach. "How did you get them here?"

"I talked to your assistant Reva," he said with a smirk

that had probably gotten him in plenty of trouble in his life. "She has a thing for the whole tatted-up bad boy thing."

She snorted. "If only she knew the truth about you."

Zach, being Zach, ignored her comment because the man loved ignoring things he didn't want to acknowledge and got off his stool. He was standing and reaching for his wallet in his back pocket by the time her girls got to them.

"Thanks for making the call," Fallon said, looking at him like she wanted to double down on what the jerk Zach had punched had said but she was trying to keep it friendly as a favor to Lucy.

"No problem," he said, tossing more bills than necessary on the bar. "Just make sure she gets home okay."

"I'm right here, you know," Lucy grumbled. "I can hear you."

Zach just shrugged, tipped an imaginary hat at her, and walked out—his step definitely lighter now, probably because he no longer had to deal with Lucy. She couldn't blame him. She didn't really want to deal with herself, either.

"Please tell me you were giving him advice about how to play so we actually make the playoffs next year," Gina said.

"Amen," Fallon added, her relief at finally being able to get that off her chest evident in how her shoulders sagged with relief.

Nope. They weren't going to distract her from the topic at hand that easily. "Never mind Zach, what are you guys doing here?"

"Where else would we be?" Fallon asked.

And this was exactly why she hadn't called them. "I don't want to put you in a weird position. Frankie's your brother."

Fallon threw back her head and laughed. "You think I've never wanted to knock his head off before? Oh, the sweet imaginings of an only child."

Lucy turned to Gina, needing to make her friend

understand that the last thing she wanted was to put anyone in an awkward situation. "And he's going to be your brother-in-law."

Gina gave her a quick hug. "But you're my best friend."

Turning to Tess, Lucy gave it one last shot. "You don't feel weird stuck in the middle?"

"Have we met?" Tess asked, her voice quiet like it always was in crowded places but still filled with warmth. "I feel weird all the time because I *am* weird. Seriously, this is my starting point for life."

That closed Lucy's trap. Looking around at her friends, who'd automatically formed a protective half circle around her barstool as if there were attackers coming at her from all sides, she let out the breath it felt like she'd been holding for sixty years. She had the most stubborn, pigheaded, fabulous people as her best friends in the whole wide world. And it wasn't just the vodka that had her tearing up a little at the thought. "You guys are the fucking best."

"We also have an Uber out front waiting," Tess said, already shifting toward the door, obviously more than ready to get somewhere less crowded.

Sure, she'd been imbibing, but her girls all looked stone cold sober. "Why?"

Gina rolled her eyes and all but yelled out *duh*. "Because we can't drive around with a body in the back of our own car."

Finally. She was with her people who understood. God, she loved her friends.

"Come on," Fallon said, patting the backpack she had slung over one shoulder. "I got a bottle of the extra spicy, set-your-mouth-on-fire vodka from the craft vodka bar on Fifth."

"Plus we have ice cream," Tess said.

"And shovels," Gina finished.

Lucy stood up and pulled all of her girls in for a group

hug. "I love you guys."

"We love you, too," Fallon said, cutting right to the point. "Now let's go."

They may have scared the Uber driver with their loud laughter and detailed plans for removing most of the men from the planet. That was okay, Lucy could live with it, because they made it to her apartment building faster than normal. LeRoy, the world's best doorman, tipped his hat in greeting as they made their way to the elevators in one giggling mass of estrogen and booze. They'd opened up the vodka bottle in the Uber. Hey, dire times called for dire measures.

"Thank God you have a real TV," Tess said as they spilled into Lucy's apartment, heading straight into the living room and ignoring the floor-to-ceiling windows that provided an amazing view of Harbor City's sparkling skyline across the water. "Doing this at Gina's house when Ford temporarily lost his mind was a giant pain in the ass."

Lucy gasped and clapped her hands before flopping down onto her couch and kicking off her heels. "You got angry chick flicks for me?"

"Even better," Gina said, holding up the tub of ice cream as if it were the Stanley Cup. "We got kickass sci-fi chicks!"

Lucy's jaw dropped. "You didn't." They understood how much she was hurting without her having to explain a single thing to them. She really could not have better friends.

"Yes!" Gina and Tess hollered at the same time.

"I'm scared to ask, but what are you guys freaking out about?" Fallon asked, looking at the three of them as if they were totally clueless.

"It's tradition, sort of like Paint and Sip," Lucy said, relaxing for the first time in days. "When something shitty happens, we regroup with some of our favorite chick flicks."

"And the sci-fi scream dance thing you just did?" Fallon asked.

Gina grabbed the remote and pulled up Netflix on the smart TV before going straight to the strong female leads section. "We only break out *Aliens* and *Mad Max: Fury Road* for the most dire of situations, because if you can watch Ripley or Furiosa and not walk away feeling like you can kick ass, then you are watching a different movie than I am."

"But first we need ice cream and glasses." Tess hooked her arm through Fallon's and started tugging her toward the hallway that led to the kitchen. "Come help me with supplies."

As Tess strong-armed Fallon into the hallway with all the subtlety of a moose in a field of fluffy white bunnies, Lucy shook her head and turned to Gina. "So you drew the short straw, huh?"

"More like they thought I might know what in the hell to say." Gina sat down on the couch and laid her head down on Lucy's shoulder.

"Do you?" Damn, she hated sounding so hopeful.

"I might, if you tell me what happened."

Yeah, that part. That was what she didn't want to do. It hurt too much. It made her really think about what went down when she wasn't overwhelmed with embarrassment and hurt. So she shoved that away and went with the awful part on the surface.

"He told some guys in the bar that he was doing the fat girl fuck party."

Gina gasped, and her eyes rounded. A red blotch of anger bloomed on her throat as she reached for the vodka bottle, snatched it from Lucy's grasp, and took a swig straight from it. Then she gasped again because that vodka was no joke.

"Two things," Gina said, her eyes watering a little as she thumped her palm against her chest. "One, did he use those words? Two, what does that mean?"

"No." There went that string of guilt tightening around her stomach and making her shift in her seat. "But that's what they were talking about—how fat girls work harder for it in bed because we have to be freaks in the sheets or we'd never get laid."

"That's awful." Gina put the vodka down on the coffee table and wrapped her arms around Lucy in a tight hug. "I can't believe Frankie would agree to something like that. I'm not saying you're wrong, I'm just having to really process that."

"Well, I never heard him agree, but he didn't deny it, either."

Gina cocked her head to the side. "So, he didn't say it, and he didn't say he didn't say it?"

Lucy had played and replayed the conversation in her head a million times, and she couldn't shake the idea that her initial reaction may have been more about the shoe she'd been waiting to drop rather than anything that Frankie had really done. But if she admitted that, even to herself, what did she have to think about other than what he'd said to her?

"It wasn't just that," she said, taking in a shaky breath as the guilt of knowing she wasn't giving up the whole story ate at her. "He told me I was projecting all of my emotional baggage on him."

Gina lifted her head and looked her dead in the eyes. There wasn't any judgement there, but there wasn't any coddling, either. They'd been through too much together as friends for all of that.

"Do you think that might be possible?"

"No!"

She wasn't holding her parents' sins against him. *She wasn't.* She was just being cautious, smart. She'd seen how love could fuck someone over. What kind of an idiot would she be not to protect herself from that by being realistic about how things really worked?

"Look, I love you," Gina said, which was never a message followed by "and you're totally right about everything."

"There is no one else in the world like you, and I'd be lost without you, so don't take this the wrong way… But you have been known to try to take control of a situation by embracing the worst of it and forcing it to do your bidding."

"Well yeah, it's what makes me so good at my job."

"True." Gina gave her a patient smile. "But those skills aren't always the ones you want to break out when it comes to relationships."

Lucy sat up, anger streaking its way up her spine so fast she was kind of surprised it didn't shoot out her fingertips. "So I should just roll over and accept what I can get?"

"Absolutely not." Gina shook her head, sending her brown waves flying. "You deserve to have someone who loves you for who you are, which is a pretty human being who is equal parts fierce and amazing."

Fuck. It was really hard to stay pissed when her bestie said something like that and actually meant it. Still, she grumbled, "I'm not fishing for compliments."

Gina rolled her eyes. "Please remind me of a time when you ever needed to do that with me or Tess, or Fallon for that matter. We love you because of who you are, as should anyone with half a brain. And I'm not telling you that Frankie was in the right." She paused and took Lucy's hand in hers before letting out a deep breath and continuing on. "But here's my question: Is it possible that he may not be the only one in the wrong?"

She was saved from having to think too much about that because Fallon and Tess came back into the living room armed with shot glasses and bowls of ice cream.

"We would have given you more time, but the ice cream's melting," Tess said.

"Yeah, and I couldn't eavesdrop at all," Fallon said. "Your kitchen is too far away for that."

Blunt as always, Fallon cracked her up—even with all of

the questions swirling around in her because Gina's words echoed that little voice in her head that she'd been doing her best to drown out. Tonight wasn't about that, though. Looking at her friends gathered around her, she knew that this was about the one relationship she could always depend on no matter what happened—her friendship with this kick-ass bunch of women.

"Well, if there's ice cream and booze, then I declare it movie time," Lucy said, getting into the spirit of the night whether she felt it all the way to her toes or not.

"*Aliens* or *Mad Max*?" Gina asked, aiming the remote at the big screen.

"Let me think about that," Lucy said, shaking her head at the other woman. "I can ogle Tom Hardy *and* cheer on the most badass gang of motorcycle grandmas ever? How is there even a thought about which one should go first?"

"Point," Gina said and hit start on *Mad Max: Fury Road*.

Everyone settled in on the couch to watch the awesomeness, but no matter how loud the cars' engines or the screaming guitar, Lucy couldn't quiet the question Gina asked. And if her bestie and that annoying voice in her head were right, what in the hell was she going to do about it?

Because unlike when her clients came into her office, Lucy had no go-to plan for how to fix the mess she'd made of her own life.

Chapter Twenty-Two

In all his years as a firefighter, Frankie had never called in sick—not once—until the morning after the fight with Lucy. That was days ago. He'd spent the ensuing time binge-watching crap shows on Netflix and picking fights with Finn, hoping to provoke his twin into a little brotherly brawl to get some of his pissed-off energy out.

Unfortunately, it was impossible to get under his twin's skin. The man was Mr. Even Keel. It was annoying as shit.

"Another day of sitting on your ass?" Finn asked in a tone that perfectly expressed the fact that even if he wasn't going to get annoyed, he wasn't going to pussyfoot around the situation.

Yeah, his twin was quieter than he was, but he was no less of a pain in the ass. Frankie just flipped his brother off and kept scrolling through the never-ending list of B-list horror movies.

"You're lucky you still have that leave time to burn off," Finn continued, not taking the hint to shut the fuck up.

"Hansen took the extra shifts to pick up the slack for

Washington being out," Frankie said.

"Oh, as long as that's taken care of," Finn said as he collapsed onto the couch. He kept his mouth shut for a whole five point three seconds, long enough to do a dramatic sniff of the air around Frankie, and went on, "I guess there's no reason for you to take a shower."

Okay, so it had been a day. Or two. Who in the hell was counting and who gave a fuck? "Do you need something? Or can you shut up, because I'm trying to find something to watch."

Keeping his mouth shut, for once, Finn sat back and propped his feet up on the coffee table next to all the empty Mountain Dew cans.

There were a lot of them. Frankie had gotten a case for Lucy and then had proceeded to drink his way through in record time to get rid of any memory of her. The only thing was that he'd failed to get the empty cans from the coffee table to the recycling bin, and he'd growled—literally—when his twin had tried to do it for him yesterday. Some people might have read something into that. Frankie just chalked it up to him wanting people to leave him the hell alone.

"Are you going to get your ugly mug up and go apologize to Lucy for whatever it is that you fucked up?" Finn asked.

Frankie punched the arrow button on the remote harder. "What makes you think it was me?"

"Because you only sit around and beat yourself up when you do something wrong."

He glared at his twin, not appreciating the truth of the statement. "Screw you."

Finn reached over and swiped the remote from Frankie. "Come on in," he hollered toward the kitchen. "But I'll warn you, he smells, so stay as far away as possible."

That's when Ford walked into the living room, along with their dad. Of all the people in the world Frankie didn't want to see, those two were at the top of the list. Ford because he was so fucking in love, it was hard to be around him. And his dad? Because that's the reason why Frankie wasn't walking around with the same idiot-in-love grin that Ford was. The apple never fell far from the tree.

"What is this, some kind of touchy-feely intervention?" he asked, putting plenty of snarl in the question.

None of the other men in the room flinched. They just looked at him with matching you-big-dumbass expressions. That's the way they wanted this to go down? Fine. He didn't give a shit.

Finally, Ford broke the silent pissing contest. "So what's it going to take to get you to go after her?"

Yeah, because it would be just that easy. "She doesn't want me."

Ford crossed his arms over his chest and rolled back on his heels, like he couldn't decide if he was good cop or bad cop in this interrogation. "From what I've heard from Gina, that's a bunch of shit."

"Yeah, well, it doesn't matter anyway," Frankie said, sinking back into the couch and giving into the agony eating away at his gut that made him feel like a man who was suffering from the flu, a hangover, and the mother of all migraines at the same time. "It's all over."

Finished.

Done.

Kaput.

"So you're just giving up?" his dad asked.

Up until that moment, Frankie had been doing his best to pretend his old man wasn't in the room. He didn't see any reason to change tactics now, so he ignored the question.

"Son," Frank Sr. said. "I raised you better than to act like that to someone you care about."

To act better than that? The words hit him like a lead

weight dropped overboard. *To act better than that?* Years' worth of denied resentment, of bottled-up anger, boiled over, rushing through him like a back draft. He turned his attention to his dad but forced himself to keep his ass on the couch or else he wasn't sure what would happen.

"You are the last person," he said, not bothering to hide the disgust in his voice, "the *very last person* in the world I want to have this conversation with."

His old man didn't say shit after that. He just sat there like a stone, staring at Frankie with an inscrutable expression on his face. Frankie didn't need to say any more. His dad knew exactly what he meant.

"Whoa," Ford said, looking between Frankie and their dad as if he'd never seen either man before. "What's all that about?"

"Why don't you ask him?" Because Frankie was done keeping his old man's secrets.

Finn and Ford both turned their dad, who sat leaning forward in his chair, his elbows planted on his thighs in an exact replica of how Frankie was sitting. Like father, like son.

Finally, he let out a long, weary sigh. "Is this about Becky Rimwald?"

The way he said it, as if it was just some silly thing, made something snap in Frankie and made his pulse roar in his ears. He jumped off the couch. "It's about the fact that you couldn't keep your dick in your pants even though Mom loved you more than anything and you always acted like you loved her."

Everyone in the room tensed. Wild, frenetic energy pulsed through Frankie, and he had to move. It wasn't a choice. He started pacing the length of the living room from the front door to the far wall.

"What. The. Fuck. Is. Going. On," Ford asked, his voice low and deadly.

Finn let out an annoyed snort. "Dad didn't screw Becky Rimwald."

Of course that's what his twin would say, Frankie had sent him away to the store the second he'd turned the corner and seen Becky and his dad.

"You didn't see what I did. I protected you from that."

Finn got up from the couch and stalked over to Frankie. Mr. Even Keel's cover was finally blown. His hands were curled into fists, and his entire body radiated wrath. But he didn't take a swing. Instead, he got right up into Frankie's face.

"You are such a moron," Finn said. "I'm surprised you can chew gum and walk at the same time."

"Wait." Ford shoved himself between the twins, giving each of them a hard shove in opposite directions. "Rewind. Who is Becky Rimwald, and why in the hell would Frankie think that about Dad?"

"Because Frankie saw me kissing her," their dad said, his voice uncharacteristically flat.

Whatever Frankie had been expecting when he'd imagined this moment, his father finally admitting his transgression, it hadn't been this. There was no relief. There was no happiness. There was only a sick, gut-churning wave of disappointment that knocked his knees out and forced him to lean his ass against the windowsill or go down for the count. And that's when he realized there'd always been a part of him that hadn't believed, had hoped that he hadn't seen what he'd seen.

"When?" Ford asked, breaking the heavy silence.

Finn shoved his fingers through his thick, dark hair and sat down on the couch. "Our senior year in high school."

"I tried to tell you then, and I'll tell you now," Frank Sr. said. "It wasn't what it looked like."

"Really?" Frankie all but snarled. "Her tongue wasn't

stuffed down your throat?"

His dad looked like there was nothing more in the world that he'd like to do at that moment than reach out and cuff his oldest—the Hartigan temper was as legendary as their ability to go wild—but he didn't. Instead, he closed his eyes, let out a breath, and then focused his attention on Frankie.

"Do you remember the string of warehouse fires we had that year? Andy Rimwald was one of the firefighters who died in them before we caught the firebug."

That summer had been awful. Ten firefighters had been killed in the fires, which had been rigged to do the most damage once everyone was on the scene. Katie Hartigan had spent most of the nights their dad was on shift sitting at the kitchen table polishing and polishing the set of silver utensils her great-great-grandmother had managed to sneak out of Ireland when she'd run off because the English had threatened to hang her for stealing. Frankie had organized it so that there was always one Hartigan kid sitting up with her, at least until she sent them to bed in the wee hours of the morning. He wasn't sure if she ever slept while Frank Sr. was working that summer. The second he'd walk through the door, though, she'd collapse against him and allow herself thirty seconds of holding him before straightening up and starting a huge breakfast with all of his favorites. They'd all been keyed up and on edge.

After a few seconds, no doubt to make sure everyone was thinking the same thing as Frankie, his dad went on. "Well, you've been on the job for some time now, Junior. You must have seen families go through hell after something like that happens. They cry. They scream. They fight against the darkness. They go a little crazy."

Maybe there were other jobs where things were like that—the military, cops—but in the firehouse they really were a family. When one went down, they all mourned. And the wives and kids of the fallen firefighter? They did whatever it took to make sure they were taken care of, something that occasionally crossed some lines. Something started the tingle on the back of Frankie's neck, that oh-shit signal that had saved him more than once in the middle of a fire.

"Becky came into the firehouse to collect Andy's things even though we told her we'd take them out to her," Frank Sr. said, his shoulders hunching forward as if even this many years later he needed to ward off the blow of what came next. "She said she wanted to take a look at the place he loved. And before she left, I gave her a hug. She was a lost widow grieving, and I was a friendly port in a storm. She didn't mean it. I had been just extricating myself when you walked in."

Frankie pulled up the memory of walking into that firehouse. His dad had been against the wall, his hands at his sides. It was Becky who'd been plastered against his old man.

"That's a pretty convenient story that you didn't share all those years ago," he said as he kept running it over and over in his head.

"Junior," his dad said with a frustrated sigh. "I love you, but don't think for a minute that I need to explain myself to you when I haven't done a damn thing wrong."

Maybe the explanation wouldn't have mattered when Frankie was seventeen, but after years as a firefighter, he'd seen that agonizing place when someone went down in a blaze, where a spouse was experiencing so much pain that became so overwhelming that all they wanted to do was just be rid of it for a little while. Still, he'd been so sure then and had never let go of it, even when the doubts started creeping in.

"He's telling the truth," Finn said, his voice sounding as tired as Frankie felt at the moment. "I ran into Becky outside of the firehouse when I came back from that bullshit errand you sent me on. She was talking to Mom, who'd come by to drop off lunch for Dad since it was a Saturday and she wasn't working. Becky was crying to Mom, hanging onto her as if her whole world had been blown away. She kept telling Mom she was sorry, that she didn't mean to kiss him. Mom just held Becky tight and told her it was okay, that it was all going to be okay. So I gotta ask you, do you really think you know more than Mom?"

The question landed like a two-by-four to the side of the head. There wasn't a Hartigan sibling alive who would dare think they knew more than Katie Hartigan, because his mama didn't raise any stupid kids. He turned to his dad, still half-processing what in the hell he'd just learned, almost afraid to hope that he'd been wrong.

"Is that really what happened?" Frankie asked.

His dad didn't blink, didn't hesitate. "Yes."

All those years, all those times that he thought he was protecting everyone, he'd just been digging a hole for himself because he thought he knew best. Instead of talking it out and asking questions, he'd given up and walked away from a man who up until that moment had been his real-life hero.

He'd been a fucking idiot.

"I gave up too easily," he said, realization sucker punching him in the gut.

Ford snorted. "That's because everything always came easy to you. School. Friends. Women. Life. So when something didn't fit within your accepted parameters, you didn't have a damn clue what to do about it. That's why you fucked shit up with Lucy, because you thought you could blast in like some knight in shining armor when that was the last thing she needed or wanted."

Frankie, Finn, and Frank Sr. all turned to look at Ford, wearing almost identical expressions of shock and horror.

"When did you turn into some crackpot TV doctor?" Finn asked, blinking in surprise.

Ford glared at them. "Gina has recommended some books."

Who in the hell had taken over his emotionally clueless brother's body? Looking around, he saw he wasn't the only one with that reaction. Frank Sr. and Finn were staring at Ford like he was one of the Pod People, too. For his part, Ford just tapped his thumb to his fingers as the tips of his ears turned red.

"The thing is," Ford said, zeroing in on Frankie, "I'm not wrong and you know it."

What Frankie wouldn't give to tell Ford to fuck straight off. Maybe he could even draw his baby brother into tossing down like they had the night Frankie had enlightened Ford about what an idiot he was being when it came to Gina. Sure, he'd walk away with a few bruises, but that was better than the guilt jabbing into him like an electric cattle prod.

Because he hadn't just seen something and gone into automatic protector mode when it came to what had happened with his dad. He'd done it with Lucy, too. When that guy at the bar had gone off like a moron, he should have walked away. Instead, he'd given in to the need to try to be her knight on a white horse. Lucy didn't need that. She didn't want a protector, she wanted someone she knew would always be at her side. He'd had the opportunity to show her that he would be with her, always. But he'd fucked it up.

"Shit. I fucked up." He looked around at his brothers and dad. "What in the hell am I going to do now?"

Finn shrugged. "Don't look at me, I'm happily single."

True enough. He turned to Ford.

His youngest brother rolled his eyes. "To paraphrase what a giant jackass told me recently on the deck of this house, go get your girl."

None of this was helpful, so he faced the man who would be totally within his rights to tell Frankie to go jump off a bridge. "What do I say?"

"You gotta figure that one out for yourself, Junior, but whatever you do, go big. A woman like Lucy isn't someone you just sweet-talk your way back to. You're going to have to work for that job."

The last word jumped out at him. That's what Lucy had asked him about on the floating deck back in Antioch. Sure, she'd been joking, but he wasn't—not then and definitely not now.

"Can you help me arrange a thing tomorrow and help me get Lucy to it? Maybe tell her it's a wedding thing?" he asked Ford.

"Have you ever planned a wedding?" His brother looked at him like he was the Pod Person now. "That shit is complicated. There are color-coded spreadsheets."

"What if it's not related to the wedding?" Finn asked. "What if it's just family and close friends?"

That would be perfect.

Ford grumbled something under his breath before answering. "This had better work, because otherwise Gina is going to kill me for messing with her scheduling."

A few minutes of planning later and Ford and his dad were heading toward the front door, but Frankie couldn't let his dad walk out without apologizing.

"I'm sorry for thinking the worst, Dad," he said, emotion making it hard to get the words out. "Can you forgive me?"

His dad gave him the same easygoing grin that Frankie saw in the mirror.

"For doing what you thought was the best thing to protect this family?" Frank Sr. asked. "There's nothing to forgive. You responded the way a man should—not by thinking of yourself, but by thinking of those around you that you loved." Then he pulled Frankie into a full-on man hug with hard back-patting. "Just try not to jump the gun quite so fast next time. Now, don't mess this up, or I'll never hear the end of it from your mother."

"She knows about me and Lucy?"

His old man gave him a look that screamed out *duh*. "She's Katie Hartigan, isn't she? The woman knows everything."

It was true. The woman always did. And that should have been his first clue that what he'd thought he'd walked in on all those years ago wasn't what it had looked like. Instead, he'd been so determined to protect her that he hadn't even given it a thought. He wouldn't make that mistake again, not with family and definitely not with Lucy.

Now it was time to get to work. Number one on his list? Sweet-talk Fallon into committing a kidnapping.

Chapter Twenty-Three

That morning, Lucy called her dad as soon as she could, considering the one-hour time difference and her hangover. Vodka and Mountain Dew were both dead to her for the next good long while.

He picked up on the third ring. "Hey there, Muf—Lucy." He paused and sighed. "Sorry about that. Old habits die hard."

But he was trying to change, and that meant something. "It's okay, Dad."

"So what do I owe this surprise call to?"

She squeezed her eyes shut against the sun streaming in through her bedroom window like a laser beam aimed right at all of her most tender spots—especially the emotional ones. "I need your help."

"Anything."

"I messed up with Frankie." And that was the undersell of the year.

After her girls had left, she'd stayed up way too long thinking about everything that Gina, Zach, and, most importantly, Frankie had said to her, stripping away her own natural defensiveness to see what they were all trying to tell her. All three of them had zeroed in on the same thing. She was so sure Frankie was going to eventually grow bored with her, she'd picked a breakup fight with him out of nothing. It seemed like something at the time, granted, but after hours of reliving the moment, she realized she didn't even give him a chance that night. Had she ever?

She thought she was being smart by prepping for disaster. In reality, she had been expecting everyone to carry her own emotional baggage.

"What happened with Frankie?" her dad asked, his voice soft with concern.

She inhaled a deep breath and told him everything—well, at least the G-rated version. About how she'd spent most of her time with Frankie waiting for everything to go to hell, just like it had with her parents. They hadn't lost their chance to be together—she'd never allowed them to have one in the first place.

"You think you're the reason why your mother and I got divorced?"

She nodded even though her dad couldn't see her, but it didn't seem to matter.

"Lucy," he said, managing somehow to put enough love in her name that it sounded like a hug. "That couldn't be further from the truth. There were many factors that went into why our marriage didn't work, but you were never on that list. Understand?"

Sniffling a little, she nodded and said, "Yeah."

"But even if you had been, holding that against Frankie wouldn't be fair. We all bring our emotional histories to relationships, and no one is perfect. However, it's how well your imperfections fit together that makes a relationship work. Do you love him?"

She didn't even have to think about it. "I do."

"Then why are you wasting time talking to me?"

"Because I don't know how to fix this." Her entire career had been built around moving beyond a crisis point, but when it came to her own personal disaster she didn't have any tools.

"What do you think you should do?"

She swallowed her first response of, *If I knew I wouldn't have asked for your help.* "Get in my time machine and go back to when we were in Antioch."

Her dad's chuckle set off Gussie, whose whiny let's-play bark carried over the line. "That's not exactly an option."

"Science really needs to catch up with what people really need." She settled back against her pillows, already feeling a little better just by talking things out with her dad.

"Or you could just go apologize and try to work things out like adults."

Ow. Truth hurts. "Harsh."

"Tough love has its place, and I do love you, Lucy. You'll figure this out. You always do."

"Love you too, Dad."

After saying their goodbyes, she hung up and got into the shower. She didn't know what in the world she was going to do next, but whatever it was, it would probably go over better if she didn't smell like vodka. By the time she was standing bent at the waist so she could blow her hair dry upside down, she had half a plan worked out.

Her dad was right. She needed to apologize for going right for Frankie's vulnerable underbelly with a rusty shank. But she'd been hurt and mad and afraid when she'd gone for the one thing she knew would hurt him the most. He'd pegged her right that first night in Marino's, she *had* been scared—not just of going to her high school reunion, but of giving people a chance. There was a reason why she led with the insults. The whole time she'd thought she'd been taking others power over her away from them, but all she'd been doing was taking it away from herself. And Frankie had paid the price because she'd put all of her baggage on him when he hadn't done anything to deserve it. Just the opposite. He'd done everything to show he cared about and respected her just the way she was.

She had to make this right.

Half an hour later, she was wearing her favorite red dress with her strappy sandals, determined to do what it would take to find Frankie and make him listen to her. She grabbed her purse, flung open her door, and stopped dead in her tracks.

Fallon, Gina, and Tess stood in the hallway wearing identical guilty faces. Gina was holding a petal pink pillowcase.

"What's going on and why are you holding a pillowcase?" The question flew out of Lucy's mouth.

"We couldn't find any potato sacks," Tess said as if that made any sense at all.

Fallon rolled her eyes. "We're here to kidnap you."

Not surprisingly, that didn't make anything any more clear. Another time she would have wanted to play along, but not right now.

"I love you, but I have to go find Frankie."

"Oh," Tess said, her shoulders sinking with relief. "That makes things so much easier."

"Unless she's looking for him just to try to whack him," Gina responded with a melodramatic evil laugh.

"She wouldn't be the first, and I'm just speaking for me *and* my siblings," Fallon said.

Lucy looked from one of her friends to the other. They had seriously all lost it. "How many Bloody Marys have you had today?"

Gina's face lit up. "None, but that's a great idea."

Fallon and Tess nodded in agreement.

Okay, there was no way she was getting dragged into whatever shenanigans this was. She was a woman on a mission. "You go ahead without me. I have to get to Frankie."

She loved her girls, but there was no way she was letting them slow her down. She pulled her front door shut behind her, dodged the threesome, and hightailed it for the elevator.

"You're not going anywhere without us," Gina said

The woman moved much more like a ninja than Lucy had expected.

Nerves plucked to the very last fiber, she turned to her girls, who were walking onto the elevator with her. She counted to twenty and exhaled, reminding herself that she loved these absolutely annoying women. "Seriously, I have to get to Frankie."

"We know, that's who we were kidnapping you for," Tess said. "And that's all we're telling you about that until we get to Marino's. Don't worry, Frankie will be there."

And that was the last the evil little threesome would say about it, no matter how much she asked, begged, or threatened. Even when they had to drive around the block Marino's was on three times to find a parking spot.

Whatever was going on, the bar was packed at ten in the morning on a Sunday. Walking inside, surrounded by her girls, she scanned the crowd and saw about a million people but no sexy-as-sin, tall, ginger firefighter who could turn her panties to ash with just a look.

• • •

Frankie was going to puke his guts up.

Okay, he wasn't really going to do that—he hadn't been able to eat since the whole Frankie-is-a-dumbass intervention yesterday—but his stomach was still rocking one way and shaking the other. He'd never been nervous to talk to a woman in his life. Ford had been right, everything had come too easy for him before. But getting Lucy to agree to talk to him again, let alone to give him a second chance? He was definitely going to have to work for it.

Shannon poked her head into the supply closet. Was he hiding from Lucy so she wouldn't walk out the door as soon as she spotted him? Hell yes, he was.

"She just walked in, you ready?" she asked.

He wiped his sweaty palms on the sides of his jeans. "I don't know."

"Frankie Hartigan, you tripped and fell hard, didn't you?"

He had. So bad he probably had a concussion or twelve. "But what if you were right, and I'm not the guy anyone wants for happily ever after?"

"Honey, you may not be the kind of guy who could deliver a happily ever after to me or a dozen other Waterbury women, but you were meant to do so for Lucy."

It sounded good, but it was hard to shake off the doubt that he'd fuck things up in the end. "How do you know?"

"You get scared running into burning buildings?"

"No." Why did people always ask that question? With the right training, the fear didn't factor in. "It's more of me knowing what I need to do and doing it."

"Uh-huh." Shannon brushed back her long dark braids, which had fallen forward when she nodded her head. "And using that big saw thing they call the jaws of life?"

"Not a big deal." It was just a tool. One that could sever a limb, sure, but it was still just a tool.

"And showing up at the total insanity that is your family's version of a nice Sunday lunch?"

Okay, now that wasn't dangerous at all. "What's insane about my family's lunch?"

"Exactly. None of those things make you think twice."

She gave him a pitying smile because she must have sensed that he was totally fucking lost. "But when it comes to telling Lucy you want to be her man, you are scared out of your giant head. That's how you know it's important. That's how you know you're going to do whatever it takes to be her happily ever after—because you love her."

He let Shannon's words of wisdom wash over him and register in his brain. She was right. He was freaked the fuck out, but it was for the right reasons, not because there was some part of himself still half-convinced that he wasn't the kind of guy who could be a part of a real couple. Even more important, he was going to be a part of Lucy's happiness.

All he had to do was convince her that he was just the man for the job.

That realization cut through all the bullshit worry filling up his head, and all of the nerves sending his stomach into panic mode faded away.

"So, Frankie, are you ready?" Shannon asked, holding open the supply closet door.

Yeah, he was. Finally.

"Do you mind doing the honors?" He held up his phone.

"Who's that? And is that a dog humping a stuffed animal?"

"It's Lucy's dad. I just need you to hold this up so he can watch. The dog is Gussie, and that stuffed animal is…well, that's a discussion that requires beer."

Shannon shook her head and chuckled. "Nothing about that is weird at all."

"It's perfectly natural for all of the creatures in the animal kingdom to have sexual urges." Tom's voice came out from the phone's speaker. "And your advice right now was spot-on. I've always said that bartenders make the best therapists."

Shannon's eyes went round, but she gave Frankie a nod and followed him out of the supply closet and out into the crowded bar.

• • •

So busy looking for Frankie, it took Lucy a minute to realize Marino's wasn't exactly Marino's. As she did a slow three-sixty, her heart sped up until it was banging against her ribs like it was about to make a break for it. Processing it all was almost too much for her.

"Frankie did this?" she asked, already knowing the answer but still too awed for that fact to make an impact.

"Yeah he did." Fallon nodded.

"For you," Tess said with a dreamy sigh.

Gina linked her arm through Lucy's and led her forward into the bar. "All for you."

And it was a lot. She gawked as they walked through the crowd. There was a cornhole contest going on in the corner. A pie-eating contest was going on at the bar. A pillowcase three-legged race was happening on the stage. It was the decathlon. He'd brought it to Waterbury.

She turned to Gina. "How?"

Her bestie gave her a knowing look and leaned in close so her words would carry in the crowded bar. "When it comes the Hartigan men, I've learned that there's not anything they won't do when it comes to declaring their intentions."

A swirl of emotions whipped through her, and she nearly collapsed in the chair marked *Lucy Kavanagh* at an empty table in front of the stage, which had been vacated by the racers. "That's what this is?"

"Don't start crying now," Tess said, giving Lucy's back a quick pat before sitting down beside her.

"Crying? I'm not…" She reached up and touched her cheeks, her fingers coming back damp.

Shit. She never cried. But here she was, crying because

Frankie Hartigan loved her.

That's when her shit-is-about-to-go-down alarms started blaring. She opened her mouth to ask more questions, but then the bar lights dimmed and a single spotlight illuminated the stage. She was still trying to unravel what was going on when Frankie walked into the circle of light.

Damn he looked good. Was it wrong that that was her first thought when she saw him? Well, too bad, because it was. He wore the same suit he'd worn the night of the high school reunion dance but had added a big round button to the lapel that read Job Applicant No. 1. Her pulse picked up, and the butterflies in her stomach went nuts, zooming and swooping and doing figure eights.

"Don't worry," he said, looking right at her. "I'm not gonna sing."

Someone from the clump of Hartigans standing behind her table yelled out a good-natured "Thank God."

Frankie didn't even give a half-second glance at the people behind her. He just kept looking at her. "I'm here for a job interview."

At his words, she clamped her jaw shut tight enough that her molars hurt, because she was not going to cry even more in front of all these people. But it wasn't sadness making her blink faster to keep the tears away. It was the realization that if Frankie was willing to do what she thought he was about to, history—neither hers nor his—would not repeat itself. They were going to write their own story.

Frankie crossed the stage, his long legs eating up the distance between them. Instead of jumping off and coming over to her, he reached out and handed her a piece of paper.

"That's my job application to be your guy, the one who's a keeper, the one who won't leave, who'll stay true, who will always be there to win ridiculous decathlons with you. The one who is declaring himself totally and completely in love with you in front of God and everyone. I realize my résumé is a little thin in prior experience."

Still not trusting herself to speak, and quite honestly unsure if anything more than a croak would come out, considering how tight her throat was with emotion, Lucy looked down at the paper. It was blank except for one sentence made up of three words with eight letters in total that meant more than any manifesto ever could.

"That's because there's only ever been one woman for me, I just hadn't met her until now." He took out another piece of paper from the inside of his suit jacket. This one was crumpled and torn into an irregular shape, and even from where she was sitting she could tell that things had been written and scratched out and something else written above it. "So here is what I can bring to the job of being your guy. I'm honest. I'm loyal. I can hold a fifty-pound birdbath head-high for as long as you need. I will always get your snarky sense of humor. I appreciate your ability to get right to the point of things immediately. I *am* worried about your Mountain Dew addiction, but I promise not to ever switch it out for its lesser cousin Mello Yello." He looked up from the paper to gaze directly into her eyes. "And I'll love you for the rest of my life, and I'll never stop doing whatever I can to make you happy—because getting to be the guy that puts that gorgeous smile on your face is the most important job I'll ever have."

Her hands were shaking as she got up from her seat, forgetting about Gina, Tess, and Fallon sitting at the table, Frankie's family, and the bar full of people. The only person that mattered in that entire room was the man on the stage. He'd planned this whole thing for her. Part of her couldn't help but think that she didn't deserve it, or him, but that voice was all but squashed into oblivion by the strangely new sense of optimism and hope that she'd never experienced until that moment. Before Frankie, her life had centered around expecting the worst to happen and not being surprised when she got exactly what she'd expected. Now? She could only envision the possibilities and the promise of tomorrow and all the tomorrows after that, when she'd finally get the hell out of her own way and stop spouting a prophecy of doom that she had the power to change. And a certainty that all her dreams would come true if she only dared to dream them.

She made it to the edge of the stage before reality hit. There was no way she was getting up there this way. But then two strong hands reached out and picked her up, lifting her up to the stage. Thank God Frankie didn't let go, because if he had, she might have just melted into a puddle right there. Every one of her nerves was going crazy with his nearness, screaming at her to just throw her arms around his neck and kiss him. The man was deadly to her senses, and she would gladly spend the next eon trying to learn how to not be so fluttery around him.

"I don't know what to say." Which for once in her life was the honest truth.

He grinned down at her, skimming his thumb down her jawline. "You forgot the most important interview question."

As if she could think of anything to ask him right now besides how quick they could get out of here and make up properly. "What's that?"

"My weak points. I have a lot of them." Now he was touching her, gliding the rough pad of his thumb over the shell of her ear. "My inability to sing is one of them, obviously." He lifted her hand and pressed a soft kiss to the sensitive spot on the inside of her wrist. "Then there is the fact that I get distracted whenever I'm around you because you are the most gorgeous woman, inside and out, that I've ever met."

He tugged her closer until she was pressed against him from hip to shoulder, looking up into the face of the man she loved.

"Frankie," she said, finally remembering that they weren't alone. "There are people around."

"Yes." He nodded, dipping his head down until his lips were almost kissing hers. "And they should know it'll probably only get more embarrassing the longer I go on, but I'm willing to do that, because when it comes to proving myself to you, I'll never stop. I want to be your keeper, your forever guy." He kissed the corner of her mouth, soft and gentle and not nearly enough. "For as long as I can remember, there was nothing in the world I ever wanted to be other than a firefighter. Then I met you. Now I can't imagine being anything other than the man you wake up next to."

And she could picture that, too. It wouldn't be perfect, but what in life ever was? Anyway, it would be perfect for them, and there was nothing better than that.

"I'm sorry," she said, meaning it more than she ever thought she could. "For everything. You were right. I was trying to make you carry my emotional baggage when I should have just let that shit go a long time ago. Can we start over again?"

"Hell no," he said, brushing his lips across hers. "Then we would have missed out on everything leading up to this moment, and I wouldn't skip over any of it for anything—although I might fast-forward through this past week."

"I love you, Frankie Hartigan."

"And you're everything I ever wanted and didn't realize I needed, and I want everyone in the whole world—including your dad on FaceTime—to know it."

And then he finally kissed her, a real one, the kind that promises so much and—even better—the kind that delivers a happily ever after.

Epilogue

Two Years Later...

The Ice Knights Arena was rocking, every fan in the place pumped up and ready to watch their team kick off another winning season. Lucy had practically yelled herself hoarse, and it was still warm-ups.

"Do you mind if I stand here and watch for a minute?" asked a man in head-to-toe Ice Knights apparel (seriously, right down to the team-sponsored tennis shoes).

Since Frankie was out on the concourse, leaving his seat open, she didn't see why not. "Go for it."

"Thanks." The guy moved in next to her in the front row right next to the glass. "So, you have season tickets for these seats?"

"Yeah, we're big fans." Well, that and she kept getting them as Christmas presents from her favorite client, who hardly ever needed her services anymore.

The guy next to her inched a little closer and took a deep breath. "Usually you're here with another woman, long hair, tied back in a braid."

She turned and gave the guy her full attention because that statement was just creepy.

He must have realized, because his face turned so red she could see the flush even under his Ice Knights face paint. "Sorry, I'm up about six rows and never miss a game. You start to notice the regulars." He held out his hand. "Alex."

"Lucy." She shook his hand. "Nice to meet you."

"I was wondering," he said, the words coming out quick, as if he was nervous. "Would you be interested in grabbing a drink or something after the game?"

"Oh my God, that sounds perfect," said an all-too-familiar male voice from behind her. "Don't suppose you know a good sitter?"

Alex's gaze moved from her face to something—really someone—behind her, and he visibly gulped. "Yeah, sorry, I don't."

Struggling to keep from grinning, she turned and looked at her two favorite male members of the human race. Frankie stood decked out in an Ice Knights jersey and a baby carrier containing a one-year-old with an abundance of bright red hair. Out of the corner of her eye, she caught Alex stepping over the front-row seats and into the row behind her.

"Too bad." Frankie shrugged and pulled the toddler out of the carrier, setting him down on his feet between them. "It's been forever since we've been out together. This is our first date since this little guy came along."

Alex looked from her to Frankie to the mini-me who was pressed against the glass looking out onto the ice. "Well, the game's about to start. I better get going."

Lucy glanced over at the jumbotron clock showing ten minutes left in warm-ups. "Nice to meet you," she hollered out, but Alex was already three rows up. Turning to Frankie, she rolled her eyes. "A sitter? Really? You didn't have to scare him off like that."

"What are you talking about?" he asked, his blue eyes wide as if he had no idea what she was talking about. "I'm just a friendly guy. Ask anyone at the firehouse, they love having me as their lieutenant. Also, you really need to talk to your connections with the team. Changing a baby in the men's restroom was a nightmare. They need to get more family friendly bathrooms."

"I'll ask Zach to put it in as a request on his next contract negotiation." With the way he was playing, the team would probably say yes.

Frankie dipped his head down so their faces practically touched. "Your sarcasm is duly noted."

"I hope this is, too." She leaned over and gave him a kiss that made her toes curl.

A banging on the glass pulled her back to the where and when of reality. Zach Blackburn was on the other side of the glass, a goofy grin on his face as he waved at Trey—AKA Francis Hartigan the third. Trey gave up a cute toddler giggle and smacked his palm against the glass in greeting. Then Zach winked at her and gave a manly chin lift to Frankie before skating toward the tunnel to prep for the start of the game.

Frankie grimaced, no doubt still holding a grudge for the almost-playoffs a few years ago. "That guy—"

"Is about to be a part of your family." She slapped her hand over her mouth, but it was too late. Shit. She was not supposed to say anything yet.

"What are you talking about?" Frankie asked, ruffling Trey's hair as the toddler continued to bang on the glass and wave at the exiting players.

"Well," she said, calling up all her work skills to smooth over her snafu. "He's basically my family, so that makes him your family."

Frankie lifted an eyebrow and snorted in disbelief.

"That's not what you said. What do you know?"

Shit. For someone who made her living snuffing out crisis after crisis, she sure was good at creating her own. Time to think fast. Good thing she had just the bit of news to distract him.

"So does that mean you're against naming the baby after the former Most Hated Man In Harbor City?"

His jaw dropped. "Baby?"

She nodded, her hand automatically going to her belly as her heart fluttered. This wasn't exactly how she'd planned on letting him know, but when had anything gone as expected when it came to Frankie Hartigan? No matter what she dreamed up, reality was always better than she'd imagined.

Frankie let out a yell loud enough to gain the attention of a bunch of screaming hockey fans, scooped up Trey, and pulled her in for a family hug. "I love you so much that we can name the baby whatever you want."

"I'm gonna hold you to that," she said, blinking away her tears of joy.

He brushed a kiss against her forehead. "Whatever makes you happy."

"That's easy. You make me happy." She looked down at Trey's smile, then back up at her husband's beaming face, and couldn't imagine it was possible to feel any better than she did right now at this moment with her family. "We make me happy. You really do know how to deliver a happily ever after."

"Only with you, Lucy," he said. "Only with you."

• • •

Ready For A Sneak Peek To Find Out What Happens To The Hartigans Next?

Oh You Are In Luck! Keep Reading!

Chapter One

Every part of Zach Blackburn ached as if an oversized green muscle man had plucked him up from the sidewalk and smashed him against one of Harbor City's skyscrapers.

Some of the biggest names in professional hockey had threatened to tear the defenseman's head off—several of them were even justified in doing so. Then there were the fans. The last poll of Harbor City Ice Knights fans had his approval rating at 3 percent. There were bloodthirsty dictators who ranked higher than that. And the media? They'd circled him like vultures waiting to pick the meat off his bones as soon as he'd signed his contract, reporting his every move and mistake.

But it hadn't been any of those who'd made him wish for death. Nope, that had happened thanks to food poisoning from God knew what.

Sitting up in bed hurt his tortured gut enough that he couldn't bite back his groan. At least no one was around to overhear it.

"Welcome back to the land of the living." A distinctive alto reminding him of brass knuckles wrapped in silk filtered into the room from the doorway. "You're not going to throw up on my shoes again, are you?"

Shit.

She was here. Of course she was—his own personal demon nurse.

Fallon Hartigan had arrived last night—at the insistence of his PR manager Lucy Kavanagh—right in time to watch him puke like a high schooler after their first taste of peach schnapps. And, yeah, some of it had landed on her. Even he wasn't a big enough jerk to not feel bad about that.

She'd been sent by Lucy Kavanagh, his PR savior and friend—well, as much of one as someone like him could have. Zach had argued he didn't need any help. That argument probably would have worked better if he hadn't made an offering to the porcelain gods without hanging up on Lucy first. Since Lucy was out of town, she'd called in the queen of mean who happened to be one of her best friends and an emergency room nurse.

"Go away," he grumbled, shoving his hands through his hair, pushing back the part that flopped over his forehead and got in his eyes.

"Not gonna happen," she said, taking a few steps inside his bedroom. "I promised Lucy I'd stay until I was sure you were on the mend."

"And last night was such a good time you wanted to stay here for more? That's your idea of fun?" It looked like it just might be. Nothing about her, from her no-nonsense braid to her oversized T and joggers combo, screamed party girl, puck bunny, or anything else close to the women he'd found himself surrounded by since it became apparent he was designated for hockey's big time.

"Since I usually see much worse on a daily basis, I'll live.

You look like you might today, too." Her gaze flickered down from his face before speeding back up to somewhere just north of his head, her eyes wide. "You need to pull up your covers."

That made him bristle. The last people who told him that he needed to do something were his folks. And he'd unknowingly signed huge loans they'd taken out in his name. They'd called it boring minutia he didn't need to worry about, since they were his managers and would always watch out for him. The accountant he'd finally hired called it embezzlement and financial ruin. So long, humiliating, shitty story, he could give two shits what anyone felt he "needed to do" ever again.

However, something about the pink staining her cheeks had him looking downward. The basketball shorts he'd been wearing when he'd finally collapsed onto his king-sized bed, the only piece of furniture in the huge bedroom, had worked their way down, waaaaaay down. And Fallon had noticed.

He glanced over at her and caught her snapping her attention back up to his face and keeping it there as she approached his bed. But she couldn't stop looking, even though it was obvious from her grimace that she didn't want to.

Well, this could be useful. All he wanted was to deal with the grossness of food poisoning on his own. Alone. No one seeing any crack in his defenses. That's how he lived his life now. He probably always should have.

But he couldn't kick Fallon out of his house and stay in Lucy's good graces.

However, if he got her to leave on her own…well then, that was a different story completely.

"Pull up my covers?" he asked, knowing he was about to put a skate across the line of decency even if he had absolutely zero plans of following through. Of course it wouldn't be the first time he fought dirty, as many of his opponents on the ice would attest. "If I do that, how are you going to give me a sponge bath?"

She jolted to a stop at the foot of his bed, and he practically heard the match strike the dynamite. "A. Sponge. Bath?"

He shoots. He scores. He would have lifted his arms in celebration—after she stormed out of the house, of course—but something in his gut bubbled and cramped, causing beads of sweat to pop out along his forehead. Want had nothing to do with it anymore, he needed to get her away from here.

Hello? This is karma here to fuck you up, asshole.

Ignoring the vehemence in her tone, along with the continuing fizzle and twist in his stomach, Zach shrugged his shoulders and ran one of his hands down the hard ridges of his six-pack, playing the part of a sexist jerk who would actually ask for a sponge bath. "I ran a fever yesterday. It made me all sweaty."

Closing her eyes, she tipped her pointed chin toward the ceiling and sucked in a deep breath. That gave him a chance to try to will his stomach into chilling the fuck out, which worked about as well as could be expected. Everything inside his abdomen did a shimmy-slosh thing that did not bode well. He barely got his oh-fuck expression off his face before she lowered her chin and opened her eyes, staring right at him with nothing but sweetness and light.

The air around him stilled, and the little hairs on the back of his neck stood up.

"Well, I'd hate for you—in your weakened condition—to slip in the shower and crack open your head," she said, putting enough sugar in her words to put him in a diabetic coma. "Where do you keep your sponges?"

Like the Homecoming Queen in a slasher movie, Zach bolted from his bed, managing to yank up his basketball shorts from just above his junk to his waist.

He held up his hand like she was a vampire he had to

ward off. "Don't even think about it."

Her laugh burst out, full and teasing. She'd gotten him. She'd seen right through him like he was an unshaded window.

With her eyes as big and round as an anime heroine's, she cocked her head to one side. "Do you no longer need my professional sponge bath expertise? I'll have you know that I excelled in the wax on, wax off motion of it at nursing school." She let out a deep, melodramatic sigh. "If only I could have specialized in that instead of trauma medicine."

Zach dropped his hand and closed his eyes. She was fucking with him. He clamped his jaw shut so she wouldn't see the smile fighting to get out even as his stomach started to roil again.

Finally, he opened his eyes and took in a deep breath, knowing he had to get her out of this room before he puked again if he had any hope of hustling her from his house this morning. "Point taken. I'll just get in the shower." He started edging toward the en-suite bathroom.

"Good." She crossed her arms and gave him a don't-fuck-with-me-again smirk. "Anyway, hasn't anyone ever told you that nurses aren't scared by anything?"

They hadn't, but then again, if it didn't have something to do with on-ice defensive strategies, he wouldn't have been paying attention.

And how'd that work out for you, Blackburn?

"So, are you going to play nice now, so we can make Lucy happy and she can stop worrying about her clients and enjoy her well-earned vacation?" she asked as she walked to his bedroom door.

An invisible icy wave washed over him, the kind that meant the fates were sending him a big fuck-you on the no-more-throwing-up thing. "I don't want to."

Fallon snorted. "Welcome to the real world, where we

rarely, if ever, get what we want."

And then she was gone before he could accidentally admit out loud that he'd learned that lesson all too well.

He'd wanted parents who hadn't embezzled all of his money, a hockey career that wasn't marred by scandal, a town that didn't hate him, teammates that didn't look at him like he was nothing but trash, and to end the streak of shitty playing that had plagued him since the Ice Knights traded for him. But, most of all at that moment, he wanted to keep whatever was in his stomach in place. Cold sweat broke out on the back of his neck. Fallon Hartigan may be a pushy pain in his ass, but that didn't make her wrong. He was most definitely not going to get what he wanted.

Propelled by a powerful sense of stomach-mandated urgency, Zach hustled to his bathroom to puke up his guts. Again.

This sure as hell wasn't the life he'd dreamed of when he laced up his skates for the first time, back when he'd thought his parents saw him as more than just a paycheck.

• • •

A civilian would have bolted. However, when they said that nothing scared a nurse, they weren't kidding. Plus, when one of her best friends called in an SOS, there was no way Fallon would say no. It would take more than Zach Blackburn dry heaving hours after his sponge-bath stunt to send her screaming for the exits.

And yes, that would be exits plural. The house he lived in was massive, if woefully under-furnished. Literally, it looked like the guy had just arrived in town a week ago instead of seven months—right in time to ruin the Ice Knights' run for the playoffs last season. Not that Fallon was still bitter, but she was totally still bitter.

As any fan knew—and Fallon was a die-hard—the team had overpaid to bring Zach Blackburn here, and thanks to his shitty playing and piss-poor attitude, he was now known as the most hated man in Harbor City.

Fallon might live in working-class Waterbury, but the feeling on her side of the harbor was the same. Blackburn was a selfish player. He had a huge chip on his shoulder. He punched out fans. He ignored his coach. He didn't talk to the other players on the team once they left the rink—and sometimes not while they were in it.

He also happened to be Lucy's biggest client, which was not a surprise because she was the best crisis PR management bad-boy whisperer in town. That meant when Blackburn fucked up, Lucy magically managed to make it all better.

Except not this time.

Why? Because this time he needed a nurse. So here she and Zach were, in his kitchen sharing a moment of awkward silence—one of the many since she'd arrived last night after a long shift at St. Vincent Hospital.

She'd walked in the door of his gargantuan house, and he'd promptly puked all over her. She wished she could say that was the first time that had ever happened to her but life as an emergency room nurse usually didn't work out that way.

Zach had one of those fancy kitchens where there was a cooking area, an island the size of her bathroom, an eating area big enough for a table for ten that only had a card table and a single folding chair, and a sitting area with a dark brown leather couch and a massive TV. He was sitting in the middle of the couch with a green plaid blanket wrapped around him. It would almost be comical, this hulk of a man with the dimple in his chin, the steel bar going through his eyebrow, and the hint of a vibrant tattoo on his forearm where the blanket had fallen away, if it wasn't for the fact that his skin had a sweaty, pasty, been-puking-my-guts-up sheen to it.

Poor guy.

Okay, he was still the jerk whose selfish play ended the city's playoff dreams last year, but the man was obviously hurting, and she couldn't just turn off the nurse thing. It was who she was, ever since she forced her siblings to play hospital with her growing up.

She picked up the folding chair and carried it over to the sitting area, along with a cup of warm peppermint tea. She handed him the tea and set up the chair in front of him before sitting down on it. He looked at the Ice Knights–branded mug in his hand as if were a live grenade.

Of course, if she'd been throwing up as much as it seemed like he had, she'd be a little hesitant about drinking or eating anything, too.

"It's peppermint tea," she said. "It'll help soothe your stomach."

He brought the mug up close to his face and sniffed the swirling line of steam coming up from it. "You aren't one of those touchy-feely alternative nurses, are you?"

"People have been using peppermint for eons to ease nausea symptoms," she said as she took out the little spiral notebook and pen she always had on her during a shift. "If you want to skip it because it's not a pill that came from a little brown bottle with a childproof cap, you can go right ahead."

He brought the mug up to his nose and sniffed again. Then, he took a sip. He didn't smile so much as grimace a little less. Fine. She could live with that.

"When did you first start experiencing symptoms?" She flipped open her notebook. Just because she didn't have a patient chart didn't mean she wasn't going to keep track of symptoms and vitals.

"This morning."

"Had you been feeling bad before that?"

"Nope." He closed his eyes and let his head fall back against the couch. "Everything was fine and then pow, I wanted to die."

Sure, it could be the flu, but Fallon was starting to suspect something else. "Anyone around you been sick?"

"Not that I know of," he said, as if he didn't give a shit either way.

Fallon glanced around at the kitchen. It wasn't so much clean and tidy as it was barren. No dishes in the sink. No bananas or anything else in the fruit bowl. Only a basket decorated with a golden bow and filled with tissue paper, ribbons, and muffins that was sitting in the middle of the island like it had gotten lost on the way to Martha Stewart's house.

She turned back to Zach, who was drinking the tea as if he hadn't distrusted it in the first place. "Eat anything different than usual or from a new place?"

"I don't eat out."

"Where'd the muffins come from? Do you cook?" she asked.

"A woman brought them over." He twisted on the couch, looking at the island behind it. "I had three."

Fallon could practically hear the ding-ding-ding in her head, and she scribbled down "food poisoning" and the pertinent information in her notebook. "And how soon after that did you become nauseous?"

"A few hours." He whipped back around, groaned—no doubt because of the quick movement—and closed his eyes. "Do you think she poisoned them? She did have a Cajun Rage tattoo."

Besides her family, nursing, and the trio of women she

called her best friends, there was nothing in the world Fallon cared about more than the Ice Knights. She wasn't just an everyday fan. She was a superfan. She knew every stat and every factoid, right down to the fact that Coach Peppers had a sixth toe. And the Rage? There was no bigger rivalry in sports than the one between the Knights and the Rage. The Rage played dirty, and their fans were obnoxious.

She snapped her notebook shut. "You slept with someone with a Rage tattoo?"

"Well," Zach said as he curled his lips upward into the signature smirk that had gotten him a huge endorsement deal, since it hadn't been his playing in Harbor City. "We didn't exactly sleep."

What was it with dudes always having to pull out their metaphorical dick to show how big it was? Be it hockey players or the doctors she worked with, she was so done dealing with the male ego.

"Yeah well, if it gets out that you bang Rage fans, the tri-state metro area will be lining up to poison you." She stood up and picked up her chair, carrying it back over to the card table, which was sitting underneath a for-real chandelier. It was a small one, sure, but still a chandelier.

"Like they need another reason," Zach grumbled as he got up from the couch. "So what do I have to do to get over this?"

"Unfortunately," she said with a smile that went to show exactly how not sad she was about it. Sleeping with a Cajun Rage puck bunny really was a step too far. "You just have to wait for it to clear your system. It's probably a minor case of food poisoning. You'll be fine. We just need to keep you hydrated and make sure it doesn't get worse."

"We?" he asked, crossing over to the island and, like the prima donna he was, leaving the empty mug on the coffee table by the couch.

"Yeah. We. I promised Lucy I'd stay until you were out of the woods, and I'm sticking to it." Unlike some people, she didn't have a lot, but she had her word and she didn't break it.

He kept his distance, but something in his stance changed, making him seem bigger than the team stats that listed him at six feet, three inches and two-hundred-and-thirty-eight pounds. "What was your name again?" he asked, his voice dropping to a lower register than before. "Felicia?"

"That's my sister."

Fallon couldn't believe it. He was trying to intimidate her. Maybe even trying to get her to leave again. She knew the signs. She'd grown up around men who couldn't actually express what they were feeling if someone tried to beat it out of them with a baseball bat. The Irish weren't exactly known for being in touch with and wanting to talk about their emotional wants and needs.

"Faith?" he asked.

"That's my other sister."

Sure, there were only a limited number of common names that started with F, but the fact that he'd nailed two of her sisters' names while he was supposedly trying to remember hers? Yeah, she wasn't falling for it.

He shifted, the move making the plaid blanket gap open just enough to show off a broad swatch of his ink-covered, muscular chest and the sparkle of the light hitting the silver ring through his right nipple. "Fiona?"

It took everything she had not to crack a smile. "That's sister number three."

"There are four girls in your family?" As if he didn't know. He must have gotten at least some background information about her from Lucy before he agreed to let Lucy ask her to come over. "Plus three brothers?"

"Yeah." She nodded, not letting herself react outwardly at all to his little display. "And I'm Fallon. Fallon Hartigan."

He glowered at her in silence, his eyes so dark they were practically black as they zeroed in on her as if he could scare her. That wasn't going to happen. One, she got more attitude from her pediatric patients than this. Two, Lucy trusted the guy, and Fallon trusted Lucy. Three, she was a Hartigan, and they didn't back down from anything.

Finally, he spoke. "I've got a game tomorrow. I'm taking a nap."

And without so much as even a mumbled thank-you for giving up her weekend to be his nurse, he turned and walked out of the kitchen and down a dark hallway. Most hated man in Harbor City? Yeah, she could corroborate that.

Food poisoning or not, Zach Blackburn was one prime, grade-A asshole. She glanced down at the basket of muffins and grinned. Fallon wouldn't have been surprised if the puck bunny had tried to poison the prick on purpose—God knew she was tempted right about now.

Instead, she took out her phone.

Fallon: *He'll live, and you owe me. Big time.*

Lucy: *Going that well, huh?*

Fallon: *What did you tell him about me?*

Lucy: *Just that you're my bestie, Frankie's sister, maybe some family stuff, and that you're an awesome nurse. The basics.*

Fallon: *That's a lot.*

Lucy: *He doesn't trust a lot of folks. He needed background. He has his reasons, promise you won't let him get to you.*

Fallon: *I can promise not to kill him but that's about as*

much as you'll get from me. He's the most obnoxious man I've ever met, and I work with doctors who think they're god—not a god but the actual big guy himself.

Lucy: *Just give Zach a chance. You'll love him.*

Yeah, that was so not going to happen—not even in a parallel universe.

Acknowledgments

First off, thank you so much for reading *Muffin Top*! I hope you love Frankie and Lucy as much as I do. They were a total blast to write, and that is in no small part because of the amazing people I got to work with on this book. My editor Liz, who happens to be a vampire, is a fabulous brainstorming and editing partner. Thank you! The entire team at Entangled who have taken The Hartigans series and done all of the heavy lifting to get it onto your shelf are amazing. Y'all are FABULOUS! Robin Covington and Kimberly Kincaid, my two ride or die girls (who really help inspire how the friendship between Gina, Lucy, Tess, and Fallon works), thanks for the virtual chocolate during the rough times and the kick in the ass when I need it. I really couldn't do it without you two. Of course, no book is created in a perfectly silent environment (and if they are, don't tell me, I'll die of jealousy), but a massive thank-you is going out to the Fab Mr. Flynn and the Flynn kids for your patience and understanding when I'm unshowered and in yoga pants and late for deadline (again). And for the Gussie fans out there, please know that he is based on a real pooch (Gus) belonging to Andie J. Christopher, who told a story of how he'd gone a-humping while she was on a video conference call and I almost died from laughing so hard. Thanks for letting me put Gus in a book.

The real truth is that this book would not be what it is without some amazing people who were willing to share their stories with me—especially Riki, who was kind enough to allow me to use her story of being concern-trolled at a restaurant as the opening scene of Muffin Top. Thank you so very much. Also? Fuck that guy. You're amazing.

xoxo,
Avery

About the Author

Avery Flynn has three slightly wild children, loves a hockey-addicted husband, and is desperately hoping someone invents the coffee IV drip. Find out more about Avery on her website, follow her on Twitter, like her on her Facebook page, or friend her on her Facebook profile. Join her street team, The Flynnbots, on Facebook. Also, if you figure out how to send Oreos through the internet, she'll be your best friend for life.

Don't miss book one of the Hartigans series…

BUTTERFACE

Also by Avery Flynn…

THE NEGOTIATOR

THE CHARMER

THE SCHEMER

KILLER TEMPTATION

KILLER CHARM

KILLER ATTRACTION

KILLER SEDUCTION

BETTING ON THE BILLIONAIRE

ENEMIES ON TAP

DODGING TEMPTATION

HIS UNDERCOVER PRINCESS

HER ENEMY PROTECTOR

Discover more Amara titles…

NEVER EXPECTED YOU
a *Love Unexpected* novel by Jody Holford

When Zach Mason, former army sergeant turned veterinarian for war-wounded animals, returns home, the decision to stay is easy. But convincing the only other vet in town to hire him is a good deal harder. It doesn't help that the beautiful, intelligent, and stubborn Stella Lane is determined to make his life hell. Too bad she's nothing but temptation. And now his new roommate…

HANDLE WITH CARE
a *Saddler Cove* novel by Nina Croft

First grade teacher Emily Towson always does the right thing. But in her dreams, she does bad, bad things with the town's baddest boy: Tanner O'Connor. But when he sells her grandmother a Harley, fantasy is about to meet a dose of reality. Tanner spent two hard years in prison, with only the thought of this "good girl" to keep him sane. Before either one thinks though, they're naked and making memories on his tool bench. Now Tanner's managed to knock-up the town's "good girl" and she's going to lose her job over some stupid "morality clause" if he doesn't step up.

WHAT HAPPENS IN VEGAS
a *Girls Weekend Away* novel by Shana Gray

Tough-as-nails detective Bonni Connolly is on a girls' getaway in Vegas with her friends and she splurges on a little luxury, including a VIP booth in an exclusive club. That's when she sees *him*. Professional poker player Quinn Bryant is in town for one of the largest tournaments of the year. What starts as a holiday fling soon turns into something more, as Bonni learns to see the man behind the poker face. Even though Bonni's trip has an end date and there is another tournament calling Quinn's name, their strong connection surprises them both. And by the end of the weekend they start to wonder if what happens in Vegas doesn't have to stay there…

ONE WEDDING, TWO BRIDES
a *Fairy Tale Brides* novel by Heidi Betts

Jilted bride Monica Blair can't believe it when she wakes up next to a smooth-talking cowboy with a ring on her finger. Ryder Nash would have bet that he'd never walk down the aisle. But when the city girl with pink-streaked hair hatches a plan to expose the conman who married his sister, no idea is too crazy. And even though Monica might be the worst rancher's wife he's ever seen, he can't stop thinking about the wedding night they never had. What was supposed to be a temporary marriage for revenge is starting to feel a little too real…